SAY GOODBYE

SAY GOODBYE

A RELUCTANT SLEUTH MYSTERY

BY E. J. RAND

Published by
Deadly Ink Press
PO Box 6235, Parsippany, NJ 07054
www.deadlyink.com

ISBN: 978-09787442-1-2

First Edition

~PROLOGUE~
TUESDAY, FEBRUARY 17
7:35 A.M.

I F NORMAN LYONS had known he was going to die that morning, he would have worn different clothes. After tossing all night, he rose early and switched off the alarm before it sounded. Anxiety numbed him while he dressed for work in the bedroom closet, with the door closed so he wouldn't wake Hannah. He doubted his socks matched.

It took clearing off the walk and digging out his car, working up a sweat in the falling snow, to calm down. Then, there he was, snuggled in the warmth of his little Toyota, heart racing and fear pounding at his head.

The forecast called for seven inches. Snow blew right back onto the plowed highway, and the surface was treacherous. Fat flakes slapped his windshield, limiting visibility even with headlights. His glasses remained wet. He drove carefully in the right lane while he fretted about his discovery.

The car rocked as his driver-side wheels thump-thumped into a pothole hidden beneath the snow. He tensed, but the tires held, and he thanked Hannah for pressuring him to buy new ones. The jolts shocked him out of his distress. He needed to calm down. More auditors get fired than murdered, and no one would shoot him in the office. If he had to, he could find another job.

He lifted his right hand off the steering wheel, flexed stiff fingers and braked as he approached a construction site where the highway rose above another and curved sharply to the left.

As he slowed, the large black SUV hanging behind him pulled forward. It must have four-wheel drive and want to pass, Norm thought, and might stray out of its lane on the curve. Sure enough, it crowded him. Its dark-tinted windows towered above.

He honked his horn. *I am here. Go away, please.* He hugged the edge of the roadway and slowed further, so the truck could ease back into its own lane or fly by and choose whichever lane it wanted

His car jerked, the steering wheel bucked in his hands when the larger vehicle rammed him. The impact shoved the Toyota sideways, bouncing him in the seat belt. He fought for control.

Orange warning cones shot past. The black wall of the SUV forced him toward the wood barrier as the curve ran him out of room. Norm mashed the horn, jammed the brake and swung away from the edge. But the heavier vehicle slowed with him, pushing relentlessly. He couldn't stop.

Hannah appeared. She smiled, and her image collided with scattering cones. For a moment, he thought the barrier might hold. Seat-belted in, hands on the wheel, eyes wide, Norman Lyons hurled off the road and into space. The Toyota plunged toward a highway far below, horn wailing in distress.

PART ONE
§
FORCED AWAKE

~1~
TUESDAY, FEBRUARY 17
10:06 A.M.

"KITCHEN, make coffee!" Gary Kemmerman waved his right arm around the room like a magic wand, and laughed at himself. The refrigerator always laughed at him; this time he heard the stovetop laughing, too. Again the wizard had forgotten to put up water.

Both arms were stiff after shoveling the front walk. At age fifty-eight, he was losing flexibility, and that was not all.

He almost called out, "Done shoveling, Sarah. Come on down." Tea for her, coffee for him, had been a ritual after he shoveled. He glanced toward her favorite tan sweater, still hanging over her chair in the eat-in area. He did not want to dwell on that.

Leaning back against the kitchen island, he brushed snow off his jeans and punched the Lyons' code into his cell phone, returning Hannah's call-me message. Norm usually called. The last time he'd spoken with Hannah had been weeks before. Norm's birthday was coming up; maybe she was planning a party.

She answered on the first ring. "Gary?"

"Howdy, Hannah."

"Can you come over? I really need to talk to you right now."

She sounded stressed. Could it have to do with what Norm had said? "What's up?"

"I'll tell you when you get here."

"Okay. I'm on my way."

She'd never asked him to her house alone; she treated men as if she needed a safe distance. Sometimes, that included her husband. He recalled Norm's random visits, the two of them talking sports, investments, movies ... there were times he wondered if the man wanted to move in.

Before Gary left, he washed his bowl, cup, and spoon. That took a moment, and since he lived alone he tried to make minimal mess. He carried the cereal box into the pantry closet. Its shelves were laden with Sarah's sauce jars and pasta boxes, muffin mixes, canned fruits, and decaf teas. He set the cereal in its place. He was tired of cold cereal, and that meant he needed to buy eggs. If he could remember.

"Eggs, buy eggs," he said aloud as he pulled on his heavy coat. He waved his arms for emphasis. It was too quiet. His own voice, when he talked to himself, provided no relief.

The snow was winding down, but folded clouds kept it gray, gave the day an eight o'clock feel, rather than mid-morning. A diet of dismal weather had made him irritable—maybe Norm, too, based on this morning's chat.

He decided against wearing boots, skipped the snow-covered sidewalk and walked rapidly in the plowed street. In his twenty-four years on the block, he and Sarah had always done that. He felt odd, heading for the Lyons house and not holding Sarah's hand, helping her in the snow. It was a little thing, holding a hand you loved. Everywhere he turned, he found little things.

Hannah opened the door before he could push the bell. She stepped back and swung it wide, drawing him in. He wiped his shoes. The Lyons' living room was painted off-white and furnished with small, basic pieces that lacked cohesiveness. It wasn't a warm space. Norm was a prickly guy, bright and unpredictable. You could respect him, but he was probably hard to love. He and Hannah seemed to live at arm's length, and their rooms echoed that distance.

Gary shrugged out of his coat, laid it over the couch near the door, and turned to say hello. Hannah was slender, with straight brown hair she wore in bangs, and large, sad eyes covered by larger glasses. He'd never seen her left eye twitch before.

"Thank you for coming." She spoke in a near-whisper. She was

8

dressed in black, head-to-toe. She favored pastels; he'd never seen her in black.

"What's wrong, Hannah?"

"My Norman is dead."

That stunned him—both the news and Hannah expressing it as if she'd broken a fingernail. She continued before he could react.

"The police told me his car went off the road. They said he died in the car. They said it was an accident. They suggested I get a friend to stay with me, and they gave me a number to call about the body when I made funeral arrangements."

He wanted to comfort her, but she stood stiffly, demanding physical distance as her words screamed caution.

"You call anyone yet? Besides me?"

"I spoke with Naomi as soon as I learned. She'll be here any minute now."

Naomi, Norm's younger sister, lived down the block with her husband and two kids, and she and Hannah were close. Naomi worked at a graphics company three days a week. She must have gone to work today.

"Did the police ask you to identify a body?"

Hannah crossed her arms and hugged herself. "Naomi works near where they said Norman is. She said she'd check."

"You want, I'll drive us."

Hannah stared into the abyss, swayed and righted herself. It couldn't have been easy, but she went back to matter-of-fact. "I just can't. Naomi will do it." She breathed in deeply. "They said the accident left him disfigured."

That word. He leaned back against the couch, gripped the nubby fabric and concentrated on texture. Hannah's left eye was twitching rapidly.

"Do the police know Naomi's coming?"

Hannah nodded, exaggerating the movement. "I called them back. The sergeant seemed very sorry. He asked me about our marriage, and if anything was worrying Norman." Her words petered out, and she withdrew.

So would I, so did I when Sarah died, he thought. Had Hannah told them what Norm was worried about? Did she even know?

Better he said nothing about the talk in Norm's car. "They tell you how it happened?"

Hannah's eyes zeroed in on him, the force that held her together behind that look. "I'm sure my Norman was murdered. I told that to the policeman. He asked questions, and I couldn't answer them. He asked if I had facts, evidence. When I didn't know what to say, he cut me off. That policeman won't believe me. Please help me, Gary," she whispered. She stared, waiting.

So she knew. She'd told them. They still said it was an accident.

He was squeezing his thumbs, then forced himself to stop. What could he do? His head rang with Sarah's words: "Don't be Mr. Logic with friends. Friends help friends."

He lifted his eyes back to hers. "Of course I'll help."

The doorbell rang.

Hannah stood rooted, as if she hadn't heard it. "My Norman was murdered," she repeated.

Torn between her and the bell, he moved and opened the door. Naomi was leaning forward, ready to sprint inside. For a moment, she looked like a chubby Norm in a curly wig. Her eyes were red-rimmed. She acknowledged him with a touch as she bolted past. He turned and saw her squeeze Hannah in a desperate hug.

He wished he'd talked Norm into taking a snow day.

He was about to close the door when another woman approached, climbed the steps and stopped in front of him. The stranger was almost his height, with auburn hair pulled into a ponytail, pale skin, soft features, and expressive eyes. She wore a long blue wool coat and had a pair of gloves in her clasped hands. He saw a wedding ring and guessed she was in her forties.

"Is this the Lyons house?" she asked.

"Yes."

"Are you a relative?"

How could she know? He glanced back, and found Hannah and Naomi had gone elsewhere in the house.

"Please come in. It's cold out here. We can talk inside." She followed him. He closed the door. Her bearing told him not to ask for her coat.

"I really can't stay long," she said. "I was in the neighborhood and …." Her hands tugged at the gloves. "I thought the family might want me to answer questions."

"Answer questions?"

They both heard a painful gasp from somewhere back in the house.

Affected by the sound, the woman lowered her voice. "I saw it— the auto accident. The police already talked to me." She bit her lower lip. "I thought speaking with the family might provide comfort. But now seems a really bad time."

"You are …?" He had matched her near-whisper.

"Natalie Strassberg. I'm a nurse at Ridgetop Hospital, so I was in the neighborhood. Who are you?"

"Gary Kemmerman. A friend and neighbor."

A heart-breaking moan floated in.

The sound further distressed her. "I'd better go. If the family wants, we can speak another time."

"Please. Let me tell Norm's wife you're here." Norm's widow, he should have said. That would take getting used to.

"I'll wait, if—"

"I'll be quick."

He walked into the empty kitchen, turned left, and found both women in the dining room. Hannah was sitting in a chair, weeping almost soundlessly, shoulders shaking and tears squeezing through closed eyes. Naomi had knelt before her, distraught but providing what comfort Hannah would accept. It was not the time to interrupt. He moved unnoticed through the dining room and out its other side, circling back to the witness, who had remained exactly where he left her.

He observed her in profile before she heard his approach and turned. Hannah believed Norm had been murdered. If so, the accident might have been staged, and this woman might have useful information.

"She's sort of in shock," he said.

"I'd really better go."

"Mrs. Strassberg, please. She'll want to know about the accident. You're here, and your memory's fresh. Would you discuss what you saw with me?"

"Do you mean right now?"

"Not here. She needs space. How about my place? I'm down the block."

She frowned. "I think not."

Did she believe he was coming on to her? "I understand. Have you had lunch? Let me buy you lunch. Anywhere you choose." With lots of people around, he almost said.

She looked at him closely. "I really do have to get back to the hospital."

"Later, then? Dinner? There's a diner nearby. You pick the time."

Her expression changed. He had her attention, but he wasn't winning her trust. For the first time in a year, he wished he were clean-shaven.

"Don't you usually have dinner with your wife?" she asked.

She'd seen his wedding ring. "Sarah died of cancer last February. I promised I'd wear our ring for a year."

"I'm sorry."

"No need. I'm almost whole." He edited "pick you up" from what he was about to ask. "Can I meet you after work? Drive us to the diner, bring you back to your car?"

The woman quarter-turned, inclined to leave. "I don't get into cars with strangers."

Or houses. What had happened in her past? "What if I said I was trustworthy?"

"Would you have wanted your wife to agree to what you ask, if she were me?"

This woman was direct and intelligent: lucky Mr. Strassberg. "Sarah didn't need to clear things. She'd leave a message if she was gonna be late. I'd rather interview you in person, but we can do it by phone. Don't want to keep you from your husband."

She surprised him when she chuckled. "Why don't we compromise? Each of us can drive, and we'll go dutch. I can meet you at the Red Maple at eight. Is that the place you meant?"

He nodded, watching her eyes.

"I'm divorced," she said. "This ring"—she wagged the finger—"is for defense. And dinner is about the accident, not a date."

He followed her out. From the front stoop, before he moved, he watched her get into a gray Chevrolet and drive off.

When he went to say goodbye, he found Naomi sobbing along with Hannah. He wasn't sure what to do until Naomi caught his eye and shook her head once, a clear not now. His regrets, his questions, would have to wait. He closed the door behind him.

Gary paused on the sidewalk in front of his house, saddened and confused. A cold wind had fractured the clouds. He turned up his collar, hunched in the coat. Here was the curb where Norm had stopped hours before in the snow, the walkway he'd shoveled, and his home filled with memories.

Whether he was ready or not, his soft "of course" had been a commitment to Hannah and to Norm. He'd have to dust off his professional skills and rejoin the world, at least for a bit. He stared at his house and knew if he went right in he might change his mind, put on his robe, and dive back into the wallow.

He paced, crunching snow, turned to face the Lyons' house, and then his own. A gust blew snow down his neck. What steps must he take? Naomi would tell him when it was safe to question Hannah. In the meantime, he had a date—or whatever—to interview the crash witness. It would also be good to interview the investigating officer.

He pulled out his phone and punched in the number for his friend Vincent Alegretti, a lieutenant on the town police department. Vincent and his wife Angela had not been close with Norm and Hannah, but they'd been block-neighbors for a dozen years. They would be upset.

His exposed hands grew cold, but the chill air felt good. Vincent answered on the third ring.

"Hi, Vinnie. It's Gary."

"Gary who?"

"Oh, come on. I need to speak to you." He flattened a lump of snow with his left shoe.

"Beef stroganoff, chicken sorrentino, veal parmigiana, Angela's ready to cook all those things for us, and you're mister no-show. You deserve a kick in the ass."

13

"True. But not now."

Vincent's sigh was audible. "Did you shave today?"

"No."

"Yesterday?" He waited a bit. "We talk, you shave. Deal, my reclusive buddy?"

The sun broke through the clouds, illuminating the street. It seemed wrong, sunlight and phone calls, life going on as if nothing had happened. "Norm's dead," he said, causing a silence.

"Norm Lyons?"

"Yeah." He imagined his friend bent forward, bushy brows knitted, the phone folded in his thick hand.

"How? When?"

"This morning. Apparently in an auto accident. Can we meet about it?"

Lieutenant Alegretti handled Homicide.

~2~
11:13 A.M.

Reminded of the perp walk from countless TV shows, Gary felt uneasy as he followed Vincent through the police station. First level held reception, squad rooms and cells; above that were offices and a large open space with partitions, desks, file cabinets, phones, and detectives—guns on hips, or in chest holsters.

At least he'd had time for a quick shave.

Printer, phone and voice noise stilled when the lieutenant shut the door to his small office. The vault-like space had no outside window and no inside glass. Fluorescent lighting left a buttery sheen on everything it touched. The computer monitor beside the cluttered desk caught Gary's attention: bars moved slowly across the screen, left to right. Probably cop humor.

The lieutenant wore a grey suit he was growing out of, a white shirt unbuttoned at the collar, and a blue-and-yellow tie hinting at years of coffee stains. He motioned to the chairs in front of the desk, and they sat.

Ignoring his discomfort, Gary unzipped his coat and launched into what Hannah had told him about her husband's death.

"Where'd it happen?" Vincent asked when he finished.

"Norm went off I-287 and down onto some local road in Passaic County, at a construction site near a town that sounded like Haskell Falls."

Thus, out of Vincent's jurisdiction.

The lieutenant leaned back, shook his head as if willing the event away. "Shit."

"There's more. Hannah insists Norm was murdered."

Vincent returned a police look. "Is that why you're here? You believe that?"

He paused, but Gary remained still. Vincent was average height, muscular from the waist up, built like a fireplug. His ears stuck out and his hair was graying. Blinking buttons on the phone console caught Gary's attention.

When he didn't respond, the lieutenant went on. "Didn't Hannah tell you the investigating officer ruled the crash an accident?" He spoke as if that conclusion made it so. "Bereaved families often claim foul play. Do you know *why* she says Norm was murdered? She have anything to back that up?"

The frozen viewpoint irritated Gary, but there was no point in saying so when he wanted to achieve something. "She's in shock, Vinnie, but she asked for my help. So I'll help."

The man waved dismissively. "What can you do?"

"I'll speak with Hannah. If she has anything solid, I'll get back to you." He held up a hand for attention before Vincent could interrupt. "There's more. A few minutes after seven this morning, when I was out collecting the paper, Norm stopped at the curb and motioned me into his car."

"In the snow on his way to work?" The lieutenant leaned forward and rubbed his chin.

"Yeah. Norm never did that before. He waves, he doesn't stop. But he had a reason. He mentioned a situation at his company, and said—this is a quote—'They'll probably kill the messenger.' Meaning him."

That got Vincent's attention. "Describe the conversation."

Gary shook his head, remembering. "Norm lowered his window and asked me to get in. I was in a robe, for God's sake."

"That ratty maroon thing?"

"Yeah. I told him I wasn't going to work with him. He said, 'Get in just for a minute.' I closed the door, tried to hold my robe together, turned to him, and he told me I needed a shave and did I know I was wearing flip-flops in the snow. Even that early in the morning he was True Norm."

"Flip-flops?" Vincent asked.

"Well, yeah. I was only bringing in the paper. He said, 'Sarah would never have let you out like that.'" Gary saw Vincent's expression. "He was right, I know. Don't you get on my case. Oh, God, don't tell Angela. I found my boots, really."

"You telling me Norm didn't dump on you for that shearing you got?" The lieutenant waved toward Gary's hair. "It looks like you cut it yourself."

He had cut his own graying hair, using scissors and a clipper. It was easier to manage. He could use his hand as a comb—and who gave a damn how he looked? "Maybe Norm got used to it, waving to me every morning last week. You beating up on me again?"

"You won't visit, you're losing weight, you bite your nails—you never did that before—and your ambition left with Sarah. You drinking?"

"No, I'm not. But I do talk to myself a lot."

Vincent offered a flat smile. "What is it you want for yourself, Gary? You're too young to give up."

"What's got you pissed?"

"This isn't about me," the lieutenant said.

"Me neither," Gary fired back. "Let's deal with Norm's death. Can I finish?" So many strangers he'd helped for money—this time, he needed to help a friend.

Vincent looked like he'd been slapped. "You're irritable. You're beginning to fit a profile."

"Okay, what I want is to look into Norm's death. As far as I can take it, whichever way it goes." He toyed with the coat's zipper. "That'll make you happy—it'll give me something to do."

Vincent considered, and nodded. "Why not? We can call you the Thin Man." He sat back and laid his hands on his thighs, though they looked uncomfortable at rest. "Go on, tell me what happened."

"Vinnie, Norm was vague. He said he'd only stopped because Hannah asked him to. I asked who was going to kill him and why. He said we should meet when he got home." A noise from out in the hallway distracted Gary.

"What else?"

He shook his head again. "I told him we could meet wherever

17

he wanted, but only if Hannah was with us to translate his tech-speak."

Vincent frowned; the hands slid to his knees as he leaned forward. "You know she knows nothin' at all about that stuff."

An angry conversation in the corridor filtered through the door. They stopped talking and listened while it came closer. "You *can't* bring him in," they heard—and abruptly the voices stilled. In a bit, Gary went on.

"Yeah, but I was zapping him for the flip-flop comment. I get enough grief from Sarah in my dreams. Gotta hand it to Norm. He laughed, said okay, why not make it a social occasion."

Vincent rubbed his left eye like there was something in it. "Bet you didn't give up."

"Hell, no. I asked him if he was serious about a death threat, or just venting."

"And he said?"

"He was serious, though he hadn't been threatened. That's when I guessed what must be bothering him, and suggested he take a snow day."

The lieutenant tilted his head the way Gary knew he did when he sensed trouble. His ears looked like wings. "Oh?"

"Only a guess. Norm was an internal auditor for Consolidated Brokerage, so I figure he stumbled across something illegal." Gary gripped the chair and bent closer. "He was worried and wanted to talk, but not then. You know Norm. Work comes—came—first."

Vincent's brow furrowed. He surprised Gary by not asking about death or theft, and when he spoke, his voice had grown deeper. "Consolidated Brokerage?"

"Yeah."

The lieutenant looked right at him. "You could've let me know this by phone. Why'd you come here?"

Gary smiled. "I walk into another police station, they don't know me. Be good if you could arrange for me to speak with the officer looking into Norm's crash, and have him tell me more than he's sorry, it was an accident."

There was no need to talk about his interview with the crash witness. Vincent's involvement in that would depend on whether anything surfaced worth mentioning.

The lieutenant tented his fingers and looked down at them.

Gary sat back and glanced around the vault. Two gray metal, four-drawer file cabinets stood to the left of the desk. The office was all work and no play, except for the screen-saver and three framed photos of Angela and Vincent, somewhere on vacation, above the files.

He turned back when Vincent spoke.

"I'll do that for you, if you'll meet a man for me."

That touched a nerve: his friend had been trying to get him involved for months. "Does it relate?"

"It might."

"How?"

Vincent sighed, and his fingers separated. "Our parents pushed our carriages together, that's how long I've known Merle. You know how we all have one really successful friend? He's mine. Merle Kingsley got to be president of a major company." The lieutenant leaned closer. "Lest you think this is BS, guess which company he headed."

The first choice was easy, probably wrong, but Gary offered it up with a shrug. "Consolidated Brokerage."

"You always know."

Well, now. "He still there?"

"Naa. He retired a year ago with a good reputation and lotsa bucks. Even got the board to promote his guy, Morgan Westbrook, into the top slot. I'll bet Merle can help you with questions about Norm and the company."

What did that mean? "Why do you *really* want me to meet him?"

His friend squirmed in the chair. "I think you can help him, too."

"I was a crisis consultant. If your friend has problems, he should go to the police, a private detective, a shrink, or a gun dealer." But then, Vincent *was* the police.

"Always the logical one."

Gary didn't reply, because he knew how random life could be.

"Merle has hired a PI, a good one," the lieutenant said, and Gary blinked and focused.

"For what?"

"He won't say." Vincent's hands came out, palms up. "Made a joke about it when I asked. Maybe 'cause I'm a cop."

"You have a guess why the PI?"

"Probably some financial decision he made years ago. They're charging corporate leaders with crimes these days—convicting them, too."

"Then he'd need an attorney, not a PI." He felt like he was back at work, wanted a forbidden martini, dryer the better, olives, onions, didn't matter.

The lieutenant frowned, and for a moment Gary feared his martini wish had gone public. But Vincent said, "Maybe he has an attorney."

"Are you sure this isn't one more neighborhood help-Gary project?"

Vincent laughed. "I don't arrange blind dates. That's Angela's job. We got chicken with mushrooms tonight. You like that. Just the three of us. Pasta, any kind you want. Come on over."

Gary didn't want to mention his own date—it would just fuel Vincent's speculation, and Angela would be all over him. "Don't bullshit me."

That didn't get his friend's back up. "You were good at helping clients while … you worked."

Gary heard Vincent's tap-dancing to avoid saying "while Sarah was alive." He'd left his practice, retired to be with her during the final months.

The lieutenant added, "I do know a bit more."

"Also related, huh?"

"Not a word to anyone, especially Merle, that I'm tellin' you this."

"You didn't need to say that."

"I know, but this is serious to me." His eyes flicked, as if checking that no one else was within earshot, and he lowered his voice. "Merle asked if I knew anyone who was good at working through situations."

"Situations?"

"Draw your own conclusion." His hands shifted to the armrests, tapped at them. "And he gave me an envelope. He said I'm to open it if he dies. We all die, but most of us leave important stuff in a bank vault, not a police station." Vincent squirmed again. "Now you know what I know."

"For all you know, the envelope might hold his will."

"Whatever it holds doesn't matter. I want you to meet him."

Gary felt the cop stare. "I'm retired." That came out weaker than he'd intended.

The lieutenant sat back. This interrogation was over, and Gary wondered how many years he'd serve.

"But you want to help Hannah," Vincent said. "Gary, I understand how you dig into a situation. I can't see you offering Merle more than guidance, and there's probably nothing to your Norm-was-murdered concern. But just in case you wind up playing with fire, I don't want to find *you* on a slab."

Gary had seen Vincent-The-Lieutenant before, but never like this.

"You keep me informed. If I say back off, you do that." Vincent found those words inadequate. "Are we agreed?"

Gary nodded.

"Now, you wanna meet that officer, or not?"

~3~
12:30 P.M.

"WALK through the food court, turn left into the first corridor, and it will be on your right," Vincent had said when he arranged Gary's lunch with Merle Kingsley. Gary checked again: Smithie's Ale House.

Fascinating. It was not what he expected in a shopping mall. The dark-stained wooden door was strapped with black iron hinges and rested in a stone surround that rose into a graceful arch above his head.

As he admired the effect, the door opened with a deep growl, and two middle-aged men emerged. One sported a beer belly, and both wore black trousers and matching T-shirts from a Toyota dealership.

When he pulled on the bulky handle, the door opened easily. The giddy brightness, canned music, and metallic air of the regional mall faded behind him.

He stopped, blinded by darkness, the air he'd let in replaced by a chill beyond shopper comfort. He caught a pleasant bouquet of beer and grilled meat. Subdued conversations, clinks of glass and silverware, came from everywhere.

Once his eyes adjusted, he found a long wooden bar to his left. It either was an import from Edinburgh or made to look it. The mirror behind the bar was cloudy; in the gloom, customers on the stools looked as if they were sketched in charcoal. The walls were dark, right up to the black ceiling. He found the setting agreeable.

He passed the bar and reached the restaurant behind it, seven high-backed booths laid out four to the right, three to the left. It was darker and quieter here. The exit sign flickered.

His destination was the last booth to the right. A man was waiting, facing him. Gary slid onto the unoccupied bench. "Merle Kingsley?"

The man nodded; light glinted off his glasses but he was sitting in shadow, folded into the gloom.

The end booth offered Gary a view of a dark-paneled wall broken by grainy old photos of men in kilts. "Interesting place," he said.

Kingsley was staring. To give him time, Gary lifted the menu. He could barely read it. It must be the lack of light. He wasn't prepared to need reading glasses for menus.

"I lose anyone following me," the man finally said, "and choose a convenient meeting place where I'm least expected."

Gary held up his left hand. He had to start somewhere. "Where *would* they expect you to be?"

Kingsley shifted to his right on the bench and leaned closer, emerging from the shadows. "Somewhere more upscale." Said flatly, not to impress.

He was casually dressed but something, his haircut or thick glasses or natural manner, suggested privilege. Short and slight, Kingsley had lively dark eyes, close-cropped brown hair that might have been dyed, an ageless face, and a body that looked well exercised.

"Do you know who's following you?" Gary set the menu down.

"No comment."

"... Why do you consider this place convenient?"

"It's attached to a crowded mall with parking on three sides—three ways to get out, and two major intersecting highways."

"You have experience shaking tails?"

Kingsley pushed his menu aside without taking eyes off Gary. "I've gotten advice."

That must be the private detective Vincent had mentioned. "You sure you're being followed?"

"Order the hamburger deluxe, any way you want it."

He caught the man's drift and waited for the waitress.

The woman who appeared looked as if she belonged in a performance of Brigadoon. She wore a small plaid hat and a matching tartan dress in a red, black, and green pattern. The bodice was low-cut, and the dress ended in a short, flared skirt. But the costume hung on her. Even the high tartan socks drooped. The outfit was meant for another woman.

She took their orders indifferently and left.

"They aren't always subtle," Kingsley said in answer to Gary's question.

"What have you done to bring this on yourself?" He leaned forward, hands flat on the table, trying to read the man.

Kingsley grinned. "I like that. You didn't ask if I was making it up or push to learn what I won't tell you."

"So what have you done, which will suggest what I might do for you?"

"Ah." The small man wrapped his hands around his water glass. It was wet with condensation. He made patterns on it before he looked up. "Do you carry a gun?"

"No."

"That doesn't matter." He dropped his eyes and shook his head, but his fingers still worked the glass; obviously, the gun did matter. "Vincent says you keep secrets," he said, and waited until it became clear Gary would not respond. "You're not an attorney or a PI. I have no immunity here."

"Then let's go dutch-treat on the burgers."

That took Kingsley aback. He recovered and grinned, looking like a wolf in the shadows. "You've done this before."

"Vincent must have briefed you."

"He said you'd been pining for your dead wife and doing pretty much nothing else for a year."

Gary went cold. Why would Kingsley throw that at him? Probably, to force a reaction. He didn't reach across and punch the little man. Instead, it was his turn to grin. "Does that change whatever you might want me to do?"

The small man nodded, his expression impassive. "I lost a wife, too."

"To cancer?"

"To another man. She said I was a bigamist, that I'd married the business." Without waiting for Gary's reaction, his hands came off the glass and he leaned closer. "I can tell you this. The statute of limitations has passed. Back when I was a junior everything, my family needed serious emergency money. It was a health crisis for the son of my younger brother. I was always the go-to guy in my family, the achiever with the odd name. So ...."

He paused again, slid his water glass to the side, and, predictably, the waitress appeared with their orders. She brought large portions with good smells.

"Need ketchup?" she asked. Kingsley nodded. She gathered a bottle from the next table, slapped it down in front of them, and ambled off, but neither of them paid attention to her or the food.

"You know, after thinking about this for years, I'm not certain whether my brother asked for my help or I just bolted into action." Kingsley had lowered his voice. "I arranged a meeting with—well, all you need know is it was a criminal group—and helped them electronically raid unclaimed funds that would otherwise have gone to the State of Virginia. I felt it would be as victimless a crime as possible."

When he hesitated, Gary prompted: "They own you after that?"

But Kingsley was far away. "What value would it be in court that I meant to be honest, that my personal gain—which went to save my nephew, married now with two kids of his own—was limited to one early episode? That I demanded integrity from everyone I've ever worked with?"

"You can't be tried for that today." That dip into the dark side was not why this man was being menaced.

Kingsley sat back and smiled, but didn't reply.

So Gary asked directly, "What have you done for the criminals lately?"

The man's smile widened, as if he was pleased by what he'd heard. "Very little. Enough to keep me a plus in their ledger. I walked a fine line."

That was enough chatter for Gary. He was tired of being led by the nose. "Was that fine line easier for you after your wife left?"

Kingsley nodded.

"So you provided the crooks with the power of your good name, like introductions and referrals, rather than direct opportunity to steal from your company."

The man's surprise flickered briefly. "How do I get free of them?"

"You walking that fine line again?" Gary asked. "With them menacing you when you wander about because they won't find you at the office and you have protection at home?"

"Did you write their script?" He gripped the table edge, irritated.

Hunched like that, he looked even smaller.

"You thought retiring would free you?"

"Of course."

"So now you have no wife, no kids, no job, lots of money for protection, and their only leverage is to retire you underground if you don't comply. What do they care? That might be better for them, you not being able to tell anyone where the sleepers lie."

Kingsley glared, but didn't respond other than by sliding his knife and fork aimlessly. The pause lengthened, and he sat back.

Another connection snuck up on Gary, and he voiced it. "You must have it all hidden away for the authorities if you turn up dead. Or vanish. That could make the crooks cut you some slack."

Kingsley's expression calmed. Again, his fingertips stroked the sides of his glass.

Gary bet Vincent's envelope was not a will. "Vincent said you might be helpful regarding the death of my friend. He was an auditor with Consolidated Brokerage. He died this morning in an auto crash the police say was an accident."

Kingsley exhibited no surprise. Vincent must have told him. "I'll set up a meeting between you and Riddock Maguire. He'll explain things."

"He your private detective?"

Kingsley reached for the ketchup, played with it like the glass. "Yeah. You'll retain him. I'll pay in your name."

"So what we say through him will be legally privileged?"

The little man nodded.

"And he'll carry the gun for both of us?"

Kingsley smiled painfully. When he spoke, Gary had to lean forward to hear. "Years ago, I told a friend in the company what was going on. He was a bright guy, and I thought he'd be able to help. Whatever it was he did, I never knew. Two days after we had our heart-to-heart, he died in an auto accident. They never said anything. They didn't have to."

So Norm wasn't the first.

Kingsley set the bottle down with a thump that rattled the silverware. "You better not take getting involved in this lightly. If they see you with me, you're in the cross hairs. You have enough invested in this to risk getting killed?"

While Gary considered that, the little man pursed his lips. "There are many bad reasons to die. Better we get to pick a good one."

The comment triggered Gary's memories of Sarah, how her void had almost become his reason. *Friends help friends.* Everyone was pushing him into this. Was there a purpose he didn't grasp? The man across the table was waiting.

"If they've begun harassing you, what is it they want you to do?" Gary asked.

Kingsley acknowledged the decision with a nod. "They aren't asking much. It's just that I need to be finished with them, which they won't accept." He was about to continue. Instead, he pursed his lips again. "Ask Riddock."

"Do the people following you know about him?"

"I can't be sure." The little man frowned. "He's often with me, including times when we've been followed, so probably yes."

Gary felt uneasy. "They have no reason to bother him as long as you're compliant. If they learn he's close to you and need to impress you again, he's how they would do it."

"You read too many mystery books."

"Think I'm wrong?"

Kingsley returned to his water glass, masking concern.

"After I meet with Riddock, will I see you again?"

"Work through him. He'll update me." The man's hands continued stroking the glass, but he looked up. "And Gary ...."

Kingsley had used his name for emphasis. "Yeah?"

"There are things Vincent knows, things he doesn't. Most, he doesn't. So let's not put me on his radar. Nothing goes back unless I clear it. Can we do that?"

What had he gotten into? He could say no thanks, right now, and end it. But he owed Norm and Hannah, and Vincent, and he was growing curious. "Okay."

Time to eat. He lifted the top of the bun to add on pickle and onion. He hesitated, glanced at Kingsley, and then piled on the onions. Ketchup would wait until his companion had used it. The steak fries looked delicious.

Across the table, the little man glanced at his food, and then back. "I expect to pay you for your involvement."

"I'm doing Vincent a favor. You may never benefit." What would the PI have to add? This had a déjà vu feel. He'd often been asked for help by people unwilling to come clean about what they faced or how they'd caused it.

"You're a crisis consultant," Kingsley said. "Charge me what you feel you're worth, and pass your bills to Riddock. That avoids mail tampering. I don't want my crisis to reach the media." With that, he squeezed a waterfall of ketchup onto his burger. "Or the law."

On the way to the second meeting Vincent had arranged, Gary laughed because he was checking to see if he was being followed.

Had his gloomy year at home just ended?

One thing he did know: he looked forward to the interview with Natalie Strassberg. He glanced in the rear-view mirror. Next time, he'd have his hair cut by a professional.

~4~
3:00 P.M.

T HE police station was nothing like Vincent's. Sergeant Hermann Schroder's office was somewhere in a wing tacked on to a multi-purpose municipal building that included town hall and a senior citizen's center. There were 566 municipalities in New Jersey. There must be incredible diversity, Gary figured, in everything municipal, except for annual tax increases.

"It was easy to see what happened," the beefy sergeant said to Gary yet again.

He listened from a bench along a wall in a small reception area; it was clear he wasn't getting beyond it. He felt the same discomfort he'd had at Vincent's station—some ingrained need not to call attention to himself. Once, he'd considered his profession the reason for the reaction.

A duty officer sat ten feet away behind the counter, shuffling paperwork, ignoring them. Schroder was standing in front of him as if pleased not to have to sit. Another uniformed officer pushed open the outside door and let in a burst of cold air. The thin, blonde patrol officer wore all the paraphernalia and clanked when she moved, belt heavy with gear.

Schroder turned, nodded, then looked down and continued. "The only witness confirmed it. Combine ice, a curve, a weak barrier, a large SUV that slips out of lane, and it's a shame that little car was where it was when it was."

Gary would not get more from him: the policeman's position hardened every time he was led back over it. But he was unwilling

29

to leave with nothing gained. There was always something, he used to tell himself. For months he'd wandered about his house and felt tired, trapped in the past, sure he'd lost his edge. Now he needed it.

"Hermann"—he and the Sergeant were on a first-name basis by then—"I'd consider it a favor if you'd recap your investigation for me."

Schroder was about to resist when, as Gary hoped, the officer remembered why he was there.

"Lieutenant Alegretti said to give you what you want. So yeah, okay, but I'll be brief. The car was checked. It appeared functional, so it probably wasn't mechanical failure caused it to swerve. They didn't find automotive paint scraped onto it. The coroner doesn't have test results yet. We'll fill in the lieutenant when we know more. The widow told me their marriage was solid. They're Jewish. I called their rabbi. He said they seemed happy. He wasn't aware of unusual stress in the relationship. He has a network, he said, and he'd have heard such things."

The tone changed from monologue to conversation. "Alegretti said you know them—knew the vic. You agree with what the widow and rabbi told me?"

Gary nodded, and unzipped his coat. The smell of frying onions wafted in from somewhere, and made him hungry again.

"The vic's employer—or a woman in its human resources department—told me the company was happy with him." The officer shifted weight from one leg to the other. "Said his job was secure. She offered performance reviews, notes, reports, anything we want. Not every company volunteers that stuff."

Schroder scratched at his forehead, combed back his dark hair with his fingers, and rubbed his fleshy nose. "Then, as I said, the weather was lousy. That curve is unsafe in snow, and the temporary barrier was damned poor." He caught himself and glanced around, hoping he hadn't been overheard. "Forget I said the barrier thing."

Gary waited.

Schroder sighed. "There were no skid marks to measure. Traffic ran over the accident site before we got there, mashed the snow on the ground, and jumbled everything. We took photos, but there was nothing left of significance except the broken barrier. We interviewed a witness who saw what took place. She couldn't identify the SUV or see its license. It was probably covered with snow. She described the scene, and insisted no other vehicle was close to the green Toyota that went off the road, or to the SUV she claims bumped it, or to her own Chevy. So it's doubtful there's another witness."

Gary recalled his final session in the green Toyota and framed questions about the accident for Natalie Strassberg. He wanted to ask her other questions, too.

The officer went on: "She said she'd been behind the Toyota for a mile at least, and it was driving safely in the right lane. Toyota wasn't the problem. The big guy—she says he had dark-tinted windows—strayed into it on the curve. After the car went over the edge, the truck kept going. Driver probably didn't even know he'd made contact. Couldn't have been too hard a push, if there was no paint transfer. Maybe it didn't have to be hard, with all that snow on the road. You're startled, jerk the wheel, skid, it's over in seconds."

Still, Gary watched him. At least the odor of food had faded.

The sergeant raked hair off his forehead. It was a losing battle. Each time he raised his right arm, the motion pulled a little more of his shirt out from under the belt. "I debated whether to wait on the shoulder of the road before the next exit—24/168 it's called, same time next day and week—to watch for black SUVs and stop other vehicles to seek out witnesses. We do that when the incident involves a fatality. But there are so many black vehicles, and on a dark morning, especially with snow, green and blue ones look black."

Schroder peered down at him. "Does this sound reasonable?"

Gary nodded.

A patrolman entered the room from the rear, leaned against the counter by the duty officer. "See that *Law and Order* last night?"

The man behind the counter looked up, happy for the break. "Which one?"

Their conversation distracted Schroder. His body didn't move, but his head swiveled.

"Sleazy defense attorney," the leaning officer said.

The sergeant waved at them. "Guys …."

"Sure," said the talker. As he vanished the way he'd come, he threw back, "They're all sleazy."

31

Schroder frowned and concentrated, as if he had to recapture where he'd left off. "If the truck driver had an inkling of what he'd done and didn't stop, he—or she—is gonna give the section of road a wide berth for a long time. No point checking auto repair shops. So much snow, everyone's gotten dinged. I-287's a major artery. We get commuters from New York, Pennsylvania, and Delaware." He shook his head. "Even Connecticut. And we don't know what we're looking for. *Maybe* a black SUV? Come on." Again he stared at Gary. "You agree?"

"Yeah," he said, for lack of anything else.

The sergeant seemed satisfied. "That's what the Great State Of pays me to do. I wouldn't want you or the lieutenant to be unhappy." He was wrapping up.

"Hermann, step back from the accident. Were there any other odd circumstances about this incident? Before, or after?"

Schroder's brow knitted as if he did remember something. "Well, the car landed mostly on its roof. They say those are safe little cars, but no car is designed to stand up to a drop that far. The victim—"

"I don't need to know that. Did the car catch fire?"

"No—right! *This* was strange." The sergeant leaned forward, threw a foot up onto the bench beside Gary, and bent conspiratorially. "Late this morning, a visitor from the vic's company asked that same question. Then he wanted to see the contents of the guy's briefcase. Visitor's a company officer. Said the driver worked for him, and he wanted to make sure no confidential stuff was in there."

Intrigued, Gary leaned closer, and lowered his voice. "You show him?"

"Sure did. Those papers are in the accident file. Wouldn't turn 'em over. They go to the widow. But I broke out the file and let him flip through what was in the briefcase." Schroder paused, then added, "I watched him."

Gary understood: the sergeant was confirming, through Gary but for the lieutenant, that the visitor took nothing from the file.

Schroder turned his palms up, revealing rough, cracked skin, and shrugged. "Papers were computer printouts. Columns of figures. I haven't a clue what that stuff means. Only geeks can decipher it." He put his foot back down, wanting to be done.

"What'd the visitor say?" Gary asked.

"No problem. That's what he said, 'no problem,' those papers weren't important. He said the driver wasn't supposed to carry confidential work home anyway."

Logical so far. "Why'd you say 'strange'?"

Schroder did not like to be prodded. "Just after 12:30 today, Consolidated called again. Either they're confused or really efficient. An assistant with a youthful voice, and quite an accent, said he was writing up a report of the first guy's visit. He asked me to restate what the exec had found. I told him."

"Accent?"

"Russian, maybe." The sergeant hiked his trousers and tucked the shirt.

Gary found it strange that someone else wanted to learn what the visitor had discovered, but without asking. Maybe the caller was with the company, maybe with the crooks. If there were crooks.

"You get the caller's name?" he asked.

"'Fraid not. Other things were going on."

The possibility he'd missed a useful detail worked at Schroder. He squinted. "The widow claimed the vic was onto some crime at work, that we were wrong and the crash wasn't an accident." He emphasized the word 'wrong.' "I asked if she had proof. She didn't."

The officer's voice softened. "I took her seriously, asked several questions and repeated a few when she seemed confused. She'd had quite a shock, I know. If she'd come up with even one good reason. She mentioned printout pages. If she meant the papers in the briefcase, she'll get 'em back. She sounded stressed, but okay. It's just she wouldn't believe the evidence."

Schroder's expression dared Gary to disagree. "You got any reason the crash wasn't an accident?" His hands went to his hips, palms back, flattening the bloused shirt.

Here, Gary knew, was where it got dicey. "Fresh angles, but no hard facts."

"Give," Schroder said. "I thought the lieutenant sent you for a reason."

Gary sat back, putting space between them, and described his early-morning meeting in Norm's car. Then, without mentioning

Kingsley, he suggested other Consolidated executives might have been killed in the past, in what had been ruled auto accidents.

Schroder's eyes frosted. "You know that because …?"

Gary shrugged. If he hadn't arrived under Vincent's umbrella, he might have been in trouble.

Schroder moved his lips in irritation but nodded. "Interesting. Thank the lieutenant. Tell him I'll be in touch." He thought of something else. "You'll be around if we need you?"

"I'm Vincent's friend and neighbor. Yeah, I'll be around. You'll—"

"Told you I was interested."

"One final question, Hermann." That stopped Schroder before he turned away, though his impatience showed. "What was your visitor's name?"

The sergeant considered, held up a finger for Gary to wait, went behind the reception desk, and returned with a binder log. He sat beside Gary on the bench, opened the book in his lap, and flipped pages.

Morgan Westbrook, Gary expected. That was the only Consolidated name he knew beside Norm's.

"Arman Pavlic," said Schroder, pointing at the sign-in listing.

Vice President, Safety and Security, Gary read.

~5~
8:00 P.M.

GARY got to the diner early, hoping she'd show. He'd changed into grey slacks, a white shirt, and a black crew-neck sweater with blocks of color. He'd even used conditioner on his hair—it'd been so long, he'd had to root around in the cabinet to find it. He asked the hostess for a table with privacy and stood off to the side where he could watch the entrance.

Natalie Strassberg arrived promptly on the hour, in her blue coat. She acknowledged him with a nod barely short of formal, and they were led to a table in the back room. The snow had paused, replaced by arctic air while a next storm blew in from the Northwest. On that Tuesday evening, the place was not crowded.

The owners had spared no expense to make the back room comfortable and upscale. No glass, bright fluorescent, chrome, and laminate ingredients; it featured hardwood flooring, dark paneling, art deco light fixtures, real wooden tables—larger, to attract families, with padded seats, and draperies framing the windows.

The picture windows offered fine views of yet another highway. Outside, clouds hid the stars and whatever phase of the moon. Red taillights flicked like fireflies, constantly in motion. He believed a highway view was central to the New Jersey diner experience, the sine qua non even in the elegant dining room.

Once the waitress walked off with their orders, his guest avoided social chitchat. "Shall I describe the accident?"

"Uh, yeah, please. Everything you remember."

She started, then stopped. "This is difficult for me, even with …."

35

She was tugging at her linen napkin much as she had worked the gloves earlier. "I saw a man die this morning." She paused again, and decided what it was that she had to tell him. "I've seen death and suffering professionally, and ...."

When she hesitated, without meaning to, he said, "Personally?"

"Yes. You can't be a good nurse without learning to separate your emotions from what's happening, what you need to do."

So that's why she'd alerted the police and returned to be interviewed after the accident. He said nothing.

"That's why I'm not all weepy. I'm upset. I feel terrible for the poor man and his widow." She breathed in. "But it's not my way to fall apart. I hope you understand."

She looked at him with sorrow and determination—one tough lady, a study in contradictions. She had been honest and probably conveyed more than she intended. She expected a reply.

"Thank you," he said.

She accepted his comment, and leaned toward him as if the two words had freed her to talk. She rested her hands on the table, holding her left in her right in a natural way that covered her ring.

"It was windy and snowing this morning, at least it was on 287. My Chevy usually handles well in snow, and I was doing fine. The Toyota, the truck, and my car had headlights on, because the cloud cover kept it dark."

She paused to smooth her napkin and put it on her lap. She used the pause to collect her thoughts. "I wouldn't have noticed anything, except the little Toyota was driving slowly in the right lane in front of me, and the black SUV was close behind it in the left lane." She had spoken at the tablecloth. When she reached her point, she looked up. "They were too close to one another for me to pass. They drove so slowly that I wanted to." She twisted the wedding ring. "I watched because I was getting annoyed."

Without needing to prod, Gary looked at her. Still in a ponytail, her auburn hair lightly sprinkled with gray. It suited her complexion. She had not covered the scattering of freckles around her eyes with what little makeup she wore. Her eyes almost matched her hair, with flecks of green. Little lines at her mouth in search of direction. She wore a thick maroon sweater that fell to her waist. Her jewelry consisted of the wedding ring and a thin gold chain around her neck.

When he didn't speak, she continued: "I was heading home from a double shift, helping a friend. I don't do that often, and I was really tired. I didn't tell the police about being tired or wanting to pass. Was that wrong?"

He held up a hand. Something bothered him. "The hospital's here. Your home isn't, not if you were on I-287 and witnessed Norm's accident. How come, if you were heading home, you showed up at the Lyons' house?"

He earned a frown. "Could you sleep if you'd witnessed that? I tried, but I just tossed. So I gave up, dressed, and headed back to the hospital. I needed to be busy." She raised her water glass but set it right down. "Before I left, I thought maybe I could be helpful to the poor man's family. The policeman had mentioned his name and town. The Lyons' are in the phone book. When I stopped there, I met you."

He nodded and went back to what she'd asked him. "Would it have made a difference if you'd told the police you wanted to pass?"

"I doubt it." She finally sipped the water.

He resisted staring but he'd forgotten his questions. "Please go on."

"Before the highway curved, the truck pulled forward. Finally, I thought. That's when I really focused. After the SUV passed the Toyota, I'd be able to get around it. But it swerved to the right instead and pushed into the side of the car. It didn't pull back."

Her brow furrowed at the memory. Distracted, she wiped wet fingers on her napkin. "The driver had to know he'd hit that car. But he kept pushing. He forced the Toyota to the edge. They both braked. I told that to the police. I braked, too, or I'd have hit them. The Toyota went right through the construction barrier and over the edge. It … vanished." She shook her head. "That truck driver was negligent. His vehicle was so much larger than the little car."

She stepped back from her narrative by taking another sip, then a deep breath. "The truck drove off. I kept going 'cause there was no shoulder. If I'd stopped, the next car along would've piled into me. I got off the highway and called the police."

"You tell them anything beyond what you've told me?" he asked.

Before she replied, she pursed her lips in thought. "They asked whether the Toyota was driving safely, which it was. They also asked whether anyone else could have witnessed the accident. No one else was close. I looked around right away, hoping there'd be a police car. I'd slowed with them, then in alarm, and the truck drove off like I was standing still. I was alone on the road. It was like nothing had happened."

He saw her brief fight for control. She grounded herself with another detail. "Oh, and they asked if I'd seen the license plate. I tried, but it looked black, too dirty to read."

Black? Odd. "Let's stay with the SUV. Anything unusual about it?"

She shuddered at the scene in her head and again scrunched her lips. That scrunch claimed his attention. He forced himself to concentrate on her words.

"Where it hit the Toyota, when it pulled away there seemed to be something protruding, or flapping, from its side."

"Like what?"

She found the image she sought: "Like the welcome mat outside my home. Only black." Her left hand circled the glass.

"Where along the side?"

"It was over the front passenger-side fender. The one that pushed the Toyota. I could see it because I was behind on that side."

"Could it have been damage from the collision?"

She considered briefly, and shook her head.

"Did you tell the police about it?" He was betting that she hadn't. He ran through reasons why what she'd seen might have been there.

The woman hesitated. "No. I didn't think of it. I was stunned. The policeman asking questions sat in my car on that road, in the snow, and lights were flashing everywhere." She sighed. "It was surreal." She grew quiet, and then spoke into the pause. "You're easy to talk to." Her expression might have been a smile if they were speaking of other things.

"I'm not a policeman."

She didn't react to that, but to her own thought: "Why would such a … mat-thing be there?"

They fell silent as the waitress brought them both tuna sandwiches, with hot chocolate for her and coffee for him. Minutes ago, she'd ordered first. He was surprised by his appetite and would have preferred a real meal, but he'd asked for what she was having, except for the coffee. "What? I like tuna," he had said, when she looked at him oddly. "That's not much of a dinner, so you may want to move things along. If so, I won't hold you up."

He must have guessed right, because she'd chuckled. He liked the sound, and what it did to her expression. Now he bet, because of their sudden silence, the two of them wearing wedding rings, the waitress figured they were one more married couple going through a bad patch. Or an affair gone awry.

He watched his guest lift a stuffed half-sandwich with both hands. She had long fingers and was delicate with food. He would get fat quickly eating in diners. Did she diet, like every other woman on the planet?

"Ms. Strassberg, can I share what the family thinks?"

"Of course, but please call me Becca."

How had Natalie become Becca? "Is that because no one else does?"

She fought a laugh. "My middle name's Rebecca. I hate Natalie—no one's gonna call me Nat—so it's Becca." Her expression changed. "Unless you'd be more comfortable with Natalie."

What sensitivity had he triggered? "Becca's fine. Thanks. I'm Gary."

She hesitated before taking the first bite of her sandwich. "Though my daughter, Melanie, doesn't mind being called a man's name." The sandwich did not move.

Had other men fled before the specter of a single mother? She gazed at him, waiting, until the silence almost became embarrassing. But he needed to raise other matters before he broached that subject. "Take a bite and put the tuna down before I tell you the rest."

She looked at him and set it down.

He put a hand on the table and leaned forward so he could speak quietly. "Norm Lyons' widow told me she's certain he was murdered. I don't know why, but I'll find out. If so, what you witnessed might not have been an accident. I was in Norm's car, speaking with him, only this morning ...."

He paused, because he had recalled a large black SUV driving off behind Norm, in what now seemed pursuit.

Seeing his expression, she reached across and placed a hand over his. "How terrible for you."

He'd best not acknowledge how good her touch felt. "I have a friend who's a police lieutenant. Would you tell him this?"

"I guess that would make sense."

"Maybe we can do it over dinner with Vincent and his wife Angela, at their home. She's a good cook. That way it's not a solemn occasion."

He'd spoken without thinking. He did not want to frighten her away, but he was as afraid to take his invitation back as to leave it hanging out there between them.

She hesitated, and withdrew her hand. "Really, how official is this? Are you asking me on a date?"

He sidestepped. "Other than my wife, I haven't asked a woman out in decades. I wouldn't know how."

"Well, you've just done it better than the so-called gentlemen I've met lately." She fussed with her napkin, without looking at it.

"Okay then. I could use a home-cooked meal."

"Don't you cook for yourself?"

"I do take-out." He smiled at her and shook his head. "I'm a pitiful cook."

She chuckled, but she was serious when she asked, "Do you often joke about yourself?"

"Are you always so direct?"

"I am." He knew he'd have to deal with the daughter when she studied her hands, looked up and added, "Ask Melanie."

"May I do that?"

She smiled. It was everything he'd imagined.

"Perhaps." She pushed the sandwich plate inches away, concentrating on him. "You can count on her to answer. She's getting an MS in psych, and she has answers for everything. Now, please answer my question."

He understood funny, serious, whatever, she wanted him to talk about himself. For more than a year, he had been neither funny nor upbeat. This one was easy. "Then no. I haven't had a conversation with anyone Sarah didn't know in a long time. Or a home-cooked meal. Friends ask, and I decline. They want me to meet women."

She looked puzzled. "Don't you date?"

"I haven't been." Let's go somewhere else with this, he thought. "But you have, and judging from your 'so-called gentlemen' comment, not always with great results."

She ignored that and, without hesitation, as if she planned the question, startled him by asking, "What'd you like best about your wife?"

He translated the question into no date until she learned more about him. She must have asked it of other men. Kept it ready, some sort of test. If he wanted to take it to the next level, evasion wouldn't do.

"I found Sarah bright, caring, and fun to be with. And challenging. She wouldn't let me get away with anything." True as that was, why had he said it? "I trusted her. We could be intimate with a glance, a word."

She surprised him again. "You were lucky. I'll bet she could trust you, too."

He realized he'd been holding his breath. The fire in her eyes calmed. Her marriage must have been different from his. "How often have you asked that question?"

She grinned. "About four times."

"Four out of how many?"

"I don't know. We're talking years here." Her right hand toyed with the chain, and she tilted her head as if a thought had come to her. "Why?"

"Am I closer to that date?"

She checked whether he was serious before she smiled. "You could still screw it up."

"You didn't expect honesty when you asked the wife question, did you?"

She bounced it back. "Why were you?"

"You demand it."

"You mean so you can get me on that date?"

That made him feel like an octopus reaching for her in the front seat of a car. He spoke softly. "Because I want honesty from you."

She smiled again and nodded, but she wasn't done. "You answered so easily. I mean about your late wife. How could you? My question surprised you."

"You surprised me because you asked it. Not many people ask that. It's revealing, isn't it?" He held up a hand to still her. "It was easy because I've had lots of time to think about what Sarah and I had, and what I miss, trying to make sense of it."

He watched her shift the plate again, the small movement lending importance to her question: "Do you miss her?"

"Of course. That won't bring her back. I also miss what we had together. Maybe I can find that again. Anyone try to explain such things to you before?"

"The way you expressed it is a first." She raised her cup, sipped hot chocolate, but she was involved in the conversation. Her eyes stayed on him.

"While we're onto tough questions, it's your turn to answer mine," he said.

"What was it?"

"You repressed it? Dating is *that* bad?"

She laughed. She hadn't forgotten.

The waitress, hovering nearby, smiled and turned away.

Becca took a deep breath and wound up for an answer that she, too, must have often considered. "Too many men think dates with a divorced woman—especially a nurse and mother—mean sex. They don't."

He bit back a line about her flashing eyes. Or that he'd forgotten what sex was, which might be funny and had also been true. "Deal."

WEDNESDAY, FEBRUARY 18

~6~
10:30 A.M.

"I'M PLEASED you went to this trouble," Morgan Westbrook said to Sergeant Schroder. The president was in his imposing corner office, sitting behind a stately wooden desk that looked as if it belonged in a cathedral. Its bulk, and the workmanship of its angular planes, conferred power on him, as it once might have endowed God's servants.

"You're pleased I'm here?" the cop asked.

Corporate officers usually weren't when the police appeared unannounced. Schroder had waited less than three minutes at Consolidated Brokerage before an aide led him up an elevator, down a corridor, and into the president's office.

The glossy desktop was bare but for a high-tech phone, a folder filled with papers, and a glass bell enclosing an antique stock-ticker machine, the kind that once spewed paper tape.

Westbrook leaned forward on his elbows and clasped his hands as if he were praying, eyes fixed on his visitor. "If there's anything suspicious about Norman Lyons' death, I'd like the police to get to the bottom of it. We're all disturbed. Are you the officer investigating the accident?"

"I am." The sergeant couldn't resist. "I'm trying to see whether it *was* an accident." Schroder stared back across the desk and knew that Westbrook—tall and thin, with a long face, intense eyes, and a thatch of gray hair that somehow made him look younger—was masking his emotions.

The sergeant pressed his boots into the thick, cream-colored carpeting and wished his station had something like it.

Westbrook parted his hands, and his face registered surprise. "We're relying on you for that determination. If we can help, we will." His probe was gentle. "You must be here to gather additional information."

To Schroder's left, a window wall overlooked more acres than his whole town. An oversized antique globe stood in a corner. Two large photos hung on the interior walls—one of a trading floor packed with crazed, waving people; the other of a stone bull in front of a columned building he assumed was the New York Stock Exchange.

He hadn't called Alegretti or cleared being there with his own boss. There was no reason to, yet. He had only a gut feeling, based on what Gary Kemmerman had told him, and police work wasn't about gut feelings. Once he had gone the extra mile, he'd call the lieutenant.

"I'll get to it and get out of your hair," Schroder said. "I'd like to meet with Lyons' supervisor, a friend of his here, and a few of your old-timers." No point in asking for the volunteered reports that—guaranteed—would show nothing suspicious; the hunch was insufficient for warrants.

"Do you suspect ... foul play?"

The man had a way with words. At least he'd said it conversationally, not in a pulp-fiction rasp. "No. Just doing background checks."

"Why did you ask to meet our associates with seniority?"

Schroder had been briefed that Westbrook was ex-army, served in Vietnam, and was a stand-up guy. "You ever have other executives who died in auto accidents?"

Westbrook didn't hesitate. "Of course. We employ 832 people in New Jersey. We've been here a long time. Like the rest of the population, we've had associates die of heart attacks in and out of our offices, and of cancer. We've suffered a drowning at—"

Schroder held up a hand.

Westbrook got to the point. "I can get you a list of every

Consolidated employee who's died in the past ten years. Name, title, office worked at, place and cause of death. That suffice?"

"Great."

"It'll take a few hours to collect. I can have it emailed."

"Appreciate it." Schroder pushed up, leaned forward, and reached across the desk to hand Westbrook his card.

Westbrook also had to reach to take it. "You still need to speak to our old timers?"

Schroder nodded.

A flash of irritation crossed Westbrook's face but didn't reach his reply. "We can set that up. My office will email the list. Lyons' manager—the man he used to work for—can arrange the personal meetings you want." The president rose from his chair and moved around the desk. Over his shoulder, without slowing, he said, "Whatever else you need, we'll be happy to help."

The sergeant stepped through the door Westbrook held open, and trailed after him down the corridor, wondering why the man hadn't asked to be kept informed. Whether the people Schroder questioned were innocent or guilty, that was the usual parting comment. He'd check the list to confirm if it omitted a fatality. That might be telling, even if they attributed the slip to clerical error.

Three minutes waiting, five minutes with the leader. He'd be out of there soon. He wondered who he was about to meet.

Westbrook was not happy. Better to let Pavlic deal with the policeman. He led Schroder to Pavlic's office, made introductions, and bowed out. The short trip back to his office took longer because he was deep in thought. Before he closed the door behind him, he asked his secretary to hold calls.

It was his third brush with risk this week, and he didn't like it, not for him, not for the company, and not for the Washington-based bank that owned it.

Two days before, on Monday afternoon, Arman's programmer Suresh Rahman had asked for an appointment. Junior programmers almost never sought private meetings with the president. He'd agreed partly because Rahman, along with several others, were his division's answer to the corporate mandate for global diversity in the workforce. Such hires had proven productive, though he had been told Rahman was not among the best.

He'd welcomed the youngster—a thin, pimply boy who needed a haircut and wore an ill-fitting black suit and a shirt with a frayed collar-top. Westbrook had noted this without judgment; he'd once fit that description.

He'd expected Rahman would make some request he could sympathize with, and then pass along to the boy's boss, or to Human Resources. That afternoon, leading-edge clouds had filtered the low sun, and a strange, yellow-tinged haze had suffused the office. The forecast had called for snow overnight, intensifying by morning.

What Rahman said had been upsetting—garbage about not knowing who else to go to, not wanting to speak out of turn or be disloyal. Westbrook had little patience for that crap.

When pressed, Rahman insisted on reading from a piece of paper, to get it right. Westbrook knew the words by heart, because he'd kept that scrap.

"Norman Lyons spoke with Teo Medved before lunch today. They didn't know I was sitting nearby. Arman Pavlic came, and Lyons left. Teo told Arman that Lyons had seen some report. Arman got angry. He said, You fool. You jeopardize millions of dollars by showing him that. You risk everything we've done here."

Rahman's concern, although he didn't actually say so, was that Pavlic had been talking about theft. Westbrook had gotten him to keep the incident to himself. Such words could refer to legitimate activities, and if so, Rahman would be in trouble for speaking out. Besides, if there *had* been a theft, Rahman had better not alert those the company might need to investigate.

When Westbrook thanked Rahman for coming forward and said the company might reward him for his integrity, the boy had come alive, unable to hide his pleasure. So greed had prompted his appearance.

After Rahman left, Westbrook hadn't told Pavlic. The next morning, Lyons had died. And today a police officer, asking pointed questions about Lyons and prior auto fatalities.

We cannot have people looking at the company as if it has

criminal problems. Westbrook knew whom to call. Later, he would learn from Pavlic what the policeman wanted.

"Again we meet," said Arman Pavlic.

Schroder remembered the man from the station. He'd been direct, but somehow ... unctuous. The sergeant had no stomach for small talk. "Did Norman Lyons work for you?"

"He did."

"In layman's terms, what did he do?"

Pavlic's office was half the size of Westbrook's. It had the same view, but Schroder found it devoid of character—no antiques or wood grain, nothing to tie the man to good taste, a successful career, or the touch of a woman.

The desk was black metal, the chairs black leather, the carpet gray, the half-dozen wall photos black-and-white. The photos were different views of the same crumbling industrial building. They might contain a personal ingredient, but if they did it wasn't pretty. Schroder wondered where the ruined building was until he caught a glimpse of the Pulaski Skyway along the edge of a photo.

Were these on Pavlic's wall because he liked dismal, or did he have business in the Meadowlands? The sergeant imagined buried bodies and cut off that line of thought. He glanced across the desk as the man prepared to answer.

Pavlic seemed to find the question funny. "Lyons kept people honest." He looked as if he were happy with the response.

"How so?" Schroder knew his impatience was forcing his words out clipped.

"He audited money flows—revenues, disbursements, investments, account balances." Without looking down, Pavlic squared the small pile of papers on the desktop.

"Did he ever find theft?"

Pavlic's looks and accent seemed Slavic. His eyes were narrowed in a perpetual squint, as if he'd peered too long through binoculars in the sun. Once a military man, Schroder guessed.

He wore a dark gray suit, a gray shirt and an electric-blue tie. He matched his office except for that tie, his gray-blue eyes and blonde hair. When he turned away to replace a folder in a desk drawer, the sergeant saw an ugly scar running across the back of his neck.

"Of course," Pavlic answered. "Stupid people try to steal. Small time. We prosecute. We praise Lyons in our newsletter. Show others crime does not pay." He offered a wide smile. He'd liked those words, too.

Schroder would remember the generalities he was being fed. No need to take notes. Whether or not Pavlic's reaction fit the situation, it took all kinds. "Was Lyons involved in any current problems?"

"That I asked Monday. The day before his accident. He told me the latest figures—for January—were solid."

"Can anyone confirm that?"

Pavlic smiled at Schroder through hooded eyes. His hands slipped down behind the desk.

Schroder wanted to draw his weapon.

"I do not lie, officer. Lyons and I discuss such matters alone, but there was witness. I will call Teodors Medved."

After Medved had left the office, Pavlic said, "We look for best everywhere in world. That boy is genius, a prize for Consolidated."

"How'd you find him?"

"I bring him, from Latvia."

The awkward youngster had difficulty with English, but he had conveyed to Schroder that he'd been present at the conversation Pavlic described, and that Lyons had responded as Pavlic reported. Further, he had said—if haltingly—that he'd socialized with Lyons, been to his home, met his wife, and the man liked his job.

Schroder wasn't about to play INS agent. The lieutenant would be satisfied with his due diligence. No one would dispute his call. The situation didn't smell right but offered little he could use to move forward. He decided against meeting other employees, at least for the moment. He'd closely check the list of employee deaths, and that should be it. Unless Alegretti came up with something else.

Schroder had trouble smiling at Pavlic, so he didn't try. He stood, wanting to get away from the man. "Thank you," was all he said. He left the building without waiting for an escort, waved to the receptionist as he passed her, and when he breathed the air outside, it may have been too close to the Bayway Refinery, but it smelled very good.

On the way back to the station, Schroder stopped at a Starbucks for coffee. He liked the smell of the place, ordered the java strong, nursed it for hours, didn't mind when it got cold.

"Here you go," said the girl behind the counter, handing him the insulated cup.

She was young and slender, her short brown hair tinged with pink, and she had multiple piercing—several small gold bands through her left ear and one at the outside of her left eyebrow. He wondered if it hurt having that done, wearing those things. Once, he had dated a woman with a nipple ring. She'd had nice breasts, but the metal was unnatural, and had frightened him. He hadn't been able to touch her there, or even ask about it.

The cup felt warm; he could taste it already. He offered the girl a five-dollar bill with his left hand. Then he saw her freeze. Her mouth dropped open. She stared through him, in shock.

From behind him, a voice with an accent screamed, "Give us money!"

He turned, a uniformed police sergeant with coffee in one hand and a five-dollar bill in the other. He faced a tall man and a short man. Both wore ski masks. Both held pistols.

He dropped the cup and reached for his holster.

They shot him six times, point blank.

~7~
12:55 P.M.

MOMENTS after Gary arrived, a FedEx man slid awkwardly into the other side of the booth. He took off his hat, smoothing back his dark hair. "Speedy delivery," he said, smiling across the table.

Gary couldn't recall deliverymen wearing hats. "Riddock?"

"You saw through my disguise."

The PI was taller than Gary and rangy, with wide shoulders, dark curly hair, and eyes that radiated intelligence. The uniform was his only disguise. It was enough. He put the hat on the bench beside him and leaned forward, looking pleased.

Merle Kingsley had asked Gary to return to Smithie's Ale House, and sit in the same seat as he'd been in yesterday. He'd been waved right through when he told a waiter that he was to meet someone in the end booth. Both benches had been empty, but a ketchup-stained plate and utensils lay on one side of the table. The kilted men in the photos needed dusting.

"Kingsley describe me?" he asked the PI.

Riddock nodded toward a table across the room. "I was on that bench when you met him yesterday."

"Didn't see you." Menus leaned against the wall, but he knew what he was going to order. With Sarah, he'd eaten healthy—not since.

"It's a gift. If you passed Merle's muster, I knew we'd meet. Thought you would—I asked our mutual friend about you.

Merle has hired a PI, a good one, he remembered Vincent saying. "You know Lieutenant Alegretti?"

Riddock's eyes crinkled when he smiled. "I've worked with Merle for years, and he and Vincent are very old buddies. The lieutenant and me, we just happened."

Gary knew how carefully Vincent cultivated sources. "Bet Kingsley ate lunch here with you, and left before I was due. He likes burgers. The plate that was just cleared had his ketchup stains. You told the staff you'd be right back, someone was meeting you, so they should leave the booth alone." He watched for a reaction.

"Call him Merle."

Gary leaned toward the FedEx man. "What am I being set up for?"

Riddock put a paper napkin onto his lap before responding. "No setup, it's your choice—but it can be dangerous."

"You carrying?"

The PI shrugged, which Gary took as a yes.

Riddock shifted his frame, and Gary noted the same awkward movement as he'd seen when the man sat down. "I'm ex-FBI. I limp from the wound that retired me. Could've stayed at a desk, but that's not me. Private work was a way to pass time, but then my family got involved. Now it's livelihood for the three of us."

"Family?"

"Brother Everett came first. Then his fiancée, Kathryn. Most of what we do isn't dangerous."

Gary took off his coat and laid it onto the bench to his right. "Until yesterday morning, neither was what I did."

Riddock moved his hands toward Gary, fingers apart. "Your turn."

Until yesterday, the only questions about him had come from the reflection in his bathroom mirror. "I worked in management consulting and public relations. That led to handling crises of all kinds."

"Vincent called you a crisis consultant. What *is* that?"

"Product tampering, oil spills, drug recalls, community resistance—faced with problems, companies hire crisis consultants."

Riddock frowned. "That can't be what you meant by crises of all kinds."

Gary stroked his water glass as Kingsley had done. "A client's life was threatened. He and I were close. I figured his way out. He referred me. Never had to hold a sales meeting after that."

"Sounds like you help worthy people out of desperate jams."

Gary heard the PI's skepticism. "Naa."

Riddock chuckled. "How'd your clients know what you'd do for them?"

"Same way you will." He smiled, and sipped water before he finished. "If not, no charge."

The big man nodded. "Why not get a PI license?"

"I'm not a tough guy."

Riddock's brows knitted, but he let it pass. "Any kids?"

Gary found he could talk about it. "Sarah couldn't."

"You never adopted?"

His hands were at the glass again; this time he realized it and pulled them back. "She wanted to. I never had time." It'd been one of her sorrows. Finally, he'd retired for her, offered himself instead. Guilt he'd carry forever.

The PI nodded as if he'd understood. "Everett and Kathryn are devoted. Madly in love. Maybe it'll happen to me."

He and Sarah had lived what Riddock described. He tried to recall Sarah's face.

"So how can I help you?" The PI's question brought Gary back and, for a moment, confused him. Riddock couldn't help him with this. "Or, how can you help me?" the man went on. "Merle was vague."

"You have a list of the favors Merle's done for those threatening him? I need what relates to Consolidated."

The PI beamed, leaned on an elbow, right hand on his cheek. "This could be the beginning of a beautiful friendship. How might such names be useful?"

"Because I'm separately involved in what I believe is the homicide of a friend—who was an employee of Consolidated."

"A homicide?" Riddock sat up straight.

"Lyons died yesterday morning in a car crash the police say was an accident. Sound familiar?" Again, he watched for a reaction.

The PI's head tilted sideways—Gary noted concern in his eyes, but the big man shifted the subject. "You hungry?"

"You didn't eat with Merle?"

"I waited."

"Like the burgers?"

The FedEx man raised his arm and motioned for the waitress. This time the costume was meant for the woman who took their orders. Gary turned away; cleavage was good, but not while discussing murder, and not when Becca's face flickered into his mind.

Once the waitress left, Riddock caught his eye. "Why do you think your friend was murdered?"

"He asked me into his car yesterday morning, and joked about getting killed. I took him seriously. He didn't."

Riddock sipped water, revealing nothing. "You see the accident report?"

"Better. I got to the investigating officer."

"Learn anything?"

Gary shook his head. "He heard me out, said he'd pursue it further." He took another step in the cat-and-mouse game. "Did you know Lyons' widow insists he was murdered?"

The PI didn't react. Between Kingsley and Vincent, Riddock must have been well briefed. "Maybe she heard what he told you?"

"I'll know later today. There's a gathering at her house." Gary wondered if he'd ask about the gathering—but then, Vincent knew about it.

Riddock licked his lower lip and tilted his head again. "What else do you know?"

He decided to tell him. "I spoke with the crash witness. After I left Lyons' car, I may have seen the black SUV she described. It followed him right from his driveway." He reached for the thick paper napkin and opened it into his lap, but never took his eyes off Riddock, who was staring with a poker face. "That in keeping with the people after Merle?"

The PI nodded, eyes opaque. "How'd you get to her? Vincent arrange that?"

He shook his head. "She visited the widow while I was there. To express condolences."

Riddock also did the napkin thing, concern returned to his expression. "If the criminals suspect she saw anything, the lady may be at risk. They're not nice guys."

The waitress brought food, and left, before Gary spoke. "Could they find her?"

The PI shrugged. "You did."

Gary had been about to describe Becca's recollections: Now he wanted her out of the loop. "She didn't see enough to make a difference. I'll ask her to be careful." He raised the fork, but Riddock wasn't done, so he held it without looking down, and listened.

"How does your friend's death relate to Merle's situation?"

"Lyons audited Consolidated's financials. He may have uncovered theft." Gary held out the hand with the fork to forestall Riddock's comment. "If Merle helped plant a man—that's the kind of thing he told me he did—there may be a connection."

The PI nodded and fussed with his plate. "How would this help Merle?"

Gary put down the fork. "You go first."

Riddock shook his head. "He won't let me shoot anyone."

"You want to?"

"Might work."

Gary glanced at the food, then back. "We need another way. We have an edge with the police. Maybe we can get behind the scenes, manipulate the players and the action, expose them, and get cops to do the heavy lifting."

Instead of words, Riddock responded by starting on his lunch. He used only a little ketchup and he chewed with impatience, thoughts elsewhere. In the semi-darkness, people were eating or talking business—no one paid attention to them. Gary reached for the bottle and joined in, holding the burger in his right hand, picking at onions, pickle, and French fries with the fork, but watching the PI. He finally gave up and focused on the food.

Riddock finished first, wiped his lips with the napkin, and then his fingers. "I'll call you tonight," he said. "After you meet the widow."

"Make it tomorrow. Early as you want."

"A bachelor like you doesn't have a wild night planned?"

Gary smiled. "Tell me, what do the crooks want Merle to do now?"

Riddock looked like he hadn't expected that. "You don't need to know."

Enough cat-and-mouse. "Then I'm gonna finish my burger, walk out of here, and you'll never have to see me again. I'll leave the tip."

"You'd do that?" The PI seemed surprised.

"Leave the tip?"

Riddock couldn't meet his eyes. "Walk away from this."

"You'd do the same in my shoes. I'll bet what you have to say fits what I told you. You really concentrated on that burger."

Riddock nodded, and leaned closer. "It might. They want Merle to recommend their candidate as the company's new director of computer systems—Merle still has clout with Morgan Westbrook, Consolidated's president. The position would be a line function in charge of the financial systems your late friend audited."

It made it more likely Norm had been murdered, and that Merle was somehow linked. "What's the candidate's name?"

"I need Merle's okay to tell you that." He grinned and spoke before Gary could react. "I'll ask, let you know when we speak."

"Any guess *why* they want a new man in?"

Riddock stuck a greasy finger into his water glass and used a corner of the napkin. "You've been busy. I'd hate to see you become a target. You're not connected to the company, so killing you would make no waves."

"Waves?"

Riddock sipped coffee and shrugged. "Years ago, they told Merle that they'd get what they wanted, but with as few waves as possible, because waves draw attention."

Gary filed that. "Maybe we can take this further. Someone at Consolidated may be dipping into the till. Why introduce fresh blood?"

Riddock tossed the napkin onto his plate. "You tell me."

Gary wasn't aware he gripped the fork, swinging it in short arcs. "Backup for the one who engineered the scheme to move on? Replacement for someone they need to get rid of? Taking what they may be doing now to another level?"

He was deep in thought when the PI changed the subject. "You want Merle to ask anything of Westbrook?"

Gary blinked and set down the utensil. "Let's first find out what Norm's widow has to say."

The big man put his right fist in his left hand and worked it nervously, then glanced back at Gary. "There's something else."

"What?"

"I also do work for Consolidated."

"That how Merle found you?"

Riddock leaned back into the shadows. "The other way around. Merle introduced me to Westbrook."

"How'd that work?"

"He was Merle's protégé at Consolidated. They've always been close." The PI put his hands onto the table, palms down. "You'll like him."

"Does Westbrook know about Merle and the crooks?"

"Hell, no. Passing the word would be dangerous."

A thought stopped Gary from reaching for the water glass. "He doesn't know from Merle. But he might from the crooks."

Riddock's face set. "Morgan's a straight arrow."

"You doing anything for him now?"

"No. He phoned for me before lunch. I haven't returned it."

Gary rubbed his chin, glad he'd shaved. "If Westbrook hears Lyon's death is suspicious, would he hire you to look into it?"

"Probably. If he's honest."

Gary shook his head. "He'd do it either way."

Riddock thought through that.

"You have friends in law enforcement?" Gary asked.

"With the FBI, a few assistant prosecutors—that's what they call ADAs in Jersey—and Vincent. Why?"

"May be useful down the road. Let's talk in the morning." He caught Riddock's eye. "Brief Merle and get his okay to tell me what you already know."

The PI nodded, but without the smile Gary expected. "Don't let them discover what you're up to, or your world goes bad fast," he said. "They're like wasps. They'll ignore you until they believe you're threatening their territory."

Riddock left cash on the table. They slid out of the benches and shook hands. Mind idling, Gary walked behind the FedEx man, watching his limp. Riddock turned toward a different exit.

Beyond The Smithie's door, he was hit by a tidal wave of brightness and noise. He blinked and let his eyes adjust before he turned left, back through the food court with its competing smells. The aisles were crowded. When he shouldered open the mall exit and stepped outside, the wind pushed him sideways, and the temperature dropped by forty degrees.

Riddock's wasps were not affected by weather. They were by waves, so Gary needed to make waves.

~8~
2:55 P.M.

A POLICE car sat in front of Gary's house, and as he pulled into the driveway, an officer climbed out and followed him. He was the target, no missing that. He left the tan Infiniti on the asphalt and walked back.

"Officer?"

"Mr. Kemmerman?" She stopped a few paces away, strands of upswept brown hair sneaking out from her cap.

"Yes."

"You're to come with me, sir. Lieutenant Alegretti wants to speak with you."

"Right now?"

"Right now, sir." She smiled, reading his concern. "I'm to bring you back when you're done. Follow me, please."

Vincent was waiting when they got there, and without any greeting led him up the stairs, across the busy second floor, and into his office.

This time there were no bars on the computer screen. The room looked the same as it had yesterday, except for a small aloe plant in a brick-colored pot beside a vacation photo. Angela liked indoor plants. She'd given Sarah a few that hadn't survived.

The lieutenant closed the door. Gary refused to sit, and hung back. "Was all this necessary? In a police car? Least you didn't

58

handcuff me. A simple call and I'd have come in, told you what Schroder told me."

Vincent sank into the same chair he'd used the day before. He looked weary, kept his eyes on the floor. "Hermann Schroder is dead."

"*What?* What happened?" He took an involuntary step closer.

"Why do you always ask me questions?"

Gary waited.

Alegretti shifted something on the small table beside the chairs, and then looked up. "He was at a Starbucks this morning, got shot in an attempted robbery. He was payin' for coffee, for God's sakes. Two men in ski masks demanded money from the cashier. Schroder made a mistake." Vincent paused, and cracked his knuckles, something Gary had never seen him do.

"Mistake?"

"He couldn't have identified them with masks on. Might be alive if he hadn't gone for his weapon. Soon as he reached, they shot him and fled. Wrong place, wrong time."

"When did this happen?"

"I'm told his coffee bill reads 11:27."

Gary walked over and leaned on the back of the chair meant for him, facing his friend. "Schroder's people know where he was before Starbucks?"

Vincent shook his head. "It's not uncommon. He'd report after." He pulled down the knot of his tie—gray suit, maroon tie, clean this time—and opened the top shirt button.

"Where'd it happen?" Gary asked.

The lieutenant rubbed his cheek and frowned. "Somerset County. Not our jurisdiction."

"At which Starbucks?"

Vincent clasped his hands and leaned forward. "You goin' somewhere with this?"

"Got a map?"

The lieutenant resisted, staring forward, sitting motionless, but finally looked toward his desk and nodded. When he pulled one from a drawer and spread it on the desktop, Gary stepped beside him.

The location Vincent pointed out was between the Consolidated office and Schroder's station. Gary unclipped his cell phone, held up a finger for quiet, and speed-dialed a number he'd programmed in years before.

"Consolidated Brokerage," a woman said.

"You the receptionist?" He leaned against the desk, turned away from the lieutenant's glare.

"Among other things. Can I help you?"

"I'm looking for Sergeant Schroder."

"Who?"

"You know, the policeman who was there this morning."

"Oh, he's gone."

"But he met your people, right?" Gary stepped forward, unable not to pace.

"Oh, yes." She sounded very impressed. "With our president."

"When did he leave?"

"Elevenish. I was back from a break. He nodded on his way out. Policemen aren't normal visitors here. Least not in uniform."

"What's your name?" he asked. As he turned away from the door, he saw Vincent had moved into the chair behind the desk, and was watching.

"Abby," the woman said. When he didn't speak, she added, "Abigail Reicher. Can I connect you to anyone?"

"No. Thanks for the help." He flipped the phone closed, lifted one of the chairs, set it in front of the desk and sat facing his friend.

"Yeah, I met Schroder yesterday," he said. "You can guess what he told me. I raised my meet with Norm, and I suggested other Consolidated execs might have died in auto accidents."

"Is that a fact?" The lieutenant's look was similar to the one Schroder had laid on him.

"Um, a guess ... if whatever Norm uncovered was worth killing for, others could've have gotten too close."

"Go on."

"If you hadn't sent me, I'd have been in trouble with Schroder for guessing at the priors. He said that interested him, and I should tell you he'd be in touch. This morning, he visited Consolidated. Met, says a receptionist name of Abigail Reicher, with the company president. Left around 11:00."

Vincent noted the name and time, and stared at the map in front of him again. "Thanks." His head stayed down.

Gary read the lieutenant's grief, and his irritation faded before his friend's distress. He recalled other times. When he'd driven Vincent and his daughter Amy to the hospital after the girl had tumbled down the stairs; he'd insisted on staying with Vinnie—someone had to calm the man down. As if it were yesterday, he saw Vinnie, in uniform, pulled from some ceremony, sitting beside him on the couch, sharing his anguish after Sarah's death.

"This is worse than moving furniture from your bedroom to the basement with our wives supervising, isn't it?" Gary said.

It took a minute, but Vincent lifted his chin, looked across the desk and smiled. "I thought Angela would be a bear, but …."

"It's okay, Vinnie. Gotta admit it, Sarah was wonderful but not easy. Guess I'm into challenging women."

His friend laughed. "I'll tell Angela. Now you're in for it."

Gary imagined his blind date across the table, clad in black leather and twirling a knife. Stress had once gotten to him, sent him to the bottle. Vincent had been on his case back then; their friendship had saved him.

"Sorry I snapped at you before."

"My fault. I shouldn't have pulled you in that way. I was—"

"Upset, I know." He leaned back, draped his arms over the chair. "It's okay. Not been a good week for us."

The lieutenant rose, moved around the desk and sat on it, beside Gary's legs. He tented his fingers and looked down at his friend. "You said Schroder gave you the facts. That should do it for you. Tell Hannah, and be done tilting at windmills."

But Hannah wanted justice, and it seemed Gary was the only one on the trail. "I don't think so," he said, certain that wasn't what Vincent wanted to hear.

The lieutenant glanced sideways at the map. "Y'never told me."

"What?"

"That Schroder said he'd be in touch."

Gary sat up straight. "Senior moment."

Except for a wry look, Vincent chose not to respond; Gary took it as a comment. And looking at the map, repeated to himself, "wrong place, wrong time." Schroder had said almost the same thing about Norm Lyons. "You said attempted robbery?" he asked Vincent.

For a moment, the shift in subject confused the lieutenant. "They demanded money. Figures, after killing a cop, they'd run." Vincent frowned. "You don't agree?"

"No." He gripped the armrests and leaned closer. "Lyons and Schroder died on the way to or from Consolidated Brokerage. Both were looking into crimes at the company. I'll bet they weren't accidents."

Vincent moved back behind his desk, and spoke only after he'd sat down. "And each of them died soon after they talked to you. Another coincidence?"

"Maybe I'd better not talk to you."

~9~
3:00 P.M.

MEGAN Safrian was on break, Becca was not ready to go home, and both nurses stood in the glassed-in corridor connecting Ridgetop Hospital's Six Medford patient floor with the north elevators. The less-trafficked area was a good place to talk. Sunlight streamed through the clouds, and they might have been on a beach except for their clothing, the vinyl floor, and the air-conditioned chill.

"Oh, take a chance." Megan gazed out the window as she spoke. "Go visit the man. Make your condolence calls together." She sipped from a paper cup she'd filled with water.

"If he's like every other man I've met, we'll give each other more trouble than it's worth," Becca said.

It was Wednesday, and she expected to meet Gary for dinner on Friday. Why would she want to see him two days before that? But she did. She was pleased by the advice, and resisted it.

Hospital rooftops stretched below. On lower ledges, four gray-painted air-conditioning units hunched on metal frames set just above the surface. Large and larger air-handler pipes emerged from the machinery and stuck into the buildings like intravenous drips.

Beyond the grounds, a sea of close-packed private homes rolled away up a ridge into the distance. The hospital had been built along one of George Washington's retreat routes. Becca imagined him gazing out at the suburb.

"I know what it is." Megan turned to her. "You're suffering

postpartum blues. Melanie was your world, and she's off to college. Hey, you did a good job. She's a great kid. You can be proud." Becca saw Megan nod with some understanding. "Though I can't imagine what you're going through. My kids are way too young to leave home."

"Single-parent empty-nester syndrome is the pits," Becca said. "When your brood flies, you'll have Max."

"How 'bout you come for dinner next Monday? You cook. Max likes your cooking better than mine, that's no secret. I'll ask him what he wants and buy the food. He can bring the wine. We'll do it after the kids are upstairs. Sound like fun?" She took another sip, and looked to see what was left in the cup.

With Megan and her husband, Becca felt like a third wheel. She didn't want to disappoint, but ... "Rain check? I need a few weeks to really dig into my blues."

Megan chuckled. "You are not old-maid material. There's a Max out there somewhere for you."

This was an old joke. "Just not yours."

"Just not mine." Megan took another sip.

Becca knew that Megan and Max zapped each other, disagreed about little and big things, but looked to one another for compromise and comfort, and laughed at themselves.

It was real, what she wanted, real for some. Could it be real for her?

Megan glanced back down the corridor; when she saw no one coming, she went on. "It's not as if you're inviting Gary into your house."

Becca had told her. Five months before, the last time a man had been in her home, the guy's name was Fred, an airline pilot, tall, dark, divorced, someone she'd met at the hospital. It was supposed to have been a quiet evening, a chance to talk beyond the surrounded-by-others dating rap. She'd cooked salmon, avoided provocative clothing and perfume, and neither flirted nor offered come-hither looks. There had been no blinking "nurse" sign above her head.

He'd been respectable until he wasn't. Fending him off, she'd told him no, that she was *not* playing hard to get. But Fred had apparently considered *no* the foreplay part of consensual sex. Her struggles turned him on. She was certain the little can of pepper spray she kept close had saved her from being raped.

"I *will* be an old maid if I keep picking men like that pilot," she said to her friend.

"You can't kid me." Megan crumpled the empty cup. "You aren't dating at all. You could use some of the meds we pour into patients." She was right, but Becca didn't want to talk about it.

Megan went on, "All men aren't like that pilot, or your First Horror. Gary Kemmerman isn't like that."

"How do you know?"

One of the three elevator doors rumbled open. An older man, a volunteer who transported patients through the facility, emerged pulling an empty gurney. He saw the nurses. "I'm here for Martinez. Radiology wants him." He handed over a slip of paper. Megan grasped the note and cup in one hand, and held up the other for the man to wait. "He lives three streets away from us," she said to Becca. "I knew his wife."

Becca nodded. "He told me she died of—"

"Died?" the old man asked. "Did Martinez die?" The gray-haired fellow cupped his left hand behind his hearing aid and bent toward the nurses.

"Not a chance," Megan said. "Let's go." She waved Becca along, and led them down the corridor.

Following behind, Becca recalled the night seven years before when she had fled from Curt, driven the dark mid-western roads, heading east, every mile a victory. It'd rained like even Mother Nature wanted to pound her. The money she'd squirreled away was in her coat pocket, the valise filled with essentials on the back seat. Her teen-age daughter Melanie, the only worthwhile part left in her life, had been sitting beside her.

Mel had understood, but that hadn't made being uprooted easier. Morose, in tears, and needy, her voice shrill, when she sought reassurance, Becca had been there for her. But no one had been there for Becca—not then, not now.

She almost bumped into the slowing stretcher.

"Sue, he's here for Martinez," Megan said, pulling Becca from her trance.

They were at the nurses' station. Sue Hanson sat entering data on a computer behind the tan, chest-high countertop separating the station from the corridor. Soon as Sue heard Megan, she rose. "Got 'em."

Megan handed her the slip, and tossed the cup into a wastebasket. Sue motioned to the man. "Fifth door down on the left. Follow me, big guy."

Becca picked up where Megan had left off. "You knew her?"

"Sarah Kemmerman was a good person." Megan leaned against the counter, resting on an arm. "What happened was a shame—for both of them. Hit him hard, I'm told. But it's been, well, about a year. He should—"

A bell dinged and a call light came on. Megan turned to check. "They love us," she said to no one. To Becca, she said, "Get to know him. You might like the guy. Gloria says she sees him all the time getting take-out from Hunan Gourmet. He'll ruin his stomach that way. He'll love your cooking. Back in a few."

"Let me help you with the patient."

Megan frowned at Becca. "Thanks, but I know what she needs."

"I don't mind." It would keep her here, seal a decision.

"Go *home*, girl." Megan flicked her hands, urging Becca out. "You actually have something to do today." She took a step away, and then turned back. "When you meet him later, do me a favor? Wear something sexy. You look great in sexy." She saw the concern in Becca's eyes. "The man will not behave poorly."

"He's not interested in women, that it?"

Megan chuckled. "That's not what his wife said. Hey, you asked me about him, I'm telling you. This time, take a chance." She waved and padded off.

Becca took the elevator down, went out and into the staff lot toward her car. She tried to concentrate on the drone of the air handler. She had friends, and her work at the hospital. She exercised, dieted, took fish-oil and calcium pills. What was all this?

Her Chevy chirped hello. She got in, closed and locked the door. The air smelled stale. It was quiet, and she knew: There had to be some man out there who would want to understand her.

She felt it at night, when she found only another pillow, and when she woke in the morning. She used to say good morning out loud, but it had become too searing a ritual.

She started the engine, eased out of the lot, slowing for the speed bump, and headed toward the highway. She frightened men away, and she was not likely to change. That's who she was.

She still had time to shower, brush her hair, and pick out something attractive to wear. Poor Gary Kemmerman. She should stay home, and give him two days of grace.

~10~
4:20 P.M.

WHEN he heard the doorbell, Gary was standing before the closet mirror, trying to knot his tie. Before he reached the stairs, the bell rang a second time. Was it the police again? He hurried down the steps, opened his front door, and there was Becca.

"Hi," he said, surprised. Her hair was down. It framed her face, shoulder length, and his surprise did not conceal his pleasure.

They stood that way until she said, "May I come in?"

It broke the spell, but not his delight. "Sure." He stepped aside.

"I see you need help with that tie." She slipped past him into the living room.

"You found my house." He locked up and followed.

"All I had to do was spell your name right," she said, facing away from him, peeking around. She turned back. "You're in the phone book."

He stepped closer. "Can I take your coat?"

Without answering, she shrugged it off and draped it over the back of the couch. Her shiny, reddish-brown hair swayed with her movement and curled onto the shoulders of a high-necked, dark green blouse clingy enough to be silk. She was wearing black slacks and black half boots. They revealed her figure. When she turned to him, he forced his eyes upward, and hoped she hadn't noticed.

Sarah had insisted a woman always knows when a man is

checking her out.

"I guess you're dressed for the gathering at Hannah's," he said. If so, they had to have a talk first.

"Right." She flipped her hair with her hands. "After what I saw, the least I can do is pay a condolence call. I didn't know anyone who'd be there until I heard you were going." Her mouth scrunched. "I'd prefer not to discuss the accident while we're there. We've covered it, and you expect me to repeat what I saw to your policeman friend."

"Want me to protect you?" He'd meant it as a joke, but it came out sounding serious.

Her expression firmed. "About the accident. If you would." Drawn by her surroundings, she glanced into the living room.

"Okay." He frowned. "You heard I'd be there? Do we run in the same circles?"

She turned back. "The hospital's Gossip Central. I asked about you, and several friends knew your wife."

"She was treated there, for a while." He looked at Becca, trying to stay clear of memories.

"A few people also know you," she said.

"Oh, my."

She chuckled. "I wouldn't be here if you failed the rumor test."

Dependent upon the kindness of strangers—that worked. "Anything I can get you to drink? Or eat? In exchange for you helping me with this tie."

"You probably don't have much food in the house." She tilted her head, and her hair swung. "You told me take-out was your specialty. Someone at the hospital saw you waiting at Hunan Gourmet, I believe."

Dinner for one, he knew. He didn't make the minimum for the free egg roll. "I bought bread, butter, and eggs this morning." The refrigerator had still laughed at him.

"Have any soda?" she asked.

"Will juice do?"

"Uh-huh."

When he returned with small glasses of cranberry juice, Becca was moving about, studying the rooms, touching the furnishings as if they spoke to her. For a moment, she stood exactly where Sarah had when she first reported the news that had changed the Kemmermans' lives and ended hers. Two women.

The blur turned back into Becca. She was distracted, and he watched as she moved. After so long, was it just hormones? She was desirable, no denying that. But he'd settle for talking with her, sharing silly things, it didn't matter. Getting to know this whole other person.

He let her examine that part of his life. She ran fingers along his memories. It felt as if she were touching him.

She brushed a hand across the top of a dining room chair and turned. "I hope you don't mind my looking around."

He shook his head.

She joined him in the living room. "These are comfortable, lived-in rooms."

"Thanks, but they haven't really been lived in for a while. They deserve better." Where did that come from? He hadn't let himself think it, no less tell another.

"Why the smile?"

"You brighten my living room."

"Do I bat my eyelashes now?" Her tone had an edge.

"Only if you're wearing false ones." She wasn't wearing false eyelashes or false anything, he bet. But his humor withered before her glance. "That was meant to be a compliment," he said, and handed her the juice.

"Thanks." She took a sip.

He led into what he knew they had to discuss. "For both our purposes, it'd be best if we went to today's gathering as if we were dating." He saw her recoil.

"Aren't we supposed to meet with your policeman friend and his wife on Friday night?" Her eyes flashed a warning.

He knew he'd crossed another borderline. "I said what I did for a reason."

Her gaze pinned him. "Are you sure you're not being like every other lonely guy?"

Too late. "Which means?"

"Let's rush into something despite problems getting over past wives, mothers, or broken relationships. Or sex troubles. Something makes your type pushy and controlling. I've seen it all."

She had it down pat. It worked like the wedding ring and test questions. "My type?"

She shook her head and held her free hand up, palm-out. "I meant lonely guys in general, not you specifically."

"Accepting invitations is not your best thing?" He wished he hadn't said it.

"Being smothered is not my best thing." She thought to say more but held it in.

"Do I get equal time?"

She looked amused. "Sure."

He spoke softly and slowly: "Do you give a damn what I might say?"

She neither backed down nor moved away, responding in the same gentle tone: "I might."

She was prickly. He found the strength of her character as appealing as it was misguided. He tried to keep irritation out of his tone. "You're right, I'm a lonely guy. It's difficult, coping with Sarah's death. I'll get past that. I had no sex problems while she was healthy. I'm told it's like riding a bicycle, but I wouldn't know yet." He found Becca appraising him. "That sufficient confessional?"

"I didn't mean to—"

"Sure you did." That led to a short silence. More calmly, he said, "You noticed me looking at you before, didn't you? At the door, when you took off your coat, while you touched the furniture. Didn't you?"

"Of course." He recognized the smile she tried to contain.

"I find you attractive—and easy to talk to, like you said about me. If that chases you away, I'll help you on with your coat. Though I'd prefer you stay. I'm not about to smother you, lie to you, or rush you into anything, Becca."

When she hesitated, he thought she might apologize.

"You said you had a reason for my going as your date."

Moving right along. How bright, he thought; what a challenge she must be. "I don't want you to be the crash witness in front of someone who might want to kill you." He paused, she was too startled to comment, and he went on. "A private investigator told

71

me at lunch you might become a target."

"*Me?*"

"The witness." He reached out, claiming the empty glass. "I gave him no name."

"Are you serious?"

"Yeah. We met on another matter that relates to what you witnessed."

"And whether or not I believe that—"

He sensed the next head of steam building, and interrupted: "I'm not being controlling, Becca. I'd rather you not take chances. If you come as my date, people might question your sanity but not shoot at you. At least I don't *think* so." He noticed her body language. "Don't worry, I won't ruin your reputation. We'll be platonic partners."

"For as long as you want?" she fired back.

"For as long as you want, Becca." He'd reacted before he understood what he was saying.

She weighed his response. He almost blushed under the scrutiny.

She breathed in. "How about we met book shopping at Barnes & Noble, then had dinner at the diner? That blends in some truth. Come on," she waved toward the kitchen, "let's put the glasses down." He led, she followed. "We don't need to tell them we had tuna sandwiches, do we?" she said, from behind.

He ran water into the glasses, left them in the sink and faced her. "Next time you'll eat real food with me?"

She could not pretend to be upset, and she laughed, hair swaying. She started to speak but changed her mind. "I wanted to learn more about you. That's why I stopped by."

Her eyes let him in; the anger was gone. He couldn't contain his smile. He wanted his friends to meet her. That led to a disquieting thought. She expected protection—from whom did she need it?

He was afraid he'd find out.

~11~
4:50 P.M.

WISPY clouds sailed across the darkening sky as they walked down the shoveled path toward the Lyons' house. Becca had pulled up her collar against the chill breeze, but his coat was unbuttoned, his hands cold. He wanted to take her hand but he didn't dare, it would mean more than keeping her from slipping.

He was wearing an old black suit that fit only because he'd lost weight. Before they'd left, Becca had said he looked good and meant it as a compliment, probably payback for her outburst.

The Lyons' front door was cracked open despite the weather. The living room, kitchen, and dining room contained clots of family, friends, and neighbors, and a larger group—probably Norm's co-workers.

He laid their coats onto the couch near the door. Becca drifted in before him, and they became separated. Conversations were hushed. Hannah had chosen not to hold Shiva; she'd have this gathering and be done with it.

"I hate this," Dalton Cabrera said, approaching Gary. "Why'd it have to happen? Hannah's too young to be a widow."

He recalled Dalton, and his wife Nadine visiting his house after Sarah's death, when he was alone. Alone—a small word. Had a year gone by? He gazed at Becca, chatting with Vincent and Angela. In an awkward situation, she displayed an ease he admired. She expected no keeper. Best leave her be and let her, when she was ready, find him.

Dalton followed Gary's look. "She the woman you're bringing to Vincent's for dinner?"

"Yeah. He tell you about that?" Gary had called Vincent earlier.

"Hell, no," Dalton whispered. "He told Angela you wanted to bring a date. She told Nadine, who told me. Angela and Nadine can't believe it. Me neither. You didn't guess that. You're slippin'."

Chubby, dark-haired Dalton, Gary knew, was a computer systems specialist. What that meant changed year to year, and Gary couldn't keep it straight. But Dalton worked from home and his services were in demand. He was good at whatever he did. Gary glanced at Becca.

Dalton tapped his arm to capture his attention. "Both our wives are excited for you. A year without a stir of interest in female companionship, and you surprise us by showing up with"—he exaggerated his expression—"a *terrific*-looking woman. I'm amazed. Did you enter a 'Date of The Year' contest? I won't ask you if she's nice, I'll ask Vincent and Angela."

"Don't read too much into it."

Dalton chuckled. "We're invited too, y'know."

"To dinner tomorrow?"

Dalton offered a shit-eating grin, and nodded.

"I didn't know, but that's great. We can all check out Becca's manners."

Gary saw Nadine heading toward them from the kitchen with a tray of hors d'oeuvres. She, Angela, and Naomi were the food brigade. When she was a few feet away, Dalton smiled and said to Gary, in a stage whisper loud enough for her to hear, "Nadine and I think you need to get laid."

"Dalton." Nadine's rebuke was soft, and she blushed. She was blonde, chunky, and pale, and her blush stood out.

Gary was fond of them both. Dalton was fortunate his wife was slow to anger. She offered Gary the tray. He declined. "That blush means the thought came from you, huh?"

"Your Becca's sweet," Nadine said. "I introduced myself."

Before Gary could thank her for the social kindness, Dalton jumped in. "So far I'm only willing to concede pretty."

"Dalton tells me you'll also be at dinner tomorrow," Gary said.

"Dalton." This time Nadine speared her husband. When he didn't respond, she turned to Gary. "Angela was going to ask if it would be all right for us to be there. We wouldn't dump us on you, especially—"

"I'm delighted you can be there. Just don't read too much into—"

"Ha!" said Dalton. "A year of nothing and suddenly—"

"I'll just take this boy away now." Nadine hooked her free hand around her husband's arm and led him off without protest.

Gary watched them, very much together. He missed it. Poor Hermann Schroder. Did he have a wife and children? He looked for Hannah. He needed to pay respects, set up a meeting to hear why she was convinced Norm had been murdered. Did she know more than what Norm had told him?

Yesterday morning. Sorrow and loss were just below the surface for both of them. Hannah had been there for Sarah. However bad he felt, he'd be there for Hannah.

"Gary?" He blinked. Becca was standing there, looking at him, concerned. "You okay?"

"I'm fine."

She wouldn't accept that. "Let's go out for a breath of fresh air. Just for a minute."

He bit his lip until he calmed, focused on her face until his eyes cleared. She waited with compassion, the other side of prickly. "I'm good now," he said when he could.

"Then let's—"

"Yeah. Let's find Hannah."

She smiled. He'd known what she wanted. He took her arm and led her toward the dining room. Hannah was standing in a far corner. Before they got near, a man stepped in front of them and extended his hand.

"I am Arman Pavlic. And you?"

Gary hadn't noticed the man earlier. He had Slavic features, sharp blue eyes, and thin blonde hair. He was tall enough to be noticed, but then he may have been elsewhere in the house. This was the man who had asked to see the papers in Norm's briefcase.

Pavlic smiled, searched Gary's face, and held his ground until Gary said, "I'm a neighbor. Name's Gary. And this is my date,

Becca." He shook the man's hand and felt him using a fraction of his strength. "How is it you know the family?"

"Lyons worked for me."

"Ah," Gary said. Pavlic wore pungent cologne, smelled like deep woods and pine needles. Not unpleasant, but he must have doused himself. He radiated self-confidence. Gary wondered what his expensive suit was hiding. This was not a man to be trifled with.

"His death was tragedy." Pavlic's eyes finished with Gary and flicked at Becca with a look that devoured. "You met widow?"

Gary responded for her. "We're going to pay our respects now." He forced Pavlic to glance at him, and took Becca's arm again.

Brushing aside his lead, Pavlic blocked her. "How Lyons' accident happen?"

"We don't know," she said. Volunteering nothing. Gary liked the "we."

Pavlic focused on her a moment longer, then nodded. "Good to meet you."

"Thanks." She did not offer a hand.

He stepped out of the way as Hannah approached, in black and gliding slowly. Ignoring Becca, whom she didn't know, she laid a hand on Gary's shoulder. "I'm so glad you're here."

He found her touch out of character. She often waved, but rarely touched. Her impassive control was frayed. She looked worse than yesterday. Platitudes would do her no good. "I'll miss Norm."

"This must be difficult for you, too," she said.

Despite her pain, she understood him. "Hannah, meet my date, Becca Strassberg."

Hannah turned to her in disbelief.

"I'm sorry for your loss," Becca said, avoiding the real reason for her presence.

"Did I hear right?" Hannah said. "You're Gary's date?"

Neither of them knew what to say. He rescued her. "We ran into each other at Barnes & Noble yesterday, then had dinner at the diner." He imagined how Dalton would run with the tuna sandwiches.

"We went dutch," Becca said to Hannah. "I'd just met the man. I wouldn't let him pay for dinner."

"I offered," Gary said.

Becca smiled, and turned toward him. "We women need our independence."

The smile caught him. "Can I pay next time?"

She chuckled, and Hannah laughed at their exchange, just once, but a laugh. "Then it's good of you to come. This isn't a typical setting for a date."

The women locked eyes. Gary remained silent.

Hannah nodded toward him but spoke to her. "He's a good man." That was too close to her loss. She wiped a tear. "Will you stay?" she asked him. "After everyone leaves?"

"Of course. I'll see Becca to her car and come right back."

Hannah nodded and said to her, "I don't mean to come between you. I hope we meet again." She was about to glide away when a couple from the company approached.

The large woman wore an expensive black pants suit, glittering jewelry and too many cosmetics. She began to speak before she stopped moving. "Mrs. Lyons, what happened is just terrible, and all of us at Consolidated are devastated." She stepped close and hugged her.

Hannah yielded, but had eyes only for the man, who bent forward attentively. "We'll miss Norman. He was a vital part of our team. He'd earned our respect as a professional and as a person." Tall, gray-haired and dignified, in a tailored dark blue suit, he held Hannah's attention almost against her will. "You have sympathies from all of us."

Gary thought he had finished when the grey-haired man added, "Let's discuss financial matters soon." He nodded once at Hannah, as if confirming his decision. "I'd like to be personally involved."

There was fear in Hannah's eyes before she buried her face against the woman's shoulder and began to cry. Gary wondered why the gray-haired man's words had caused the upset.

The man turned to him. "You are?" His eyes bored in as if they'd read his mind.

His intensity caused Gary to backpedal. "I'm a neighbor. I stopped by to pay condolences. Name's Gary." He stuck out his hand. "And you are?"

The movement broke the tall man's focus. As they shook,

Gary read his expression. Perhaps he'd been dismissed. "Morgan Westbrook," the man answered. "This is my wife, Jennifer. I head the company Norman Lyons worked for."

"Good to meet you," Gary said. So this is Riddock's friend and Merle's protégée. Now was not the time to mention it.

By then, Hannah had broken free. "Mr. Westbrook, it's kind of you to become involved. I'd prefer Gary handle the meeting you suggested. I'm not up to it yet."

The president looked at her, glanced at Gary and back at Hannah. "Then we can wait."

"I'd rather Gary met with you." Hannah was over her tears. The look she gave Westbrook was stubborn.

Westbrook's turned to him. "Are you an attorney?" His tone oozed irritation.

"No." Gary had been surprised so many times that he accepted Hannah's task stoically. It offered cover that might give him a chance to discuss other things with Westbrook.

"Please," Hannah said, not a question, and Gary saw it was directed at Westbrook.

The man nodded. He pulled a card from a suit pocket and handed it over. "Call me. Tomorrow's good, any time before two." He breathed deeply, exhaled through his mouth, and added, in a non-combative tone, "I didn't mean to offend. This episode's painful. I want to do this right, and I'll work with you to get there. What we can do isn't much in terms of what's happened, but it's the only way we can help Norman's family."

Gary suspected the man was speaking honestly. Once you got past the veneer, maybe there was a real person underneath. "Thanks. Now she needs some rest." He pocketed the card and turned to Hannah. "Let's go inside." She didn't resist.

"We'll be leaving now," said Westbrook.

Without goodbyes, Gary guided Hannah away. Becca followed them to the small table in the kitchen, where Hannah dropped into a chair with relief. Becca—ever the nurse—brought Hannah a glass of water.

The Westbrooks collected their coats and departed. Freed from their boss, the Consolidated contingent began a polite exodus. A farewell line formed in front of Hannah and briefly snaked into the dining room.

Once the crush ended, Becca said to Hannah, "I have to go now, but we'll meet again."

"I'll find our coats," he said.

"I'll send him right back."

Hannah seemed alert when she looked up at her. She was not smiling.

~12~
8:05 P.M.

WHEN Becca appeared, Gary helped her on with her coat. Once they stepped through the front door, it was dark, and much colder. The breeze crawled into their clothes, and their breath steamed. The scraped snow on the steps had frozen into a glaze, and—he couldn't avoid doing it—he took her arm and helped her down. She allowed him without comment, but separated when they reached the walk.

There were no stars. Except for a single streetlight and reddish haze from quilted clouds, the night was forbiddingly dark. They paused, acclimating to the outside and to each other, alone again.

"I'm glad you're heading home." He glanced at the wall-to-wall cloud. "It's gonna snow later, into the morning. You working tomorrow?"

"I'm off. Reward for the double shift. I'll catch up on sleep." Her hands were in her coat pockets. His were cold.

She turned her head, making sure he was close. "Thanks for letting me roam. And for getting rid of that horrid man."

"Pavlic?"

"Um-hmm." They moved slowly along the sidewalk. "Did you see how he was staring at me when he asked about the accident?"

In every way possible, he wanted to keep her away from that man. "I'll bet he just wanted to look at you."

She ignored that. "I met Angela and Vincent, and Nadine and Dalton—I think I got the names right. I like your friends."

He smiled, though she couldn't see it. "They're good people."

"So is Hannah. While you were getting our coats, she asked me if I was married."

"She shouldn't have—"

Becca laughed. "I knew why. She's lookin' out for you, Gary. I told her we'd joked about it, each wearing a wedding ring for a different reason. That relieved her. She worried I'd be trouble."

Before he responded, Becca tugged his sleeve. He glanced down and saw her hand slip back into her pocket. He wasn't brave enough to take it. He looked in the direction she'd turned, and saw her car parked a few houses down across the street.

"You deserve a thank-you, too," he said. "You were kind before."

They crossed the road. "Angela told me she's delighted to finally be able cook for you," Becca said. "She seems quite a homemaker. We discussed what she plans to serve. Five courses: How could I tell her that's more than I eat in a day? She said you've turned down a dozen of her dinner invitations. Then Vincent joked you'll cut her social life in half if she doesn't have to pester friends to find blind dates you never meet anyway."

He turned toward her, but she didn't notice, drawn by her vehicle. "I'm happy to relieve Angela of the burden. I told you I wasn't dating, blind or otherwise. And whatever Angela cooks will taste great. I'll eat it all, though it'll wind up right here." He patted his stomach.

She stopped beside her car and faced him. "You know, I needed to pay a condolence call, and I did want to see you. But I never thought there'd be any enjoyable moments in there."

His emotions were confusing him. "I wasn't looking forward to it, either. You made the whole thing easier."

Becca scrunched her mouth. "I don't want to keep you from Hannah, but would you answer a question for me?"

"Ask away."

"You've been candid about important things. Why'd you cover up about Arman?"

She'd caught him. "You gonna bludgeon me for praising you?"

"You just covered up again."

"That was honest." But she waited, immune to his evasion. "You believe I covered up because …?"

"He asked me about the accident."

"He's Consolidated's security officer. He should be asking."

"But not me. Not if I'm simply your date. He stopped us because of me, though I think he recognized you, too. He wanted to see how I'd react to his question, not to gaze into my eyes. You know that."

Gary was floored by how perceptive this woman was. "How could he know you're the witness?"

"The policeman who interviewed me took my photo. For the record, he said. I signed his consent form. Are they involved?"

So Schroder must have been as casual with the accident file as he had been with the logbook. "I don't think so. As a company officer, Pavlic must have seen the police file that contained the photo."

"You knew he met the police?" Becca was becoming upset.

"Yeah." He said that softly, unsure where she was going.

"Did you learn that from the private detective?"

"No. Vincent got me in front of the sergeant who investigated the crash. The one who interviewed you." He was not going to mention Schroder's death.

"That man told you about Pavlic?" She sounded frightened.

"Yeah."

"Would he have given Pavlic my name?"

"No. My guess is, Pavlic was surprised to find you here. Must've remembered you. You have a face that—"

"*Please.*"

This beautiful woman either did not know that, or wanted no one else to know it. "You were easy for him to recognize," is all he said.

She looked grim. "If he knows who I am, will he … come after me?"

"I don't think so. The PI said these criminals try not to make waves, and harassing you would. No one but me knows you have more information."

"Then why weren't you being honest?" Before she went on, she took a half step back, and her left hand emerged and touched the car, as if for reassurance. "Because you don't know me well enough? Or you don't trust me—maybe I'd tell your secrets?"

"Safer for you not to be involved." Would he ever be able to reassure her before she crossed the line. "I worry about you."

"Too late," she said. "He knows I'm the witness. We're in this together."

"Becca—"

"Do we give us a chance?"

She stood her ground. He wasn't sure what it was, but she wanted something. So did he; no was not an option. "Of course. Why are you doing this?"

She stared at his chest. "I can't have you making decisions for me. I've been there." She glanced up, and the streetlight trembled in her eyes. "I need you to be honest." She waited for his answer, standing by her car door.

Pulse racing, he looked at her. She looked back, and he knew she didn't want to leave but would. "I promise."

"We're full partners, then, wherever this goes?"

He took a deep breath, let it out. "In the Lyons thing."

"In … everything," she said, eyes glowing.

It took him several seconds, but he nodded.

"Is that a yes?"

He'd never get away with anything. Where had he heard that before? "Yeah."

Becca sighed. "You sure you didn't bribe your friends to say those nice things?"

He hesitated. "I don't want to smother you."

She smiled at him, and her hand came off the car. "Is there something you want to say?"

"Yeah."

"I'm listening."

He couldn't avoid asking. "I'd like to see you this weekend."

"We're already on for Friday night. The dinner, remember? I spoke about it with Vincent and Angela. We're bringing dessert. For six. Angela said Dalton and Nadine are coming." She pulled keys from a pocket. They clinked. She glanced at them for a moment. "I insisted. About us bringing dessert."

It was too dark for her to see his blush, but she must have translated his silence, because after a bit she said, "I think I understand what you asked."

"You do?"

She took two small steps forward and stood against him, a faint pressure, her head came up, and she kissed him on the lips. He was afraid to move, wary of the urge to hug her, unwilling to scare her away. He felt her everywhere. His hands had reached the waist of her thick coat when she broke the kiss.

"This is the oddest and best official first date I've ever had," she said.

He knew. "You'd better leave before …."

Her smile warmed even his hands. "You need to get back to Hannah."

Ten minutes later, he was sitting beside Hannah at the kitchen table, his hand over hers. He felt it when she shuddered.

Dalton and Nadine were the last to leave. They tried to engage Hannah, but she could barely respond—worn and pale, head down, eyes half-closed. She'd sleep soundly.

Unless talking about her husband's murder woke her up.

~13~
8:45 P.M.

EVER since he was a child, Arman Pavlic had loved the "off to work we go" refrain from the Disney movie with the dwarfs. The words had been dubbed into another language, but the tunes remained true. The refrain was playing in his head as he followed the woman's gray Chevrolet.

The tender kiss he'd observed from deep in the shadows meant he would not have to kill her. The kiss told him the woman and Kemmerman were involved with each other and had not met for purposes dangerous to him.

He'd have enjoyed killing her. An accident at work perhaps, unrelated to the others. Her figure was good. He imagined her lying helpless, Snow White with red hair and big breasts. He'd plan for a chance to use her.

His company car, the black BMW, had wide tires and handled well in snow. He glanced at its glowing dials as he followed the Chevrolet down the hill and around toward the highway, a route he'd driven before.

He recognized her as the crash witness—attractive, except for something hard-looking: pain lines on her forehead, around her eyes and mouth, faint scars on a cheek, marks that might have been made by cuts from a ring. Had others tried to get information from her?

She'd answered his question without hesitation, without seeming to hide anything. But one could never be too careful.

He pulled closer as she turned onto an access ramp for Interstate

80. She drove aggressively and squeezed right onto the highway. Four vehicles passed before he found a slot. When he caught up, he allowed a silver Acura to remain between them.

It was the second time he'd seen Kemmerman. Upsetting. Tying up loose ends, he wondered why Lyons had stopped, on his way to the office yesterday morning, and invited the man into his car. Could Lyons have given him the printouts? Unlikely. Kemmerman hadn't been carrying anything when he left the car. Could Lyons have told him about the report, his suspicions? Possibly, though their time together had been brief.

And the woman—had she been following Lyons? She must have seen what had happened. She may have seen Pavlic, even through the tinted windows. That could prove dangerous. Lovers or not, she and Kemmerman might be working together, or for others.

Serge would forbid him to kill either of them with so much else going on. Even to protect tens, ultimately hundreds of millions of dollars. But he could warn them to back off, all by himself, in a way she and the man would understand.

He veered to the left to confirm the Chevrolet still sailed along in the fast lane. He had to follow her, however long the trip. Distracted, he considered how he might kill Kemmerman, who seemed ordinary except when he focused, and who valued the woman.

And all this because, on Monday, Lyons got his hands on a report from their harvesting system. He'd had only moments with the pages from Teo's desk before Arman pulled them away. Stupid of Teo to allow that, and surprising that Lyons remembered the codes. Within the hour, he'd entered their system from his office computer.

A turn signal flashed from the silver car ahead. It swung into the right lane and slowed approaching an exit. He blew past it, but lengthened the distance between him and the Chevrolet, until a boxy Cadillac plugged the gap.

Mind idling, he hummed the tune in his head. When it's off to work we go, we always do our homework: break a difficult task into pieces, make it easy. Especially murder.

He'd driven Lyons' commuter route late Monday to locate the perfect spot for an accident. A 6,000-pound, four-wheel-drive SUV made it easy. He'd boosted it from the employee section of a mall-parking garage, returned it before lunch, before it was missed, and retrieved his car.

There was minor damage to the SUV. The owner would figure it'd been caused while he was parked. Arman had not wanted to collide with Lyons' car, but apply strong and steady pressure, as tugboats use. He'd crafted a thick rubber mat at Serge's garage and strapped it over the front passenger-side fender of the stolen car. Before dawn, the mat had been invisible, and Lyons' car wouldn't reveal telltale paint.

He'd kept the mat.

The woman had to be approaching the range for a normal commute, even in this insane state. Again he veered left to confirm she remained in line.

It had been simpler in Latvia. He'd get instructions, steal a car, enlist his team, do surveillance, and shoot the victim—if necessary, bodyguards included. Killing bodyguards was free.

Latvia ranked eighth of sixty-two nations in murders per capita. Much of that had been his doing. Here, there were so many precautions to take.

The crime-lab shows on TV made him laugh—limitless man-hours and resources. Even if such technology existed, the ability to employ it did not. Suburban police thought accident where that was the likely cause. A loose wheel, bad brakes, frayed appliance wires, grease on a stairway, a drug overdose—endless opportunity.

Even being shot during a robbery became an accident of fate. Too bad Serge wouldn't let him shoot the cop. He was to do nothing that might compromise his position. But Lyons had been Pavlic's.

The three pages the man had printed out were in neither his corporate office nor his smashed car. They must be in his home. Earlier, while people were milling and the widow was busy, he'd visited Lyons' cramped home office—but found nothing. Lyons surely used his home computer to delve into what he'd discovered, and that would leave a trail. The man might have spoken to the wife. As shocked as she was when Arman had met her, she had seemed on edge, and flinched, as if she knew something

That had been all the confirmation he needed. So he'd acted. The widow was exhausted. Soon, she would be sleeping quite soundly.

Serge had given him the option, even offered help. But he'd made his own arrangements. One loose end, neatly tied up.

The Cadillac slowed. The Chevrolet, turn signal blinking, slipped to the right and headed toward an exit. He turned behind her and the BMW skidded, slid to the left. Yanked from his thoughts, he grasped the wheel, became one with the car. The skid ended in a millisecond, a patch of black ice.

He looked to the Chevrolet. It sped on without hesitation, taillights twinkling in the cold. He was the perfect distance, just too far for his headlights to reach it. He preferred not to exceed the speed limit, but this woman drove fast.

How could he act without causing Serge's feared waves, and in a way he would enjoy—but Kemmerman would hate? It's off to work we go, he hummed, and once more wished he was the one to find Snow White. The image shifted to red-haired Becca, naked beneath him.

That was it. He unclipped his cell phone and made a call. When he finished, he turned off the BMW's heater. Warmth dulled him; he'd need to be alert. Without the fan, he could hear the tires slashing through blown snow.

He followed his quarry like a hungry cat, humming a Disney tune.

~14~
9:40 P.M.

THE last visitors had left. Hannah sat beside Gary at the table, head in her hands. In the stillness, the kitchen clock ticked. Her left hand twitched toward paper plates on the round wooden surface. "Mother would be upset."

"You mean she *liked* Norm?"

Hannah smiled. "Of course not. It's just that Father died years before Mother, and she never got over it."

"She'd want you to get on, for sure."

She spoke without looking at him. "What about your parents? You never mention them."

"Oh, Mom had a chronic illness, Dad took care of her, and when she passed, he had no reason to hang around."

Distracted, Hannah stacked dishes. "You mean he left?"

Gary captured a crumb-filled plate beyond her reach and handed it over. "He died."

She set it on top, slid the pile away and frowned. "You make it sound optional."

Never sounded right, no matter how he put it. "He gave up. Without Mom, he … just gave up."

"You weren't reason enough for him to …?"

"Apparently not."

She reached toward the plates, pushed them off another inch, giving her hands something to do. "How old were you?"

"Eight."

"What happened after?"

He leaned back, crossed arms over his chest and resisted crossing his ankles. "I lived with Aunt Ethel, one of my mother's sisters, and Uncle Gus."

"That must have been tough." She sighed and closed her eyes.

So much flooded back. Larry and Steven had been the biological children in the household. His own moody nature had kept him an outsider, picked on at home, in school, at play. He'd retreated into imaginary worlds.

"But you survived," she said.

He put his hands on the table and listened to the clock ticking. Hannah looked as if she'd gone to sleep sitting up. "Sure did. It made me the logical loon I am. Sarah taught me emotion."

"She told me *she* was the one who found *you*."

He smiled. "She had to. Back then, I steered clear of women."

Hannah laced her fingers together and faced him. "You're doing it again. You're almost a recluse."

He didn't respond.

"What about Becca?" she asked. "How'd you find *her*?"

He couldn't help chuckling. "She *also* found me."

Hannah's head dropped as if a weight had fallen on it. Her hands went to her chin. "Is this one door closing, one opening?"

"Speaking of doors, did you lock up?"

She shook her head and fixed him with a glance, knowing what he'd done. But she sighed again and pushed up from the chair. "Wait." She went upstairs. He heard her moving about, drawers opening and closing, creaks through the ceiling above.

From somewhere below, the gas furnace went on with a thump. Hot water flowed, sighed through pipes and radiators. Old house. Wind tried to sneak through the window behind him, moaning in frustration. Surrounded by ticks, creaks, sighs, and moans, he felt weary. But he needed to find out what Hannah knew. She'd be the opposite of the night Riddock had expected.

When she reappeared, she was wearing a gray sweat-outfit and white sneakers, and she had a file folder in her hands. Her face displayed her grief. Without a word, she looked around, then went down to the basement. She returned, alert.

90

"Security check?" he asked.

"The house is locked up tight." She rubbed an eye with her free hand, then closed them both and shook her head as if willing reality away.

"Wanna talk?"

She put a hand on the table, stared at the chair but pulled back, unable to sit.

"Oh, not here. I can't stand being here right now. I see mournful people, hear so-sorrys—and Norman, I'm sure he'll walk in on us."

She stood motionless, eyes closed again.

Change Norman to Sarah, how well he understood. He pushed his chair back from the table. "How about the diner? I haven't seen you eat anything. It's my duty to preserve you."

She shook her head.

"The Kemmerman manse, for sustenance and chat?"

"Why not?" She opened her eyes and smiled at him. "Though I've been told the food sucks."

He laughed. "True enough. I make coffee."

She shook her head. "I can't drink coffee. But I'm glad you reminded me."

She went into the small bathroom off the kitchen, and returned with a pill bottle. She waved him up with the hand holding the pills. They rattled.

"You're exhausted, Hannah. Are you okay … health-wise, I mean?"

She turned away but spoke as she moved. "I'm on meds for an irregular heartbeat. I have to avoid coffee and alcohol."

He followed her toward the door. "Why didn't I know about this heartbeat thing?"

"Sarah knew. You were always at work. She used to drive me to the doctor. What I have isn't serious. Maybe that's why she didn't tell you." She stopped by the coat rack along the wall—when she reached for one, he stepped up and got it for her.

"Doctor says it shouldn't bother me," she went on, as he helped her into the heavy brown coat. She pocketed the pills and switched hands with the folder. "Most times, it goes away by itself."

He pulled on his own coat. "You can handle the stress?"

She leaned against the front door, fighting memory. "I may never be okay."

"Sorry, wrong question. Let me show you the way."

She locked up. Gary helped her as he had Becca, and they walked along the sidewalk, faces lowered, shoulders hunched against the tugging wind. Hannah grasped the folder. He was aware of the curb where Becca had parked. Had she gotten home safely? What had she worn to bed?

"Did you mean to bring your date this evening?" Hannah asked, as if she'd read his thoughts.

Might as well tell her. "She brought herself. She wanted to express regrets. She witnessed Norm's accident."

Hearing that, Hannah stopped short. "Neither of you told me."

Steps beyond, Gary turned back. A glob of snow fell from a tree and smacked his chest like a snowball. "We don't want anyone else to know she's the witness." He brushed his coat.

"Why?"

The breeze flapped the folder, ruffled her hair while he considered. "She'd be fielding questions all the time. She's already told the police what she remembers."

"Did she speak to you about it?"

Hannah was so engrossed she didn't move. He took a step closer. "Uh-huh."

"Did you hear anything suspicious?"

That was another discussion he didn't want to have right now. "First, tell me your story. And inside, not out here. It's cold."

He pulled at an arm of her bulky coat and they started forward.

"Did you meet Becca because she's the witness?" she asked, a few steps later.

"Yeah."

She might have stopped again but for his pressure on her arm. "Has some good come from Norman's tragedy?"

"What'd you mean?"

"You behave with her a little like you did with Sarah. I haven't seen you so happy in a year." She'd turned toward him, and might have tripped on a snow mound but for his arm. She went on, unmindful: "It's no secret you like her."

They turned left onto Gary's front walk, him leading because there was less room between knee-high borders of snow. He wasn't sure how to deal with her observation. "She said you had a few words with her before she left. How come?"

"Did I do wrong?"

He turned the key in the lock. "You kind of helped."

Hannah stopped on the stoop. "I'm breaking my rules."

He turned back. "Right. Me, the wolf in friend's clothing."

"It's just …."

She looked stooped and so unhappy. "Life will be different, Hannah. Come on in."

She crossed the vestibule and studied the living room.

"Times I'm sure Sarah will come walking down the stairs," he said, as he helped her off with her coat. She kept the pill bottle and folder. He tossed coats onto a chair.

Hannah closed her eyes, put hands on her cheeks, dropped back on the larger couch, face lowered. "It's been a year since Sarah died. She told me what she made you promise, to get on with your life. She made me promise I'd look after you. I know she did the same with Nadine and Angela. You can't live in the past," she said, lifting her head. "Sarah will always be with you. She wanted you to have a second chance at love."

He looked down at her. "Did she say that?"

Hannah nodded.

Gary bit his lip, had to bite it again before he could speak. "Then she wouldn't be happy with me."

"Maybe now …." She paused. "Don't be upset about what I asked your friend. I don't want to see you become a bitter, lonely man."

He breathed deeply before he replied. "I'm not upset. What Sarah said is good advice for you, too."

"But you've had a year to come to terms." Her voice broke. "I've had a day."

"Is it warm enough in here?" Concern for her kept him rooted. She nodded.

"You can't have coffee—can I get you anything else?"

"Do you have a bottle of water?"

"You're in luck. The chef carries that." He brought one to her from the walk-in pantry closet. He kept it in inventory, one more familiar detail.

Hannah shook a pill into her hand, opened the water bottle and washed it down. As if water granted energy, she smiled. "You look alive with Becca."

He was standing, couldn't sit. "We've agreed to date, see where it goes … tell me, what was that business with Morgan Westbrook? He frightened you."

Hannah looked into the distance. "Yesterday, I was overwhelmed. Now I'm numb. What can either of us do to change things when the police say Norman's death was an accident?"

"Maybe nothing. But you asked me to try. Trust me to. Hang on." He went to the kitchen, got a pad and pen, and sat in a chair facing the couch. "Why do you believe Norm was murdered?"

Her voice was weak. "The police insist it was an accident, the temporary railing was inadequate, and I should sue the state. That's the end of it for them." She placed the bottle on the coffee table and stared at the rug. "I was told justice lies in suing. Take the money, forget the crime."

He hadn't made a note. "That's not why Norm might have been murdered."

She looked surprised but said nothing.

"Why were you afraid of Westbrook? He's the president."

"Norman spoke highly of him, but any of those company people could be behind it." She sat back, folding into the couch for support. "I can't meet with that man, no matter what the reason. I never want to see any of those people again."

Good reason for Hannah's insistence on a single get-together in Norm's honor rather than seven nights of visitors. "I'll try to meet him for you tomorrow," Gary said. "We'll do the best we can." She nodded. He asked again, "Why do you believe Norm was murdered?"

She lifted her hands from the cushions, locked them together in front of her. "Norman didn't discuss his work with me, but he considered himself more than a financial auditor. He told anyone who asked he was an 'information technology security specialist.' Those four words I memorized, but that's about it. He and his buddy

Teo call themselves 'IT Geeks.' When he talks about what he does, he gets so technical it's gibberish to me."

Gary made no comment about the present tense.

"After work Monday, Norman seemed anxious. Usually I leave him be, but he was so tense I asked what was wrong. Once I asked, it all came out. He said he'd uncovered massive fraud. He wanted to prove it, let management know about it, and stop it, but he didn't know whom he could safely talk to."

Gary understood the "kill the messenger" remark.

"Norman brought home three printout pages." Her right hand pulled the blue folder out from under a leg and placed it on her lap.

She stroked it as she spoke. "He came in muttering, spent an hour at his computer with the door closed, something he rarely did. He said he had to make a decision—he used the word 'dangerous'— before he got to the office tomorrow."

Gary took notes.

"Here's what he brought." She bent forward, handed him the folder. "Norman thought of taking it yesterday morning, but he told me he could duplicate it, and this would be better in a safe place. Imagine, he led me to the upstairs bathroom and slid this into the laundry hamper." She smiled at Gary. "He wrapped it in a clean towel."

Consolidated's logo was staring up at him from the folder. He opened it, flipped through the sheets it held. He had no idea what he was looking at, but this might explain Pavlic's visit to the police, and the strange following call Sergeant Schroder had described. How did the crooks know Norm had them? If they'd murdered him for them, what else might they do to get them back?

"This is gibberish to me, too, Hannah."

"I asked him to speak to you about it," she said, wringing her hands. "I didn't know what else to do."

Better not to mention his conversation in Norm's car, or what he'd learned from others—pieces that pointed to murder might not mix well with an irregular heartbeat and exhaustion. "I hate to badger you—why *else* do you feel Norm was killed?"

She leaned back, looked up and spoke at the ceiling. "He's a careful driver. He stays to the right, doesn't speed, knows the roads very well ... intimately he ... used to say. His car was small, but he said it was well rated for safety. The tires were only three months old. I remember, because he'd had a flat and when I insisted he buy new ones, we had a spat. He hated to spend money. But he bought them." Tears appeared. She lowered her head, blotted them with a sleeve, steadied herself.

"The crash happened the day he was going to report what he'd found." She nodded at the folder. "Maybe they wanted that back. But he left it here."

Gary wondered if Pavlic had considered that. "Did Norm work with anyone at Consolidated who might shed light on this?"

"His lunch buddy was Teodors Medved. He's a nice young man, quite a computer whiz. He's from some Baltic country. One night we had him over for dinner, and he ate like we were his meal for the week. He drank an entire liter of cola." She had a faraway look.

"While I served, they talked jargon. Teo was excited about invisible programs and backward codes. That sticks in my mind, because I asked if they were in the secret agent business."

"Sure Norm *wasn't* a secret agent?"

She looked at him with surprise, realized he was joking, and chuckled. "With his nerves?"

"Was this Medved fellow at the reception?"

"I didn't see him," Hannah said. "I don't think he drives. The evening he visited, Norman brought him from the office and drove him home. Most days, he works from home. Norman told me Pavlic drives him to the office a few times a week."

Hannah frowned. "Did you meet Pavlic? He's frightening." She thought back to what she'd wanted to say. "Probably Teo couldn't get a lift."

Or, with so many Consolidated employees coming from different directions, he didn't want one. Yes, Gary had met Pavlic. So it was Pavlic and Teo, just as it had been Pavlic and Norm. Meet Teo Medved, he noted, and unexpectedly connected Hannah's backward code comment with the string of numbers at the bottom of the three printout sheets. He reviewed them again. As he returned them to the folder, he noticed a phone number scribbled on the back of the first sheet.

"Did Norm write this?" He held it up so she could see.

She nodded. "I asked, too. He said it's Teo's cell phone."

Gary copied it. He scanned the notes and realized how weary he was. He had nothing left to push with, and Hannah looked as if this had been the longest day of her life.

"We can piece the rest together in the morning, Hannah. You're exhausted. I'll walk you home."

"I'm not ready for that." She shifted on the couch, digging deeper. "For Norman on the stairs, or in bed. I need …." She was quiet without being done. "I feel lost."

His hand stirred; he wanted to console her but doubted she'd prefer that. "I felt lost, too. The feeling's real, and it gets bad if you let it. But it fades. Your family, your friends, we understand, we'll be there for you. It's a bitch, but it's a process. Take it one day at a time. Things will get better. I promise."

Hannah glanced up, locked onto him. "Thanks." Her moist eyes dropped to the rug. "Can I crash on the couch?"

"Finally, a femme fatale in my house!"

She shook her head, smiling. "You dream about Becca upstairs. I'll stay here. I doubt either of us will sleep. I know where the bathroom is. Got a blanket and pillow?"

He even found her a sheet.

Hannah was right. They were both awake when they heard sirens.

~15~
11:49 P.M.

GARY dismissed the fire-truck wail. That sound often grew closer, louder, and then faded, danger rolling away along with the noise.

But this convoy wound down close enough to hear radio chatter, doors slamming, voices organizing. A police siren followed. Rotating lights beat through facing windows.

He'd been in bed barely an hour before he ran downstairs. He and Hannah, half-awake and still dressed, were outside quickly. He put her coat over her shoulders but neglected his own. Shock fueled them.

Hannah's home was ablaze. "Oh, my God," she moaned, and sagged against him. He kept her from falling, and when she began to shake and gasp for air, he motioned to a fire official. The man spoke into a radio. Two EMTs ran up. They took her, asked questions, and led her away. He followed until they waved him off. She vanished into an ambulance he hadn't even seen.

He returned to the fire official, identified Hannah and told him no person or pet had been in the house. He didn't say it was arson. The man radioed the news, relieved.

Gary joined others straggling out to watch the fire. The heat toasted him on one side; February froze the other. Firemen linked hoses to a main and snaked them around adjacent houses. Soon, water was gushing from three directions. Both neighboring homes were evacuated as firefighters worked to suppress the blaze. Trees glistened.

Many of the wood and brick homes had been built a driveway apart, seventy-plus years ago, when garages were detached. Their back yards butted the back yards of similar next-block homes. Now the houses were all colors, wore several types of siding and roofing, were cut with skylights and larger windows, and bloated by additions.

In the fire's glare, they looked vulnerable.

Water froze on the ground where the blaze couldn't warm it. The slick roadway was littered with bedraggled people moving carefully, dressed in whatever had been at hand. The setting became a nightmare of flames leaping and roaring in the breeze, collapsed wood spraying embers, firefighters shifting position. The watchers felt horrified, each secretly relieved it was not his or her home ablaze.

Police herded the crowd further back, and re-set the do-not-cross line.

Gary watched the Lyons house, with its dry dimensional lumber and decades of curling memories, disappear. It collapsed into itself while utility people were working at the curb. Glowing embers arced through the air and forced the workers back, until only blackened sticks and odd pieces of wall remained. The fire surrendered, except for a jet in front that died when gas service was cut.

Dalton reached Gary first. They stood silently until Vincent showed up. Like most nearby homeowners, they were upset and curious. Vincent wore a coat and was carrying a blanket, just in case.

He folded the blanket over Gary's shoulders. "I hear Hannah was with you."

"Know how she's doing?" Gary pulled the blanket further around.

"Naomi's with her in the ambulance. Hannah's in shock. They've medicated her, and expect she'll be fine. But she'll be at Ridgetop overnight, at least."

"Naomi taking her in?" Naomi's large home, with the beat of adults and school kids, would be a good place for Hannah. Naomi had clothes for her. And food.

"I'll bet."

The conversation stilled.

He leaned close to Dalton. "Be home tomorrow morning?"

"Sure." Dalton turned and his eyes fixed on Gary. "Somethin' up?"

He didn't want to mention the printouts to Vincent. "I'll stop by. Eight okay?"

Dalton nodded, and commented on the heavy workload he had the next day—but he'd always have time for Gary—so he needed sleep. Gary watched Vincent stare at Dalton's back. The "I'm so busy" line was the way Dalton usually took leave. Vincent had never commented about it, despite his more taxing profession. "We are what we are," he'd once said, after recognizing Gary understood what was going on.

Now Vincent gazed at the burned home. "Shit."

The wind had freshened, and a fine snow began to fall. Gusts pushed tiny flakes sideways. Gary drew the blanket tighter. "Least it held off till the firemen finished."

Vincent squinted at the sky. "More snow. Just what we need. Angela's upset. We'd better postpone tomorrow's dinner, if that's okay with you? We'll give you a second chance soon."

The thought of not seeing Becca brought a flash of disappointment. He debated whether he should tell the lieutenant all he knew about Norm's death. Then they'd have to meet Becca. But it wouldn't be the same.

Anyway, what did he have to offer? Comments made by a friend who could no longer explain them? Doubts about an auto fatality ruled an accident? An unhappy widow and three pages of unspecified significance? A policeman killed during a robbery? A house fire?

What could he do later today? Take the printouts to Dalton. Speak with Riddock. Meet with Westbrook. Meet with Norm's friend Teo, if that could be arranged. Then he might have ammunition for Vincent.

He'd have to tell Becca dinner was cancelled before she bought— or made; did she cook?—dessert for six. Maybe they could share dessert for two. Watching the smoldering ruin in front of him, joy leaked out of the weekend.

Vincent interrupted. "Sorry, Gary. I know you were looking forward to bringing her. We'll have you both over real soon. It's just—"

"It's okay."

Vincent brushed snow off his ears and jammed his hands into his coat pockets. "Is what she saw worth meeting about later?"

Gary shook his head.

"You like her, don't you?"

"We're dating." He recalled the effort it had taken. Mature romance must work differently from young love. It had to overcome the baggage of two lifetimes apart, with much more to discover. Would Sarah approve? Why did that matter? He knew it still did. She'd been the love of his life. Even as a memory, she wouldn't be easy to replace.

He glanced down and saw Vincent was wearing one sneaker and one slipper.

Vincent followed the eyes and shook his head. "I'm taking my sneaker and slipper back to bed. You try and get some sleep."

He started to turn, but Gary reached out and grasped a sleeve. "Wait a sec."

The lieutenant was facing the ruined house as he spoke: "No shoe jokes, please."

Gary bent close and spoke as softly as the wind would allow. "I'd treat this house fire as arson."

Vincent turned back, instantly alert. "You know something?"

They were inches apart. "Man dies accidentally Tuesday, his house burns accidentally Wednesday. You believe in coincidence?"

"Another hunch?" With the slipper and a sneaker, Vincent had trouble with the police stare.

"Yeah."

The lieutenant's look conveyed his disbelief, but despite that and his footwear, he walked off to the remaining patrol car.

Gary locked the house securely and fell into a nightmarish half-sleep.

Were the printouts on his coffee table the only reason for that exquisitely timed house fire? Hannah should have been asleep at home. If she had, she and everything Norm had told her, along with those papers, would be ash. He'd be mourning two friends. As it was,

Norm's office had been incinerated, along with his computer.

Merle had been right to worry.

Strange that Norm's ghost, chains clanking, had chased Hannah away and thus saved her. Somewhere in the Beyond, did Norm get to do good deeds? One day, he'd share the thought with Hannah, but not soon.

Sarah shook her head and laughed. She was laughing at him. She was younger in his dreams, healthy and full of the passion she'd brought to his life. "Oh, please," she said, "don't screw up your second chance." She sounded tired. "I need to know you'll be okay, you big lug." Her laughter morphed into the jangle of the cell phone.

It was on the dresser. He stumbled to it. With eyes closed, he whispered hello.

A woman sobbed. "Oh, Gary!"

It was Becca.

PART TWO
§
A SHORT WAR

THURSDAY, FEBRUARY 19

~16~
2:12 A.M.

ADRENALINE surged. "What's wrong?" he rasped, heart pounding. He gripped the small phone and asked again. She didn't answer. Shivering in the dark, he heard labored breathing. "*What happened?*" he demanded, and she broke down into gasps and sobs.

He had to get to her. He stumbled toward his clothes, smashed against the dresser, almost dropped the phone. She needed help *right now.*

A change in sound alarmed him, and a different voice came on the line. "Are you Gary Kemmerman?" The girl's voice was shaky.

"Yeah." He leaned against the wall.

"Mom insisted I call *you,* but I called 911 first."

It was Becca's daughter. "Are you both okay?" Becca had said Melanie lived on campus. *Why were they together?*

"I'm fine. It's *Mom.*" She paused.

He pressed into the wall, forcing himself to speak softly, trying to calm her. "Tell me what's wrong."

When she gasped, a wave of anxiety hit him, and he almost shouted at her. She spoke in a staccato beat, near panic. "Someone broke in, used chloroform … I got her to examine herself … she wasn't—oh, thank God."

The wall kept him upright. "She hurt?"

"Just upset, confused."

"What happened to her?"

"Someone took off her pajama top, carried her to a chair, in her bedroom, taped her wrists to the chair ... I found her, crying."

"Only her top?"

"Oh, yes, thank God." So this was meant as a warning. He ignored his stomach. "Melanie, were you there through all of it?" He stepped into the closet, switched on the light.

"I didn't hear a thing till Mom screamed and woke me." She sighed. "Why would someone do this? It makes no sense."

It made perfect sense. "Your mother needs you to be in charge until the police get there. Can you do that?" He pulled underwear from a shelf.

"Yes."

"I'll be there soon as I can." Leaning against the door frame, he got his legs into it, tugged the briefs up with one hand.

"We may be at a hospital."

"No!" he heard Becca shriek. "I'm okay, no hospital."

In the diner, she'd said a nurse must separate her emotions from her profession. "Melanie, if you're gonna be anywhere but home, call me. Now, I need to speak to your mom." He stopped dressing and concentrated.

The line was silent, and then he heard sniffles. He said, "How are you feeling, exactly."

She spoke slowly. "I'm dizzy. My heart's racing."

"You injured?"

"No."

"You sure?"

"I checked. Mel did, too."

She sounded half-asleep. "Does the drug have side effects?"

She took awhile to answer. Waiting, he pulled jeans from a hangar. "I don't think so. None that last."

"Are you certain, really certain, you don't need a hospital checkup?"

"No! No hospital!" Her next words were softer. "I'll be okay."

He hoped he could rely on that. If EMTs thought she needed help, they'd still be there, or on the way to a hospital with her, when he showed up.

What worried him most was the danger she'd put herself in if she described the details to the police. Ignoring the warning could mark her for death. Lyons and Schroder had crossed that line.

"Becca, police and EMTs will be there soon." He moved the phone away from his ear. "Are you dressed?"

She snorted. "Of course!"

"Listen. I believe this was a warning. Let's talk about it when I get there, before we do anything that might make us more serious targets. They're going to ask you what happened. Tell them you woke up not feeling well. Skip the rest."

"I know." She whispered the words.

She knew? He leaned, almost brought down a clothing rod.

"I ... know who," she said, and choked up again.

He filed her words. "You'd best persuade your daughter to go along with you. You hang in there. I'll be with you soon as I can."

"It's snowing. Stay home," she pleaded. "We'll be okay."

"See ya soon." He broke the connection, finished dressing and ran out, knowing he had to get there—and that she wanted him.

While he dreamed of fire and death, the flurries had turned into a blizzard. Gusts tugged at his car door, heavy flakes blew sideways and spotted the driver's seat before he could slide in. Rolling down the small hill, he grasped what he'd overlooked. He drove faster.

On Tuesday morning, if that black SUV had been waiting on Norm's street, its occupants had seen him get into Norm's car. They'd worry about what Norm might have told him. But if they were at Hannah's just hours ago, that worry had to have become alarm, finding him and the witness together: two people who had no reason for being together other than the victim. That had forced whoever killed Norm to act.

He'd doubted Becca could be identified, failed to connect the dots even after she said Arman had recognized him. He'd been blinded by his feelings.

The right lane of Route 80 was plowed until, without warning, it wasn't. At speed, he rammed a drift, and it shoved back. The right side of his car bounded off the ground and it skidded out of control. He swung the wheel, jammed the brakes and the car spun around and around, shuddering to a stop in the middle of the highway. It stalled facing the wrong way, into traffic, everything dead but headlights angled toward the median. He was road kill.

Only at 3 A.M., in this blizzard, he was alone on the road.

He listened to his racing heart and the howling wind, sat leaning against the wheel, as still and stalled as his car. Even his headlights cut out, leaving him in darkness.

An auto traveling in the other direction broke the spell. Its driver must have been coming off a night shift. It was only time until another car hit him.

Becca filled his mind. He turned the ignition and the car restarted. Back with the engine came fans blasting hot air, beating windshield wipers, headlights illuminating falling snow—and in their cocoon he circled to change direction, shaky, thankful the air bags hadn't exploded and the car hadn't flipped.

The message was clear: a warning for him to focus, to wake from his year asleep.

After that, he drove carefully. He'd be no use if he were dead. As for falling in love, there'd have to be a better time.

Only there was no point bullshitting himself. He couldn't keep away from her.

Ahead of him, the wind built a curtain of snow, and he slowed. His being with Becca would raise her risk. He had to make her safe. *Could he love again, and survive her loss?*

Without willing it, he recalled the evening and saw her talking with his friends, understanding, waiting for him, standing up to him when she needed to, pressing close on her own to kiss him.

"Sarah, what should I do?" he asked aloud. He waited, but this time there was no answer. He heard road noise, saw blackness swallowing the polka-dotted flare of his headlights.

A gust rocked the car, but what shifted was inside him. "Becca," he said, like a prayer.

Soon he was speeding again.

~17~
2:58 A.M.

THE front lights were off. Even with the snow-brightness, he couldn't make out house numbers. But he spotted the ambulance down the street, illuminating the falling snow.

He slowed, aware of drawn shades, parted blinds, neighbors awakened by the commotion checking what was going on. He pulled up behind the ambulance. Its engine rumbled; exhaust puffed from the tailpipe and was whipped away.

Becca's gray Chevy, and a small red Saturn, filled the short driveway. The cars sat in low drifts, blanketed by snow. Before he turned off his headlights, two EMTs in reflective turnout coats pulled the front door shut and slogged toward the ambulance.

He intercepted them. "Everything okay in there?" He spoke loud enough to be heard over the wind, and the two-way chatter in one man's hand. The man with the radio continued toward the ambulance.

"You'll have to ask the women inside," said the closer man.

Gary nodded. The man holding the radio yelled back, "Let's get the rig movin'. Senior residence at Pomander."

Becca's two-story had a pitched roof and window shutters, he noted mechanically as he strode to the door. He pounded on it. The ambulance pulled away with a snarl. Snow gusted into his collar. He was fearful of what he might find, alarmed at his own lack of control.

"Who's there?" Melanie asked through the door.

"It's Gary." The door opened a crack, chain still on. Part of a face peered out before the door closed and the chain came off.

He searched for Becca the moment he stepped inside. "She okay?"

Melanie had backed a step, blocking him; she nodded. She was as tall as her mother and slender, with long, dark hair and a round, pretty face. She was barefoot, and she was wearing jeans and an FDU sweatshirt. Her face was drawn, made older by anxiety and the hour. But she looked right back, appraising as he was. Her mother wanted to call him first. He sensed her interest.

"She's in the shower. She'll be down when she's done." Seeing he'd stopped, she moved aside for him and closed the door, turned the deadbolt, hooked the chain.

"What'd the EMTs say?"

"They wanted to take her to the hospital, and *boy* she got upset." The moment Melanie turned back, her eyes were on him—darker than Becca's, older than her age. Her voice was higher pitched than her mother's. She'd calmed, but her nerves were coiled below the surface.

"She told them she was a nurse, she wasn't going *any*where." She flipped her wrist like a dancer when she emphasized words. "They told her to rest, drink lots of water, you know, and she'd probably be fine by morning." The girl stepped away from the vestibule slowly, watching him as she spoke. "The taller one said if not, she'd know what to do, since she was a nurse."

He could tell Becca had annoyed them. If that was true, she was on the road to recovery. Melanie led him into a small living room, a tranquil space with an Oriental rug, a couch, and chairs with salmon, maroon, and light green fabrics. A coffee table, an antique desk, and three lamps finished the room.

"Did you tell the police—"

"Yeah, we told them what you wanted." The hand was shaking at him like she was firing a gun. "Mom insisted I go along with her, and I did because I couldn't make her *more* upset." She glanced toward the stairs, making sure her mother was not in earshot, before she went on.

"Someone broke in and *attacked* her. That's *serious*, and it needs to be reported, even though what happened was weird. Why would someone attack *her* and not bother *me*? Why bring chloroform and tape, go to all that trouble, and …?" She couldn't put words to a worse outcome. She leaned toward him. "*You* must know why this happened. She said *you* asked her to lie about it."

He doubted Becca had told her what was going on. Melanie wasn't blaming him for what had taken place, and she might well, if she knew. "Has your mother mentioned an auto accident she witnessed Tuesday morning?"

The girl's eyes clouded over. "Please, sit." He peeled off his coat and laid it over the back of the couch, as Becca had done in his house. Melanie turned a small chair around and sat facing him. "Mom told me about the crash, and that poor man dying." Her long neck made her look coltish.

"I believe what happened here is related," he said. "I'd rather she and I talk to you about it together."

The shower kept going. He bet Becca would run out of hot water before she gave up trying to scour off what the night had brought.

The eyes were on him but the girl said nothing—he spoke into the pause: "She told me you live in the dorms."

"Yeah." She bent forward, rubbing her hands along her legs below her knees, and decided to tell him despite her annoyance. "Mom called when she left you. I drove home before the storm got bad."

"Does she often ask you to visit?"

Again Melanie glanced toward the stairs. "That's *your* fault." The left hand flipped. Before he could cringe, she added, "We talked for hours, about her, and us, and things, you know, but she really asked me over so she could tell me about you." She watched him, neck curved to the left.

He heard a wind gust, a shutter rattling. "How did you find her, when she woke you?"

The young woman raised her left hand to knead her right shoulder. "She was screaming my name. Afraid I was hurt. But I didn't know that, I thought she was having a bad dream, and I ran to her."

"Does she have bad dreams?" Except for the shower, the house was still—he heard no clocks, no appliances.

Melanie frowned at him and bit her lip before deciding. "She used to. *Real* bad dreams."

The hand that flipped stayed on her shoulder. He saw her distress. "Go on."

Tension caused Melanie to fire out words without pauses. "Like I told you before, I found her with her wrists taped to the chair. Whoever did that first removed her pajama top because it was on her bed. It was folded neatly ... and that's *crazy*. She ... she was dazed and so relieved I was okay. She was crying and holding me, and I didn't know what'd happened, but what I was trying to do was check whether she'd been hurt."

The hand came off her shoulder, found its companion, she rubbed them together. "I couldn't *believe* she hadn't been hurt, I couldn't *find* anything wrong, so I got her to examine herself. I told her she's a nurse and better at that than I am. We didn't find any cuts, bruises or burns at all."

He heard the cadence of 'cuts, bruises, or burns.' She'd said it like an oft-chanted litany. Had Becca been abused, back then? Might go a long way toward explaining the difficult time she'd given him, and why trust was so vital.

Free to get out what she couldn't tell the police, Melanie went on. "We were afraid the intruder might be waiting downstairs. That scared me, Mom too, so even though she said not to, I called 911 from upstairs. She told me where she'd written your number, but she was trembling and couldn't dial.

"We didn't dare come down until the ambulance got here. It beat the police car. When we saw lights, we checked from a window, to make sure it was them." She leaned back, hands on her thighs, breathing deeply, removing herself from that scene.

"You know how the intruder got in?"

She nodded, with another frown. "An EMT asked me to get water for Mom. I found a kitchen window open. I mean, you know, the window was closed, but the lock was open. I'd checked it before we went upstairs. Mom forgets those things, and I'm all over her about locking up. I *did* check. I *know* I did."

He had to do it. "Melanie, do you know if your father or her parents ever abused your mother?"

She looked at him sharply. The hands went into fists, the neck curved. "Come on, now, I'm not gonna get into that."

"I'm not trying to upset you." He spoke softly. "I'm concerned, because that might affect how she deals with this."

The girl smiled painfully and shook her head. But she relaxed, the hands opened. "I thought *I* was the house shrink."

"That's right. Your mom told me you're close to a graduate degree in psych."

She leaned closer. "You know, you're the first man she's asked into this house in *months*. She said she felt she could trust you." She paused, but she had more to say. "I'm not sure I want to know what it was you did, or why this all had to happen. We're just so lucky." Her upset surfaced, her eyes grew moist. "I've aged a whole year tonight."

"And I'm going on a thousand."

Becca surprised them both when she added, "Not on my account, I hope."

He turned and saw her leaning on the banister, standing on the second step, in jeans and a sweatshirt, feet bare, hair damp and hanging, slightly off balance.

"Truth is," he said, staring, "I've aged centuries tonight." He could barely talk. It was impossible, what was boiling up inside. He watched her walk off the steps. Her eyes were averted. But it wasn't her fault. We'll get through this, whatever it takes. He rose.

"You two must have met." She faced her daughter, but addressed him. "You got her to stop crying."

"I told him your secrets," Melanie said, tight herself.

"I have no secrets from this man. He and I are partners." Becca turned to him, eyes on his chest. "I frightened you. I'm so sorry."

She looked up and that was it, tears flooded his eyes, and she was against him, crying herself, no gentleness in their fierce hug.

Melanie burst into sobs. Becca and Gary separated, each held out a hand, and like a child she ran into their arms.

~18~
3:11 A.M.

MELANIE was sitting in the chair and wiping her face with the sleeves of her sweatshirt when she looked up, red-eyed. "A group hug."

"A family hug," Gary said from the couch, primly distant from Becca.

Melanie's glance was intense.

"Catharsis for three," Becca said. "How'd you arrange that?" She was limp, made no effort to repair her face.

He knew he hadn't arranged anything. He resisted wiping his eyes and turned to her. "None of what happened here was your fault. But there may be more to this. I need you both to show me your bedrooms."

"Oh, God," Melanie said. "Why?"

The question revived Becca, and she chuckled. "Mel, he was married a long time. He's seen lots of messy beds and ladies' underwear." She rose and helped pull him upright.

"Can I use the bathroom first?" the girl asked.

Her mother nodded; she loped off.

When they were alone, he asked, "On the phone, you started to say …."

"That I know who did this." Her face showed concern. "I knew you'd ask. Thanks for waiting until Mel left. She knows nothing."

"About the Lyons affair. *How* do you know who?"

She breathed deeply, placed palms against his chest, and leaned

114

forward. "I tried to wash his smell off my ... that awful cologne."

He put his hands over hers. He knew what she was about to say. Inside, something hard and cold dropped, lodged in his gut, and wouldn't go away.

Once Melanie returned, Becca led them up the stairs. "Strange way to lure an eligible man into my boudoir."

Her daughter tried to laugh. "I sure do change the dynamic."

"And rightly so," Gary offered, drawing hesitant chuckles, which pleased him because things were steady and he doubted they'd stay that way.

Becca indicated a doorway. "My inner sanctum."

He entered first. The room was small and functional, walls covered in flecked paper, with narrow pink stripes over a light gray background. Closed white blinds blocked two windows. The bed was a mess. A sliding closet door was open. Two chairs stood beside a small table beneath a mirror. One still had slivers of silver duct tape stuck to the arms.

The black slacks Becca had worn hours before were draped over an arm of the other chair. Her black bra lay folded on its seat. He couldn't help imagining her body, but this was not the time.

Nothing seemed out of place. He crouched by the chair with the tape, bent, sniffed at the arms and the back. It was there—a trace, but of a well-remembered odor. "He knew the smell would reinforce the warning."

"The person who did this to us—you *know* who he is?" Melanie asked, hand flipping.

"We think so," Becca said, when Gary hesitated.

"Is that odor the reason we're here?" The girl stood behind her mother by the doorway, a hand on Becca's shoulder.

If I were trying to leave a message, Gary was thinking, I'd reach out for the soft target in the house: he'd check Melanie's room next. Then the bathrooms, kitchen, everywhere, to prevent either of them from finding something on their own. "Let's take a look at your room, Melanie."

He followed them across the hallway. They waited at the entry.

The girl's room must have been patterned after a holiday in Bermuda. The walls were blocks of washed out yellow, green, and orange pastel. The carpeting was the same light gray, and a rumpled plaid quilt covered the bed. The bed, and the matching window curtains, had ruffles. The effect was delightful. He saw a small desk and its chair, bearing a haphazard collection of garments.

He suspected he'd find something, and when he considered where to look, he saw it right away. "Do you collect little cars?"

"They're boys' things," Melanie said.

"And no boyfriend gave you that?"

Becca saw it. "Oh, God."

A matchbox-style toy car was resting on the nightstand beside the head of Melanie's bed. He lifted it, using a tissue, and folded it into a pocket. It wouldn't yield prints, but he wanted it out of sight. "You have a decision to make," he said to Becca.

"Would someone *please* explain what's going on?" Melanie asked.

Becca nodded, freeing him to respond. "I'm afraid I've put you and your mom in the sights of a violent criminal."

"It's not your fault," Becca said.

"The car is a warning for us to back off."

"Why would he leave that toy, after what he did to Mom?" Again, the girl stood behind Becca, leaning toward Gary.

"To tell your mother that next time, he'll get *you*. Think of how clever. He saw your mother with me. He must have found her attractive, and—"

"You think *everyone* finds me attractive," Becca said, taking a step into the room. Sucked into her wake, Melanie followed.

Gary smiled and shook his head. "I said that because he went out of his way to combine his warning with voyeurism. He committed an invisible crime. What could you have reported to the police? No physical evidence supports a break in. No—how'd you put it, Melanie—'cuts, bruises or burns' are on your mother."

Becca glanced at her daughter. Melanie pretended not to see it.

Gary went on, "Becca, they'd call it sleep-walking. And if you reported the crime, it would make the local papers. Would you want to be known in the community as—"

"Don't even *go* there." She took another step toward him, and her daughter followed along. "Can't we have the police get him?"

116

"For what? Nothing we can prove. We don't know if he's part of a mob."

"So he—they—can keep right on doing whatever they want?" Becca asked. "Murder, assault? Why did they kill your friend? Or need to do what they did to me?"

"Someone was *murdered*?" Melanie gasped.

They were standing in a rough circle in the middle of the girl's room, and he faced her. "The accident your mom witnessed might be a murder." He didn't mention Sergeant Schroder. He turned to Becca. "Hannah told me Norm had found evidence of embezzlement at his employer. Hours ago, her house burned down."

"Oh, *no*! Was she—"

"She's safe," he said. Both women leaned toward him, distressed. Melanie grasped her mother's shoulder. "She'd just finished telling me why she believes Norm was murdered. We were at my house. She couldn't handle the ghosts in her own."

"This is way too much." Becca's voice was soft; she was twisting her ring. "Let's tell Vincent everything."

"Dinner's been put off, Becca."

"Why? They were looking forward to it … oh, the fire."

"Yeah. Vincent feels bad. I was going to call you, so you didn't buy dessert for six. He said they'd invite us soon." Then he had a notion.

"Maybe we can still have dinner Friday, and share dessert for two," Becca said.

The thought warmed him. "Let's make it dessert for five."

"You, me, Mel …?"

"Vincent and Angela. They live close to the hospital and the university. Until we get through this, I'd be afraid if you stayed here. Stay with them, at most for a week."

"We have to move *out* of here?" Melanie asked. She pawed at the shoulder.

Her mother turned her head and patted the girl's hand. "You live in the dorms anyway. They're open between semesters."

Both women watched him shake his head. "Even so, she'll also have to stay with them. Please, just for a while."

"Your friends would put us both up?" said Becca.

"I'll ask."

"That's asking a lot."

"I'd do it for them. If not, we can make other arrangements. My treat."

"Your treat?" Melanie said.

"Money, I have. It's your mom my life was missing." He'd spoken without thinking.

Becca smiled, but Melanie frowned. "Next semester doesn't start for a week, so I've got time. Mom can still go to work, right?"

He recognized the concern about finances—his remark may have led her down that path. She was looking out for her small family. He'd provide whatever was needed, but self-respect might not let them accept. He said to Becca, "I don't want to lose you income, but I'd like you to take time off. Can you do that?"

She nodded, still smiling.

"Can't we just forget this whole thing?" Melanie asked. "You know, back off, like you said the criminals want us to do, and get on with our lives?"

"I wish." Gary stepped back and sat on the edge of her bed. "I can't trust they'll understand we're out of it. Whether they meant to or not, they've left me with no choice but to be in the game. I can't be looking over my shoulder and worrying about you."

"Will one week make a difference?" the girl asked.

He recalled Riddock's words and said, "I'm gonna hit a wasps' nest with a stick," and immediately regretted voicing it. Becca paled. Melanie backed a step.

"You're not a cop, are you?" asked Melanie, voice shrill.

"He hasn't even got a gun," Becca said, in a whisper.

"Then how can you take on these murderers?" They both looked at him.

"Leave that to me." He said it calmly, hoping not to make things more difficult. "We have to get going. Pack some stuff. I'll put the bags in my car. You'll have to leave your cars here."

"Why?" Becca asked.

"Pavlic must have followed you from Hannah's. He'd recognize both cars." Gary imagined the man hiding outside in the dark the night before, waiting for Becca. She would have been easier to kill than the policeman. But then he must have seen Becca kiss him, and the personal relationship that revealed—a reason other than Norm Lyons for them being together—might have saved her. He blinked. The kiss might have saved him, too.

"If they've killed already, and you run around swatting at them," Becca said, and her voice broke, "won't they just kill you?"

~19~
8:00 A.M.

THE early-morning sun cast angular shadows down the familiar street. Gary walked in the plowed road as he had two days before, when Hannah called, hunched over this time as if a sniper was tracking him. The folder Hannah had given him was zipped beneath his coat, jammed under his belt.

He'd already left Becca and Melanie at the Alegrettis'. After introductions, Vincent had sat them down to get details of the attack, the accident, and anything else they might know. Gary had gone first, been brief, and not mentioned Merle or Riddock.

Once again, he'd suggested the deaths of Schroder and Lyons were linked. The news of Schroder's death had upset the Strassberg women. Angela had drawn them away to help her make hot chocolate and get familiar with the kitchen.

"This is serious," Vincent had muttered as soon as the women were gone. "Remember our agreement?"

"I don't know enough yet. Give me another day."

"Hannah expects you to meet Westbrook, so you're cleared for today. For today only," he'd said, clasping his hands and working the fingers. "Then you back off, or I swear I'll lock you up until this mess settles."

"Agreed."

"Ah!" Vincent had said, hands out, head shaking, "I wish you knew how to be careful."

Then Becca had returned, wanting to say goodbye, and followed him to the door. He'd taken her hand, but she pressed close and hugged him. He'd felt her heartbeat, hands kneading his back like a cat's, heard a small moan, "Don't go." But there was so much to do.

He'd returned home and taken the pill that calmed his stomach and allowed him to eat most foods.

The last thing he'd done there was reclaim Hannah's folder, and it burned against him as a black SUV appeared in the road, the killers come to get back what was theirs. He was poised to run when he saw that the vehicle had a neighbor's vanity plate. As it passed, he waved and turned onto the Cabreras' front walk. Dalton opened at the first knock.

"On the button, Gary. ... wow, what bags under those eyes. That woman must be great in the sack." He blocked the door, waiting for an answer.

Gary couldn't see the road. The killers, firing at him, might hit Dalton. "Let me in."

"Oh, sure." He moved aside, and Gary stepped into safety.

"Want coffee?" Nadine asked, coming in from the kitchen in puffy red slippers and a thick robe, hair tangled from sleep.

"Yeah, sure," Dalton said.

"Yours is on the counter, sweetie. Good morning, Gary. I meant you. You look like you need it. You can take off your coat."

"Yes to the coffee, and thanks." Dalton took his coat to hang it, Nadine went back to the kitchen, and Gary asked, loud enough for both to hear, "How's Hannah?"

Nadine returned with two steaming coffee mugs. Gary took his with his right hand—the Consolidated folder was in his left, three sheets that weighed a ton.

"What's that?" Dalton asked, motioning toward it with his cup.

Nadine ignored her husband's question, glanced to her right as if she could see through walls to Hannah, and told Gary, "She's well as you can expect. Naomi forces her to eat, even to cook, to keep her busy. It's therapy for both of them."

Gary nodded and pulled the folder closer to prevent Dalton from grabbing it. "I need favors from both of you. But you have to keep what I tell you secret."

"Secret?" Dalton asked. "What's goin' on?"

Nadine's expression changed. "Maybe we should sit. You didn't get any sleep at all last night, did you, Gary?"

He leaned forward in the small chair beside Dalton, in the man's office. The attic had been insulated and fitted with a plug-in radiator and a through-the-wall air conditioner. It contained a covered computer tower under a table, two others displaying their guts on desktops, several flat monitors, three printers, tangles of USB busses, and bits and pieces of other gear Gary couldn't identify, wires strangling everything. Dalton was talented, not neat.

He waved the file Gary had given him, looking pensive. "Are the police handling this?"

"No. Least not 'til you say so." The office was too warm for him.

"How's Norm's death connected to it?" Dalton kept the folder airborne.

"Monday night he told Hannah these were evidence of major theft. He was pushed off the road on his way to work Tuesday morning."

Dalton nodded, and pensive turned into brooding. "Lean back. Close your eyes. Rest while I examine this stuff. Won't take long."

The chair wasn't comfortable, but the killers seemed far away, the attic was hot, and the equipment hummed like a lullaby. Gary closed his eyes and slipped back several hours in time.

They had been at Becca's. He would have preferred not to wake the Alegrettis, but there was no other way. When Angela answered the phone at 4:30 A.M., he'd asked if they'd put up Becca and her daughter. Being a police officer's wife may have prepared her for such late night requests: She'd asked why, spoken briefly with Vincent, and they'd agreed to a seven o'clock arrival.

"We can't wait to greet them. Now let us sleep," she'd said, when he tried to express gratitude.

Friends help friends, and Gary had chalked up a big one for those two.

The women had packed a few bags and he'd loaded them into his car. The mood had been somber. He'd driven carefully in the waning snow, checking that no one was following. En route, he'd offered breakfast at the diner. Becca had declined, but Melanie was hungry.

When they arrived at the restaurant, Becca had insisted they sit in the back room. They'd been led to a table and presented with the oversized menu by a waitress they must have woken up. Melanie toyed with salt and pepper shakers as she glanced around. "Wildly romantic," she said.

"Don't be a wise-ass," her mother snapped, looking up from the menu.

Becca must have told her, he realized—*and* found Tuesday evening's conversation romantic.

The waitress sidled up, pad in hand. He smelled bacon cooking on the grill, couldn't think of food. The women started with hot chocolate; he ordered coffee. They put napkins in their laps; he couldn't keep his hands still. He'd only known her for two days. He was being absurd. But he was certain.

"Can I speak freely in front of Melanie?" he asked. Becca caught gravity in his tone, studied him, and nodded. He took a deep breath. "Would you marry me?"

"Wow," Melanie said, dropping a shaker, righting it without looking.

Becca didn't move, but her eyes filled. "I can't."

He spoke to cover his shock. "You don't have to decide right now."

"I can't," she whispered, menu forgotten.

Melanie looked alarmed, bit her lip to stay still.

He gripped the table to avoid shaking. "Why not?" He barely heard himself. Maybe he'd read her, the situation, all wrong.

"I'm still married." She strangled the words.

"What?" Melanie was startled.

He flooded with relief. "That's okay. Let's live together. We have plenty of space for Melanie. I'll paint a bedroom with those terrific colors." Both women watched him. "Maybe one day?" He blinked. "I love you."

Never in his life had he seen such vivid eyes. His right hand was flat on the table and her left hand moved to cover it, but it was her only answer because she turned toward her daughter.

Melanie swung around. "Why didn't you get divorced?" The voice sounded like it ached.

Becca glanced at him, and back. "I was afraid letting him know where we were would draw him to us. I'm grateful for you, but I'm not proud of anything else with him."

"You said we had to leave 'cause he hurt you." Her deep eyes were filled with pain. "He hit you, you cried, I don't remember—is that why?"

Becca worked her lips. Her voice was raw. "I couldn't accept it when he began touching *you*."

Melanie's mouth dropped open.

Bright fluorescents had powered on elsewhere in the diner, but the women hadn't noticed. Gary had done the math. She'd been almost thirteen. Maybe it'd seemed normal affection, maybe not.

Becca had rested her other hand on her daughter's shoulder. Melanie reached for the hand, breathing deeply, blinking, had clasped it like an anchor in both of hers. She'd gazed around the diner, from side to side, and, helpless to prevent it, started to cry.

"Did Norm print these out?"

Dalton's voice pulled Gary back. He pushed up in the chair. "What'd you say?"

"Unless you get some sleep, today's a bad day for you to tackle bad guys." Dalton bent toward him. When Gary didn't respond, he went on: "I asked whether Norm printed these."

"I don't know," Gary said. "That important?"

Lost in thought, the computer man peered at the small calculator in his hand. "The scheme is clever. $2,163,837 was transferred in January, and the funds came from 7,650,000 accounts. That sounds like Consolidated's global total. The transfer equals 28-point-something cents per account. I think they were skimming the float."

"Float?"

"Money not otherwise invested," Dalton said, talking to the

calculator. "It's usually swept into a low-interest fund, so it won't be idle."

He leaned sideways and pulled a sheet from a corner of his desk. "In January, Nadine earned 2.84 percent a year on those funds. That's"—he worked the calculator—"point 00236667 times her money a month—or $5.36. Investors don't even notice that income." He looked up and smiled. "I could set this up myself, but what I'd do is round a point-five at the end to zero. That would be more than enough."

"So that's all they took?"

"That's the clever part. Who'd notice?"

"How'd Norm find it?"

Dalton set down his wife's sheet and waved the folder. "I bet Norm saw these, on a screen, a desk—he'd have had to know the code to print it." He frowned. "We're talking $26 million a year. God knows what else may be going on. You haven't told Vincent?"

"Not yet."

Dalton nodded. He shifted in his chair as if the machine on the desk was talking to him. "Some sub-routines can identify every computer that enters the system. If Norm went in, it might be why they killed him."

Gary leaned forward. "Will you go in?"

"For sure. That's the fun part."

"How?"

"Hack in—you know that. Lotta bucks made keeping things honest." He shifted the folder to his left hand and rubbed his eyes with his right. "We see what their other reports look like, how their addresses are organized and are they like this one, what protocols control money transfers and were they employed here, where the little cents came from, and especially where the big bucks went to."

He pulled away when Gary reached out. "My job. I'll give it back. How about I copy these for you?"

"Sorry I brought this to you, Dalton. I can't let you do what Norm did, and have them target you and Nadine." He reached out again.

Dalton grinned. "Wait up. How would it be if the crooks found police computers hacking into their world?"

"Can you do that?" He put his hands on his knees.

"For sure." Dalton looked like the cat that ate the canary. The folder was airborne again. "I helped Vincent's department set up its Computer Investigation and Technology Unit. My fee was so low it was almost a public service, but I get to play with their toys. Can't imagine a better use."

"It would be good to have a few days before the crooks know you're in their system," Gary said.

There was a pause while Dalton considered that. "I doubt they check the program every day."

"Sure they can't trace you?"

"If good guys find me, they'll just beef up the firewall, strengthen the biometrics, anti-virus software, intrusion detection systems. If they're thieves, we'll scare the hell out of whoever manages their system."

That got Gary's attention. "Someone has to *monitor* these programs?"

"Sure. The 'malware'—name for rogue software—was probably introduced by an insider. Consolidated defends against unauthorized access. It's easier to compromise the system from within." He waved the folder. "This is turned on to do what they want, then off as quick as they can, so anybody else who uses or protects the system won't notice it."

"How do they hide what they're doing?"

It took Dalton a full minute to frame his answer. "It's a masquerade. Without going into root kits, kernel levels, assembly language—stuff you won't understand—the malware mimics its environment to give it a legitimate footprint."

"Footprint?"

Dalton rubbed his chin and shook his head before he replied. "We run detective programs to identify the change—or footprint— unauthorized access leaves. Without that, if auditors hit upon missing funds, they might not know how they were taken, or where they went. They'd have no way of finding the report you brought."

Gary felt Dalton's excitement but didn't try to understand the explanation. "You have their output. That's your way in?"

Dalton tilted his head. "I have to sneak in and prove it. I love this stuff, especially when it's real."

Gary made the connection. "I may know the insider who monitors the invisible programs."

Dalton set the folder down and leaned toward him. "Have I told you how gorgeous your Becca is?"

"Not so far today, but it's early."

"You wanna enjoy life with her, better stay alive. Don't push this. Leave it to Vincent's troops." He reached out, tapped at Gary's knee. "They have guns, and there are lots of them."

"If you find nothing," Gary said, "don't call, I'll probably see you tonight at the Alegretti's. If it is theft, tell Vincent right away." He pushed up from the chair. "I don't need copies of the folder. Leave the sheets with the lieutenant."

And he can put them right next to Merle's envelope.

~20~
9:05 A.M.

Gary sipped coffee at a table near the Marriott GrandPointe lobby piano bar. He needed the coffee. The clouds had blown away, and morning sunlight brightened a snow-covered landscape too cold to melt. The glare penetrated even through the huge, dark-tinted lobby windows.

He felt like a secret agent, waiting for an unknown courier to pass along a coded message he had to read with transposed digits: move the first number to last. The clandestine meeting would take place in that room. At the elevator banks, he was to make sure he was alone in a car and press every floor so his evil pursuers couldn't know where he got out. Riddock hadn't told him whether the number would be written on rice paper he could swallow. He'd bring the scrap with him, give it back, and ask.

He sat among small round tables and malt-shop retro chairs on a low platform, separated from the rest of the atrium lobby by potted palms, a waterfall-pond feature and decorative railing. The hotel was twenty-four years old and the lobby, with marble floors, rounded columns, and recessed lighting, relied more on dignity than pizzazz. The piano music came courtesy of a non-union player piano.

Two mornings before, he'd have scoffed at Riddock's precautions. But not today. The PI had called while he was home retrieving Norm's pages, before he met Dalton. He'd told Riddock they needed to meet in person, quickly, the three of them. The man hadn't protested.

Gary knew in his gut that Arman had killed Norm and attacked

Becca, left his smell, threatened her young. A rock through a window was a warning—what Arman did, meant war.

There was risk in tweaking a brutal man, tied to an unknown group who operated beyond conventional morality. But he'd bury the bastard. He hadn't known he had such hatred in him.

"Excuse me."

Startled, he looked up at a bellman. The boy offered a distracted smile, as if he were here but preferred to be elsewhere. "Are you Mr. Gary?"

He nodded.

"Room 520 is ready for you."

The boy turned and left. And Gary had no rice paper to swallow.

Merle opened the door to Room 205 with a finger at his lips. Standing, the man was shorter than Gary remembered, and in bright light, the glasses gave him pop-eyes. Riddock was sitting at a group of three chairs, drawn away from the first table and placed facing each other. He waved Gary over.

It was a small meeting room. A podium faced four tables covered with white cloths, each surrounded by six chairs and set for lunch, right down to red linen napkins. The windows were hidden by drawn maroon drapes. Fluorescent lighting lent a yellowish tinge.

How many small conference rooms had he worked in, with too much coffee and chain-smoking clients? Confrontational, frightened people? It felt like another lifetime.

Merle bent behind the podium. Classical music washed over them. "We can talk now," he said as he approached.

Gary wondered why they'd chosen this place, and why Riddock—who looked worried—wore no disguise. But first he had to know if he was right. "Tell me the name," he said.

The little man sat down in the vacant chair. "What name?"

"The person you referred to Westbrook." Gary noticed Merle's right eye wandered—perhaps he had a touch of amblyopia. It seemed he was watching Gary, and everything around him, at the same time.

"The one they want me to recommend?" the little man said.

"Come on, Merle. I mean the man who's already there. The one probably involved in Lyons' death."

"You have enough to make this worthwhile?"

"Oh, yes." Gary looked away from the glasses.

Merle nodded, but Riddock answered. "Arman Pavlic."

Reason for his worry, Gary thought, and said, "Rings no bells." He watched for a reaction. The broad-shouldered PI wore a gray t-shirt and long black sweat-pants, legs cinched at the bottoms. His parka hung lopsided over the back of his chair—was the gun in a coat pocket, or in one of the two bags that lay behind the big man? Gary used a bag like that for the gym. The sweats must be Riddock's disguise: Merle must be a member of the Spa attached to the hotel.

"Don't play poker for money," the small man said with a leathery smile, glasses flashing as he shook his head.

Riddock rubbed his knee and added, "Pavlic was late for work Tuesday morning by about an hour and a half. At times he leaves during the day, but he's always there to open up. Just not on the morning Lyons died." He leaned forward, and stared at Gary. "Now, tell us why we're here."

Gary walked them through everything, from his chat with Norm in the car to his conversation with Dalton, who was by then at the police station with the purloined printouts. He included Becca's recollections, and his theory about Schroder's murder.

"Some things stand out. Arman checked the papers Norm had in his car, but then someone else—a second caller—asked what he'd discovered." Gary realized that, if he hadn't questioned Schroder, the information might have been lost. "Dalton says no one could get into the thieves' program without knowing the codes. How'd Norm get them?"

"Your thoughts?" Merle asked. Now both men leaned close.

Gary shifted in the chair and clasped his hands. "Teodors Medved could be key to this. He's the whiz-kid programmer Arman brought from abroad. Hannah said he was Norm's friend. If he's the keeper, he might have answers for us."

Riddock scribbled into a pocket notebook and looked up. "Why would *he* talk to *us*?"

Over their heads, one of the florescent tubes began to buzz like a wasp. The thought caused Gary to lower his voice.

"I'll bet he'd meet me on behalf of Norm's family. So I can use his remembrances to console his friend's widow." He stroked his chin. "Medved may be the one who phoned the police. It fits, if he knew Norm accessed those reports. If Medved was Norm's friend, he'd be upset about his death. Especially if Norm got the codes from him: That would make him responsible."

Gary slowed. "It's not something that would please the killers he works with. Medved may have called to find out if he's in trouble." He made another connection. "We might want Medved protected."

"Why?" Riddock asked, his pen and notebook frozen.

"If he's their hands-on guy, he can point fingers. If the crooks want to introduce another top-level programmer into Consolidated, that—"

Gary's phone sounded. He glanced at the screen, held a finger up for quiet, and flipped it open. "Can't talk. But I can listen."

"Bingo," said Vincent. "It was arson."

Gary rose, moved toward the podium, and faced away from the others. "That was quick."

"They're all over it when we suggest arson. Tell you why tonight. Angela's called twice, and she never does that. Your visitors are terrific."

"Thanks. You're sure because. . . ?"

"They found C4 traces on the gas line."

"I was hardly sleeping, and I didn't hear a big bang."

"Slow gas leak, timer, basement explosion as an accelerant."

"What now?"

"We're investigating Norm's death." And Schroder's, he didn't have to say.

Gary started to pace. Merle and Riddock were watching him and whispering to one another. He turned away. "Dalton there?"

"Playing with his toys."

"Speak to him."

"He connected?"

"You'll love what he may have."

"Thanks. Be careful."

"Bye, buddy."

"That was Vincent," said Merle, pointing at him. "What

happened?"

No keeping secrets from that man. Standing a few feet away, with both men looking up at him, Gary reported.

"When did the fire start?" Riddock asked.

"Around midnight." He reclaimed his seat.

The PI made another note, glanced at Gary, and said, "They must have wanted to burn up the widow."

Merle looked worried. He removed the glasses and wiped them. He looked different with them off. "So far we have two murders, an attempted murder, arson, and an attack on a witness. They're spooked." He slid the glasses up his nose. "We'll do what we can to protect Medved. You want to meet Westbrook?"

"I have his card," Gary said. "He expects me to call and visit him today. Maybe Riddock should be there with me."

"Anything you want me to ask him?"

"You're sure he's straight in all this, Merle? Not been—"

"Yes." The word was almost cut off by his teeth.

"You realize—"

The small man's reaction pushed him forward in the chair; he waved his right hand in dismissal. "I'd trust him with my life. He and I have been through a lot."

Gary nodded. "Let's keep Norm's death and the fire separate from the printouts and theft. How about we tell Westbrook all Norm's stuff was burned up? Then we can work the crash without raising the specter of theft—or the thieves may cut their losses, maybe Medved, too, and run."

"What about the C4?" Riddock asked.

"Sure. We can tell Westbrook it's triggered an investigation into Lyons's death. Let's ask Westbrook to bring his director of security on board. That way, Pavlic will know he's made waves with Norm and the fire—it's better for us if he concentrates on that."

Merle nodded. "What do we do now?"

"I'll get in front of Westbrook—I hope with Riddock—and try to visit Medved. Once the lieutenant learns what the printouts mean, I'll bet he brings in big guns." As the music paused, so did Gary. He glanced toward the lectern. Sound resumed, a louder aria, with two vocalists.

"We have to get back to the gym," Merle said, heading toward the music.

When Gary returned to the lobby, he wasn't sure he'd accomplished anything in Room 205. He glanced around, but no one seemed to be watching him. He went to the opposite side from where he'd been—it might be quieter without the tinkling piano. He had three calls to make: Medved, Westbrook, and Becca.

He sat on a bench along the front wall. Piles of luggage lay on the floor. Groups of people, many with cameras, chatted about what they'd seen yesterday, where they were going today, how they liked their rooms and food. He heard Statue of Liberty, Ellis Island, Empire State Building, Broadway.

It was too noisy and exposed for what he had to do. He moved through the lobby, back into the hotel and down a wide corridor, past banks of elevators disgorging more luggage, more guests, more noise.

Beyond the elevators to his right, double-doors were open onto an empty meeting room. It was set assembly-style, with hundreds of chairs facing an imposing dais backed by an outsized projection screen. An easel beside the doorway held a professionally done poster proclaiming the upcoming session: *Spirituality—The Path to God*, it read.

The Lord works in mysterious ways, and Gary needed all the help he could get. He turned into that room, sat in God's silence, and made his calls.

~21~
9:45 A.M.

IT annoyed Arman, having to come to Medved's rooms on a day he didn't have to drive the boy to the office. He usually waited downstairs—what he found upstairs was upsetting. Worse even than the small kitchen was the computer area, where disks, computer parts, crumpled paper, candy wrappers, even soda cans, lay scattered like piles of garbage across the table, on a chair, on the worn rug.

He scowled. "Teo!"

The boy's voice squeaked with alarm. "I know ... what is where." His brown hair was spiky and unkempt, his movements almost random as he flapped his arms, waving toward the disks. His flannel shirt was torn; he was unmindful of what he wore.

Arman wondered how the boy could live in this heat, with covered windows and poor lighting. In contrast, he imagined the palace he would build back home. Millions in profit—part his— rested in banks across the world. But he felt uneasy. If he had to flee, he wanted to duplicate this success elsewhere. To do that, he needed Teo.

He said, in Russian, "Where's the master copy? It's overdue. I'm tired of waiting."

Teo withered, and his eyes dropped. "Soon. I try—"

Arman gestured with his right hand, a practiced motion, like drawing a pistol. "Speak our language."

The boy shrugged. "What you want is complex. I have to layer in elements of the original system."

"Are you making progress?" He lifted a CD from the table and read what Teo had marked on its cover. He could translate the words but had no idea what they meant.

"Yes." The boy began to collect the disks, stooping, scooping, and looking away from his boss.

"You've said that before." Arman held out the CD in his hand, forcing the youngster to face him and reach for it. "It has to be ready soon." He didn't release it, trapping the boy. "When?"

Medved shifted his feet, pulling away from the disk like it was a hot potato. "Maybe three days."

Arman sensed his reluctance. "Make it two."

The boy sighed.

"I'll drive you tomorrow. You give me the complete program in the afternoon. Are we clear?" He offered the disk a second time.

Medved nodded, took it, and hung his head.

Arman knew if the boy could not finish, Serge's new person would. Either way, Teo would not be left to incriminate them. He smiled.

Medved lifted his eyes. The boy, thought Arman, must believe the smile was for him. "Good lad." He nodded. "You'll get a large bonus. You'll make your family very happy."

"Thank you, Arman."

Arman glanced around, and left.

Medved was aware of his heartbeat. Since Norm's death, things had changed. Only Arman knew what Norm had done. Now Arman was pushing, as if there were a deadline.

He stood against the door, glancing at the sorry rooms. Was it too late? He was already a criminal.

His computer beckoned, its 23-inch screen a window. He called up his bank account in the Caymans, reported to no government, accessed only by his passwords; the balance read $392,148.83.

For Consolidated, he monitored systems that sent a river of funds flowing among the company, financial institutions, and millions of client accounts. But not all of it was legitimate. Diverted by his sub-routine, a small portion streamed abroad for Arman. This he'd adapted, and now a small fraction snaked through the ether to his own survival account.

But he had no way to get the money, and no escape plan.

He punched off the account. Back came the Consolidated logos, with his blinking to-do list. A branch in Paris had to be tied into Consolidated's French national system, European network, and global reporting.

Would he ever see Paris? He kicked off his shoes. He couldn't concentrate. In four hours, a man named Gary was coming. No one had ever been in his rooms except Arman and Ana, the nasty old lady who owned the building, provided food, and would tell Arman if he tried to leave, if she didn't shoot him first. He'd seen her pistol.

His phone had rung just before Arman's arrival. He knew he shouldn't meet this Gary, but he'd do what he could to comfort Norm's widow.

The blinking list grabbed his attention. Where was this Paris branch? He entered Consolidated's Imagery and Mapping Agency service, pulled up the capital of France from satellite distance, zoomed in and found the branch on the Champs Elysées, near the Arc de Triomphe. Trees, bare in February, lined the sidewalks. Would he be there one day? In springtime, on vacation?

He used his fingers to fly across Europe to a neighborhood near the Old Town in Riga. Did his brothers still live in that small, dank house?

When he lived there, Mother had adored him—her youngest, with computer talent from early childhood. A brother had worked the docks, another in a steel fabricating plant. They had earned little for backbreaking labor, came home tired, often drunk.

Mother had told his brothers he was golden. At seventeen, he'd earned more than they had combined. She'd saved the best food, bought the best clothes, for him. She'd made him sit at the head of the table. She'd told his brothers they were dolts, as their father had been before he left for another woman. Teo had sensed their fury, but they could do nothing about it except drink more.

One day, Mother had been at her sister's when his brothers got home. They'd beaten him but been drunk enough for him to squirm free and run. At first, he'd stayed with a friend his family knew nothing about. It had taken weeks for the pain and bruises to fade. He couldn't go home, or back to work. His brothers had been looking for him. They needed his income.

At that moment Arman had said, "Come to America, work for me, and you'll be rich." Medved had wanted no part of the man—until his life fell apart.

His head itched. He scratched, wiped fingers on his shirt, returned them to the keyboard, and cut the Riga view. His priority must be what he'd promised Arman. But he couldn't concentrate.

He rose and found the remote to the television Arman had bought for him. When Medved learned why he had been brought here—to turn an auditing keyhole into a vehicle for theft—he'd resisted.

Arman had shredded his tourist visa, found his cash box and put the bills into his own pocket. Worst had been his smile. So Medved had become effective as an employee for Consolidated, and a thief for Arman.

But he'd spent time learning English from TV programs, starting with *Sesame Street*, sitting close, the volume low. English was the first task, and he'd hidden his ability from everyone. Escape was the second.

He knew fate owed people nothing. He'd have to make his own luck. Today, he'd done poorly. He sank onto a chair in the semi-darkness, the remote unnoticed in his hand. With his promise to Arman, he worried, had he shortened the rest of his life to thirty hours?

~22~
11:18 A.M.

Riddock Maguire sat on the edge of his desk and looked around the small office. "Shall we meet?" Everett Maguire and Kathryn Reilly—his brother and future sister-in-law—smiled. Working in one room plus a tiny kitchenette, with the bathroom in the hall and a computer on each desk, they met whenever they paid attention to one other. Their desks were three feet apart. Their coats hung on a wooden tree beside the door. Both windows in the room faced another office building; if they leaned close and peered left, a green-in-summer lawn was visible.

"The coven is now in session," Kathryn said. She was slender, with blonde hair and freckles, and her quick sense of humor complimented his brother's edgy personality.

Everett had a scrawny build, prominent nose, and Adam's apple; he didn't look like Riddock despite being his younger brother. "The adopted one," they joked. He'd followed Riddock into police work, lured by the dark sunglasses and "special agent" status of his role model. Two years before, Riddock had persuaded his brother to join him as a partner in the agency. It would be safer, he felt.

By the time Kathryn entered Everett's life, the agency had needed help. After she accepted his brother's marriage proposal, Riddock had surprised them by making her a partner. Five months later, she'd staked out roles as an intuitive researcher, an excellent photographer, and the invisible one in the crowd.

Riddock sat on the edge of his desk, facing them. "We have a job

138

for Consolidated, and I'd like your take on it."

Agency Rule One was, *NO one gets hurt.* The ex-FBI agent remembered friends who'd felt invincible behind the dark sunglasses, and hadn't been. If a job was dangerous, Riddock worked it. He'd put his partners through a version of boot camp, complete with exercise, weapons training, and courses in criminology, research, and surveillance.

"We need to keep tabs on a young Consolidated programmer who works at home three days a week and rarely goes out when he's there. He has second-floor rooms in an attached house in a bad neighborhood. He's driven to the office two days a week. He may be working for criminals. In the past three days, they may have killed an auditor on the road, torched his home, attacked the only witness to his crash, and killed the investigating policeman."

Sun-glare off the neighboring gold-glass building lit the office; they didn't need lights on sunny days in February until mid-afternoon. The eyes watching him looked bright and worried. "What do we do?" he asked.

Everett pushed back his sandy hair. "Get reinforcements."

Riddock watched his brother force himself not to glance at Kathryn. She wanted to handle fieldwork, and resented her fiancé's efforts to protect her. The last time Everett had interfered, she'd thrown a tissue box at him.

"You're right. If we tail 'em, sit on their street, try to question 'em, we might catch shit."

Everett and Kathryn were used to dealing with garden-variety employee theft, marital hanky-panky, missing children, a client category they'd named "family fund fights," and the like. This was different.

"Can we drive him to work?" Everett asked. Yesterday, he'd been involved in a missing persons case, and Kathryn had helped bring him up to speed on Internet telephone directory sites.

"His boss drives him," Riddock said. "I doubt he'd be allowed to get into anyone else's car."

Kathryn tapped a pencil against her desktop. "This for real, or are you testing us?"

"For real. Could be if the crooks sense anyone coming down on this kid, they'll kill him and we lose our best—maybe only—witness against them."

Everett said, "We can break into his home while he's at work."

At times Riddock felt itchy, contemplating mistakes that might get his family killed. He thought of the bottle in his desk. "Kathryn wouldn't like that, bro. The people downstairs are probably with the crooks. We'd find a welcoming party once we left, or we wouldn't make it out." He rose and returned to his seat. His desk was at the left; he could see them both.

"Why not save us all time?" Kathryn asked. "Just tell us."

"Sure." He leaned back, canting the chair like a rocker. "I visited the man's street this morning."

"And you were dressed as …?"

He smiled, nodding at Kathryn. "I thought of your friendly meter man, but then I bought a bottle of Thunderbird, took a pull, and stuck it in a coat pocket." He laughed, pulled the bottle out of a drawer and set it on the desk. "Anyone want a taste? Gotta tell ya, it's awful."

Kathryn grinned and shook her head. "And I'll bet you staggered and slurred."

"Both. The only way into the house is from the front. The rear backs on a razor-wire chain-link fence. So I rented a room in a house across from his place. Kathryn, I want you to get in there with the digital camera—turn off the flash."

He chose not to respond to Everett's frown, replaced the bottle, and went on, focusing on her: "Lock the door, keep the lights out, and don't make noise. Draw the shades down to three inches. Bring bottled water, a cold lunch, nothing that smells—no garlic, please— and our port-a-john; don't need strange diseases in the family."

She smiled—even Everett did, though he leaned forward, hands clenched.

"Use our best designer-label frumpy clothes," Riddock continued, "a dark wig and thick glasses, and cover those freckles. Could be the loaded knapsack, tied under the front of your coat, might make you look older, even unattractive, if that's possible."

"Good," Everett said. She laughed at him.

Riddock had more. "Photograph anyone who visits, stands on

the street, or sits in a car. If we can't break in, we can see who else comes along. Bring your cell phone." He considered, and added, "Call me every time something happens. We clear?"

She was taking notes. "Will do." She turned to Everett. "You promise me you won't jump all over your brother for this."

Her fiancé didn't meet her eyes, but his hands unclenched. He turned to Riddock: "What's your role in this, bro?"

He heard the stress in Everett's voice. "I'll meet Westbrook, protect Kingsley, and decide how to use what Kathryn comes up with." Riddock unlocked the closet, used another key to open the gun cabinet, and took out a .32 Smith & Wesson. "Kathryn, you're expert with this weapon. The work shouldn't put you in harm's way, but I'd feel more comfortable if you have it. Try not to need it. If you go up against these men, they'll kill you. But if you want to be in the big time, you have to learn to carry." He handed her the weapon and felt Everett's eyes hot on him.

"Great," Kathryn said. She held the pistol like a mound of Jell-O, but her smile was glorious.

~23~
NOON

THE secretary closed the door behind him. "Thanks for seeing me," Gary said to Westbrook, as he stepped into the impressive corner office. Walls of windows, without nearby buildings, made it feel like they were meeting in the sky; the carpet was so thick he was walking on clouds. He recalled the president's stiffness yesterday, and expected he'd have to fight hard for Hannah.

"It's Gary, right?" Westbrook asked. He stood from behind a massive, sculpted desk, in shirtsleeves and dark blue slacks, manner relaxed, tone friendly. "Call me Morgan."

Gary found the man different—and when Westbrook smiled and pointed to a group of chairs by a window, he followed his lead.

The grey-haired president stood and lifted a folder—same style and color as the one Norm had brought home—from the desk. He came over and sat in the chair beside Gary, rather than facing him.

"I gave this regrettable—that doesn't say it, does it," and he shook his head —"situation some thought, and had decisions formalized so we could turn them over to you for Hannah Lyons."

"Decisions?"

Westbrook understood. "Hear me out. I'm trying to be helpful and generous. We're side-by-side so we can examine documents together, in case you've questions."

"We appreciate that, I think."

Westbrook grinned, ran fingers inside his collar, and finally opened the button. "That's better."

When Gary just waited, the president glanced toward the folder and began: "There are three fund flows. First is life insurance. Lyons had the usual, two years compensation, double indemnity for accidental death. That's in the neighborhood of $325,000, a hefty chunk of change."

The grey-haired man opened the folder, handed Gary a sheet, and went on. "This form—which I've signed for Consolidated—together with a death certificate and an accident report from the police, both of which have to come from your side, will give you what she needs for the insurance company. Policy copy, names, phone numbers."

The president sat quietly until Gary had scanned the sheet, and returned it to the folder. Sunlight faded behind a cloud—ceiling lights brightened as soon as it became darker. The windows were heavily tinted.

"Thanks," Gary said. The windows offered a lot of blue sky. The air outside was frigid, but there would be no snow.

Westbrook pulled out a clipped sheaf of papers. "Life insurance proceeds usually aren't taxable," he said, turning to Gary and handing over the pile. "Next is the retirement plan. We use a 401k. Norman Lyons was fully vested. Holdings, value, and contacts are enclosed." Once Gary returned the sheets he'd been given, Westbrook slipped them back in, closed the folder and looked up, as if he were done.

"You mentioned three fund flows," Gary said.

Westbrook smiled at him and went on without referring to the folder. "We can keep her health insurance in our plan under COBRA, for 18 months. She'll have the same medical benefits as before, but she'll have to pay for them." He tapped the folder. "Amazing, how costly health insurance has become. To make that easier, we'll provide her late husband's full salary to her, for as long as she's on COBRA, and automatically deduct the premiums. We'll have to take out social security and estimated state and federal taxes. All this is in a memo in the file, with a copy for our accounting department."

He handed the folder to Gary and stood. "You're free to check," he said as he stretched, bending his back. "Too much sitting."

There wasn't anything for Gary to do but thank the man. He glanced up from the folder.

"You know," Westbrook said, arms behind him, his hands rubbing his lower back, "what happened to Lyons, excuse my language, sucks. I can't bring him back, but I can try to help his widow. I've been down that road." He sat down in the third chair, facing Gary, and leaned forward.

"You have?"

The president's lips curled, part smile, part grimace. "Long time ago. A small war in Asia. You get close to guys and their families." He twined his fingers, rubbed them together nervously. "Jennifer and I were kids then. You see friends die and think that's the worst."

He'd been talking to Gary; suddenly he was sinking deep inside. "Then you come home and find their wives in debt, trying to keep a job and be super-mom, hurt and lonely, unsure how to meet another man who can accept someone's else's kids and isn't just out for sex. Talk about situations that suck." The hands flew apart, went to his thighs, and he sat upright.

Gary could see why Merle and Riddock thought highly of him.

"I didn't mean to put you through that." With a deep breath, Westbrook flopped back into the chair, losing his tension.

They both turned toward the knock on the door. It opened, and Westbrook's secretary stood there. "Sorry, sir, but the exterminator said you'd called and that I was to interrupt you."

Westbrook nodded. "I did. Send him in. Thanks, Carol."

Gary turned back and riffed through the folder, saw the additional material, didn't feel he had to review it here. He looked across at Westbrook, who was distracted. "Hannah Lyons will be pleased." In apparent response, the president laughed. "Something I said?"

"Not you." Westbrook couldn't stop laughing. "Sorry."

Gary turned, and had trouble keeping a straight face, too. Riddock Maguire limped through the office, wearing the outfit and hat, carrying the gear, waving the sprayer, scanning the moldings, looking every bit like a professional killer of pests.

"I thought I'd give you the full treatment," he said, when he saw the eyes on him. "Just one of our thousand disguises."

Westbrook regained composure. He bent, continued rubbing his back. "Thanks for coming on short notice. I wanted Gary Kemmerman to hear what we had to discuss, since he's representing Norman Lyons' widow." The president nodded toward Riddock.

"Gary, this is Riddock Maguire. He's a private investigator and a friend. I've retained him to look into Lyon's death."

"I have news," Riddock said, looking from one to the other. He sat at the edge of the empty chair beside Gary and offered his hand. "Good to meet you, Mr. Kemmerman—is it?" Except for a certain liveliness in the eyes, he gave no indication they'd met before.

"Just Gary, please. If you're a PI, what's with the outfit?"

Westbrook said, "No one else knows who he is."

Riddock raised a hand to capture their attention. "The Lyons' house fire was arson. That makes his death suspicious. The police are looking at it as more than an auto accident."

"*Arson?*" Westbrook appeared surprised.

"Plastic explosive ruptured the gas line."

Gary turned to Westbrook. "Did you know that?"

"Hell, no."

"Why would your internal auditor be murdered, and then his house burn down?"

"We don't *know* he was murdered," Westbrook said, flustered.

"Why don't you take the initiative and call in the police?"

"That—that puts Consolidated under a microscope." His hands came off his back and, balled into fists, went onto the chair arms. "Then I've hammered our stock, upset the parent bank in Washington, and maybe all for nothing. With Riddock's help, we'll know where to go before taking public steps."

Appropriate presidential thinking, Gary figured. He bent closer to the man and locked eyes. "Lyons must have uncovered *something* dishonest. That's what got him killed."

"Nonsense." The word was spoken through clenched teeth.

"He probably brought something home," Gary went on, refusing to release the man's eyes, "and that's what got his house torched."

With effort, Westbrook turned to Riddock. "You think that's what caused the arson?"

The PI was following them like a ping-pong match. "Don't know." His brows furrowed. "I'm told nothing important in the house survived the fire."

Gary said, "I'd like Consolidated to pay for the COBRA tab for those 18 months. In addition to everything else."

"I thought we'd put that arrangement to bed." Westbrook's tone was bitter. This time he didn't meet Gary's gaze.

"That was before I knew about murder and arson." Gary grasped chair arms, bent, and sounded harsher than he'd expected. "Hannah's lucky the fire didn't get her."

"I don't like to revisit closed issues," Westbrook growled back.

"Then let's bring in the police and give them the same data Lyons had available." He spoke more softly, the two of them face-to-face. "The state has a corporate fraud group. They'd probably keep a look-see quiet."

Westbrook couldn't hide his anger, but his voice calmed and his fists unclenched. "We'll pay the health insurance. Because of the circumstances, not because you're blackmailing me."

"Write it out," Gary said, leaning back.

"You don't trust me for that?"

Gary realized the insult had caused little irritation. "This is Corporate America. You've given me everything else in writing."

Westbrook went behind the desk and scribbled a note, the only sound in the office the scratch of his pen. He handed it over.

The sun emerged and the ceiling lights dimmed. "Thank you," Gary said, sliding the sheet in with the others. This was not a man who would fold without good reason. "You'll share the PI's news with your head of security?"

Westbrook looked back sharply. Gary played innocent, and hoped the man was not as perceptive as Merle. "Right," the president finally said.

What else could he say? Gary hoped Riddock had noticed.

"So, just where do we start?" Riddock asked, and when Gary turned, he saw the PI had been thinking, not paying attention.

"That's why you're in the detecting business, and I'm only the client," Westbrook snapped.

Riddock's head tilted—he didn't understand. "Morgan, that was rhetorical. Got a pad and pen?" The PI waited until Westbrook was ready. "I'd like personnel files of the people running your computer system: Arman Pavlic, Teodors Medved, Suresh Rahman, and Norman Lyons."

The president's brow furrowed. "You know their names?"

"You told me to get plugged in, so I could be up and running when you needed me."

Westbrook exhaled. "Go on."

"I'd like a listing of company equipment the four men used at home. If you have them, their attendance records—when they've been out of the office. If you know it, what make and color of car, or cars, they drive, with license plates. Also, names and phones at three major financial institutions where Consolidated parks funds."

Gary turned to Riddock. He wasn't supposed to have raised the prospect of theft.

But the PI went right on. "Perhaps you make personal calls, ask those trusted people to cooperate with me. Tell 'em it's just a periodic check of your internal auditors. Prudent step after Lyons' death."

Westbrook's hands clasped, and the emotion left his face. "You're looking into fraud? Theft?" he asked Riddock, sounding confused.

Gary masked his nervousness.

"If you don't object," said Riddock. "The connection between Lyons' death and his house fire opens that avenue." He waited.

"Sounds good," Westbrook finally said, looking and sounding as if it wasn't good at all. "Please be careful."

Riddock handed Westbrook a business card. "Send the material to my pest control office, FedEx, for arrival by 10 A.M. tomorrow."

Westbrook smiled at the card.

Gary recalled Riddock's FedEx disguise, and wondered if he'd be delivering the package to himself.

"Good to meet you," Riddock said to Gary, and walked out.

After the door closed, Westbrook turned to Gary, eyes hard again, hunching as if he might leap at him.

Gary tucked the folder close.

"What do you do when you're not representing Hannah Lyons?" the president barked.

"Was I too easy on you?"

Westbrook laughed once, shook his head with a smile, and when he stood, he stepped back, leaning against the front of the desk. He waved toward the folder as if he'd read Gary's mind. "I put together a package you shouldn't refuse. You pushed because you saw the situation makes Consolidated vulnerable."

"You really care what happened to Lyons?"

Westbrook frowned. "Damn right. This is a job where you have to care about your people."

"The way Merle Kingsley did?"

"You know him?" The man's eyes grew hooded.

"His name, reputation, that he was here before you. I used to handle corporate crises," Gary said, to cover his mistake.

Westbrook considered before responding. "Ever work for him?"

"No."

The president's hands went flat on the desktop. "The crises you handled, were they like our financial negotiations, or the alleged arson and murder?"

Gary shrugged.

"Maybe I should hire you." He pushed away from the desk and went around it.

"I'm retired," Gary said, rising before Westbrook could sit.

Last time he'd said that, look what happened.

Once he was alone, Westbrook tapped a pen against his left hand, deep in thought. He lifted the phone, punched in a three-digit code without looking, and got Arman's voice mail. He scanned the internal phone list, and pressed another extension. This one rang and was answered by a young woman.

"Hello."

"Suresh Rahman there?"

"No, he's out sick today."

Westbrook tossed the pen. "You are?"

"Maggie Donovan. I'm using his computer while he's out. Want me to leave him a message?"

"No thanks, Maggie." The man hung up, and thought a while longer.

~24~
12:45 P.M.

THE offfice door banged open and smacked into a chair. The lieutenant looked up from behind his desk, startled, and found Dalton Cabrera in the doorway.

Dalton had a stack of printouts in his hands and began speaking before he walked in. "Gary asked me to give you my best guess soon as I could."

Vincent wasn't sure he knew someone else was there. "Detective Tim Colangelo, Dalton Cabrera. Dalton helped set up our computer investigation unit."

Colangelo, in jeans and a scruffy sweatshirt, reached up with his right hand. "Good to meet you."

Dalton tried to shake and dropped the printouts onto the desk. "Oh, sorry." He bent around the detective and shuffled the papers into a mound, forgetting the handshake, never really looking at the man.

The policemen glanced at one another. Vincent shrugged. Colangelo shook his head. "I'll leave you guys. See ya later, Lieutenant."

When he closed the door, it grew quiet.

Vincent studied Dalton. Every time the man showed up, he was excited. He was wearing a short-sleeved, partly tucked Hawaiian-print shirt that February day. Dalton lifted the restored pile, sat in the seat Colangelo had vacated, and the papers teetered.

Vincent leaned forward onto his arms. "You found something

149

you want to tell me?"

"Oh, yes. Can I set this stuff down?" When Vincent nodded, Dalton elbowed work out of the way, and laid his pages in the cleared space. He looked up, making eye contact for the first time. "Gary tell you about our meeting?"

"No."

"Okay." He waved his left hand. "We have a sub-routine in—"

"Keep it simple."

Dalton began to speak, then thought better of it. "Let's get Larry in."

"He knows about this?" Larry Goldstein headed the CIT Unit.

"I dealt with it as training for him," Dalton said.

"I'll get him." Vincent rose, pausing as he reached his neighbor. "Coffee?"

Dalton turned with a big smile. "Sure."

"How you take it?"

"Black. Don't lieutenants have assistants to get coffee?"

Vincent bit back his first reply. "Only captains."

Minutes later, the door had been closed and coffees rested before the three men. "This *is* a big deal," said Larry, a chubby older man with curly gray hair, a bushy moustache and deep-set eyes, who looked as if he should be selling oatmeal on television. The neck of his uniform shirt was unbuttoned, and he flowed over it. He was sitting beside Dalton, wriggling to find comfort in a chair that barely contained him, and speaking to Vincent. "You don't need to know computer details. This crime is a natural for the AG's Fraud Unit in Edison."

Maybe all computer people started in the middle, Vincent thought. "What crime?"

"Oh, sorry. Our first take is that twenty-six million a year is being skimmed from Consolidated accounts."

"No one noticed that much flying away?" Vincent caught the look of consternation on Larry's face. "Okay. I asked you in, the least I can do is listen." He took a sip of coffee. Still too hot.

"Dalton did an amazing job with this," Larry said.

The lieutenant asked, "Should we tape this for Edison?"

Larry shook his head, as if Vincent didn't understand. "They are the big time. This much money, they'll want Dalton to repeat it in front of them."

"You never told me about Edison," Dalton said to Larry. "What's in Edison?"

"State police." Larry rubbed at his moustache. "The ones with the manpower, the big bucks, and the prosecutors. They try to keep crooks out of corporate coffers."

Dalton twisted to face the chubby man. "What'd you mean by 'big time'?"

Larry shifted again before responding. "They make your home toys, and what we have here, look Stone Age."

"Oh, wow." Dalton began rocking with excitement. "Can I see?"

Vincent held up a hand. "Talk to me, Larry."

The big man nodded. "We'd never have discovered this, except for the pages Dalton brought in."

"Those pages," Vincent asked Dalton. "You get them from Gary Kemmerman?"

"Sure. He got 'em from Hannah Lyons, who had 'em because Norm Lyons brought 'em home Monday night and didn't want to take them to work Tuesday morning." Dalton nodded with his points like a bobble-head doll. "Gary said if I found anything suspicious, I was to tell you, that you'd know what to do."

"So the Consolidated crew knew the papers weren't in Norm's car. That's why he must have warned me to check for arson."

"Pages might've caused a murder," Larry said.

"How'd Norm get 'em?" Vincent asked, and they both looked at the man in the Hawaiian shirt.

"Without the code, there's no way you could access this." Dalton raised his left hand and shook it with urgency. "That's why Gary wouldn't let me hack from home. When Norm printed these, it made him a target."

"They know you've broken into their system?" Vincent asked, frowning, leaning forward again.

"Maybe." The hand came down, slowly, forgotten. "I told Gary it would scare the hell out of 'em."

Vincent sucked on a tooth.

"Lieutenant," Larry said, "this could be happenin' elsewhere. Totals could be staggering. Funds sent abroad electronically could train and equip terrorists. Doesn't mean it's goin' on, just that it could." He shook his head. "America fundin' our enemies again, like we already do payin' for all that oil."

Vincent felt like he was riding a volcano. "You sure about this?"

Larry nodded. "The Staties will love it. And we got reason for speed. Crooks shut the operation down and we don't learn who they are, they move on and do it again. If it was worth killin' for Tuesday, it still is today. Dalton says Gary's searching for the killers."

"Hey," Dalton said to Vincent, "Gary said he knew their gatekeeper." He gripped the chair, looking worried.

"I hear Gary's morning started real early," the chubby man said.

"Dalton told you?" Vincent leaned closer and glared at Dalton, who drew back.

"Says I'm trustworthy," Larry added.

Dalton's mouth opened and closed twice before he said, "You are," while looking at no one in particular.

"What I'm sayin' is," Larry went on, "Gary's tryin' to find people who'll be happy to kill him."

"The State of New Jersey needs you for a while," Vincent said to Dalton.

"Great! I'm ready." The smile returned. "Just feed me some lunch."

"Larry, have someone get him a sandwich. I'll pay. I need to set a session with Franklyn Warnke. We'll be out of here within the half hour."

Vincent reached for the phone, but the chubby policeman interrupted. "To Edison?"

The lieutenant nodded, phone hand in the air.

"It's almost two. You got an estimated return?"

Vincent smiled. "Need to ask?"

"Right." Larry rose, holding the chair down so it wouldn't come with him. "Anything you want me to bring?"

"Dalton, and every piece of paper he has."

"What do you want from the deli?" Larry asked Dalton. He lifted the printouts from the desk, carried them himself, and guided

Dalton out of the office.

Vincent was holding for the assistant prosecutor. He thought maybe he should have called Gary first.

~25~
2:15 P.M.

GARY waited through two rings, the alert he and Medved had arranged during the morning's phone conversation, and ended the call.

The street the boy lived on was seedy, the houses lining it dilapidated, and he worried about his car being stolen. The tan Infiniti was eight years old, hardly a target of choice. But it held memories and had kept him alive twelve hours before. He locked it, left with a pat, and found the house.

The front door opened the moment he reached the stoop. A gangly young man in jeans and a flannel shirt stood waiting.

"Your face says you are surprised?" The boy phrased it as a question.

"You're so young." He stopped before the entry.

"I am nineteen." The boy pointed at himself, hands constantly in motion. "I am Teodors Medved. You are Gary Kemmerman?"

Gary extended his hand. "That's me." The boy's voice was thin, high pitched, accented. It fit Schroder's recollection of the second caller. He was among the wolves.

Medved shook his hand, drew him in and closed the heavy front door behind them. He led the way up a dark flight of stairs. There was no lock on the door to the dismal rooms: thick, drawn drapes, dark paneling, frayed oriental carpets, weak lighting except for a daylight-type lamp at a computer station, surrounded by a clutter of disks. The walls were fitted with useless gas-lamp fixtures that looked

154

like oarlocks; he felt he was in the belly of a slave ship.

The boy stood by the door, as if unsure what to do. "Can I take you out for lunch?" Gary asked, as much for himself as Medved.

"Better we stay." The kid stepped close to the computer—its screen held the Consolidated logos—and put a hand on it.

"Where'd you come from, Teodors?"

"Please, I am Teo. From Latvia. Why is it I surprise you?"

He motioned Gary to an overstuffed chair, then cleared disks off a smaller one so he could sit. Gary sank in too far and felt itchy, embraced by sticky velour. "I thought you'd be closer to Norm's age."

Medved waved at himself. "You see, I'm not."

There was intelligence in the kid's bright eyes, and anxiety difficult for a nineteen-year-old to hide. Be careful, Vincent had said. How careful could he be? He had to confront the boy. He wouldn't get a second chance. "We've a lot to talk about—Norm Lyons, and other things. I'll be truthful, if you will."

The boy frowned. "What other things? You are careful."

"You too have learned that." Good Lord, Gary thought—he was beginning to phrase his speech like the boy's.

Medved flapped his arms, taking in his surroundings. "Not well." Then, as an afterthought, "Want water?"

Gary smiled. "If you'd asked when we first spoke, I would've brought cola."

The boy leaned toward him. "How you know I like it?"

"Hannah Lyons told me many things, because she's concerned about how her husband died." He put hands on knees and bent closer. A pipe screeched as someone in the house turned on water. The boy didn't notice. "She told me of your discussion about invisible programs and backward codes. Like the codes on the three sheets Norm Lyons brought home."

Medved paled, said nothing.

"Norm liked you," Gary said.

The boy sat up straight. "I liked him, and Hannah is nice woman. They took trouble to drive me, cook dinner. I enjoy that."

"Do you know their house—the place you visited—was burned down the day after Norm died?"

"No!"

Gary saw the boy's shock. "The people you work for didn't want you to know. The fire was set by someone to destroy the computer report. The one Norm brought home. The one with the backward code."

Medved couldn't hide his alarm. "Was Hannah hurt?" His fingers scrabbled at his jeans.

"No. She was at my house, talking about Norm's murder." He waited; it took a few seconds before the boy corrected him.

"Accident—" Medved flinched, interrupted by banging that sounded like gunshots when the water was turned off and pressure hammered the pipes.

"You know Norm was murdered. And you know why." The boy wouldn't meet his eyes. "You called the police the next day. You wanted to know what Norm was carrying in his car. You were hoping he wasn't killed for the report from your secret program."

Color drained from Medved's face. His fingers stilled and his head dropped.

"And the police traced the call, know you made it … Teo, I can see Norm really was your friend. You couldn't have prevented what happened. I want to tell you two things you don't know, because you have to make an important decision."

The boy looked up, stunned.

Gary spoke softly. "Police computers have hacked into your secret program. An investigation is underway. And your handlers want Consolidated's president to appoint someone else as director of programming." The boy looked dazed. Gary reached out and tapped his knee, got his attention back. "If you're the one who runs their system, your life may be in danger."

~26~
2:18 P.M.

Pavlic saw who was calling, turned away from his closed office door and barked into his cell phone, "What?"

"He has visitor upstairs," said Ana, the old lady who ran the safe house.

Who was there? It was after two, the mid-winter sun low and weak. Outside, the air seemed hostile. Far below, at a construction site, he watched a crane lift a bucket of concrete.

"How many?"

"One man," she said.

"The vehicle?" His office phone sounded, the beep of an internal call—he ignored it.

"An old car. He drive alone, park on street."

The front door was always locked, Arman knew. "You let him in?"

"No."

"Uniform?"

"No," she said. "I doubt he is police. Or one of us."

"You know him?"

"Tall, with gray hair. I have not seen before."

Foolish not to have bugged Teo's rooms. Arman knew too many tall, gray-haired men—including Westbrook. He'd have to go himself.

"Call when visitor leaves." Arman broke the connection. He selected a black leather jacket. His gear was in the BMW.

* * *

The boy's shocked expression told Gary he'd gotten through. "Teo, what do you do for Consolidated?"

"Is secret." The boy tucked his fingers, leaned on his knuckles.

He caught Medved's eye. "Are you in this country legally?"

"Would you …?" Teo blurted, then grew silent with fear, eyes wide. This was the worst shock yet and he stared back.

"I'll help you, if you'll help me."

The boy slumped, and his response was close to a whisper. "How can anyone help?"

Gary touched Medved's knee again, held the contact as he spoke. "I'm here because I am a friend of the Lyons family. But also because I've been sent by the policeman investigating Norm's murder, and the arson."

The boy jerked his leg away and his hands came up, pleading. "What if I … do things … not honest?"

Gary leaned close without reaching. "They know you're doing unlawful things." He paused to let it sink in. "But I believe you're being forced to do them. You had no part in what happened to Lyons, or his house. If you answer some questions honestly, you may not be charged with crimes."

It brought a washed-out smile. Then Medved stiffened. "But I want to stay. Here in America."

"How about we make that part of your deal?"

His eyebrows rose. "A deal with prosecutor? Like on *Law and Order*?"

Gary laughed. "Exactly. We can discuss several things: protection, a real job, a place to live, eventual citizenship."

The boy's eyes narrowed. "I know immigration law … you say those things so I do what you want."

For a moment, Gary was unsure. "Let's handle it this way. I'll go to the police lieutenant and ask him. I'll tell you what he says. You can make up your own mind."

Medved's left hand rubbed his right wrist, and the pause grew before he looked back at Gary. "That is fair."

"If you agree and we come pick you up, you can pack and take anything you want. We'd like you to bring all your disks and hard drives, because they're part of what we want to ask you about, and because we don't want others using what you've worked on. Once we leave, you'll never come back."

"Where will I stay?" The boy coddled his right wrist. Gary wondered if it had once been broken.

"We'll work it out. I'll see you're pleased with where you live."

Medved smiled, then pulled away. His hands gripped the chair. Something made him afraid. "Have your policeman say yes, quickly."

"Let's call him right now." Gary pulled out his cell phone and punched in Vincent's code. The connection was weak, with static and noise in the background, but he answered.

"Gary, I want you home. *Right now.*"

"What happened?"

"Dalton found it. You can't play policeman anymore. Drop what you're up to and get back here. Your ass is grass if they find you."

"Slow down. I'm with Medved, the one running that secret program. If he becomes our witness, could we protect him, keep him in the country?"

Vincent didn't speak without thinking it through. Gary took a chance, rose and held the phone so Teo could also listen.

At first there was only static. Then, "I'll ask the AP. I believe we can, but I won't commit without approval. I'll know by tomorrow morning. He'd have to come clean."

Gary smiled and straightened. "Thanks, Vinnie. I'll be home before dinnertime."

"Leave *now*. When you get to my house, knock, don't ring."

"Later," Gary said, and put the phone away. He couldn't bring himself to sit in the chair.

"That was your policeman?" The boy's color had returned.

"Yeah. He's worried about me. Because of your other friends."

"About becoming a citizen … you were honest?" Distracted, Medved rose and almost dropped back into the chair before gaining his legs.

"If that's what you want, we'll find a way." The kid looked so damned earnest. "I promise we'll try. One request. Don't tell anyone about my visit, or what we've discussed. If you do— "

"I will be killed." The boy thought of something else, waved two fingers at Gary like guns. "You will be, too."

Gary pulled out a card, found a pen. "Here's my cell number."

Medved put it in the shirt pocket.

"If anything happens, call and we'll pick you up. If I get news, I'll call you." He thought of something else: "Put your phone on vibrate."

The kid smiled. "It is, all time. You are kind."

"As you were to Norm."

Medved went soft. "I may have been reason he was killed."

Gary reached out and grasped the boy's shoulder. The movement was so friendly, Teo didn't flinch. "That's not true. Whatever happened was between Norm and others, some of whom you know." He'd heard the boy's guilt, hoped it would become motivation to turn him against his criminal handlers.

He started for the door.

"Wait," Medved said as Gary reached for the knob. "The woman downstairs. She is with them."

Gary turned back to him. The boy's hands were clasped tightly. He was waiting for a decision. "Show me to the front door, and I'll thank you for telling me what a nice person Norm Lyons was, so I can relay it to his family," Gary said. "Would that help?"

Medved smiled, and clapped his hands without making noise.

~27~
2:37 P.M.

Pavlic slipped into the alley beside the house. He moved a garbage can out of the tall shed, built to hold several cans, and stooped so he could step in, careful not to dirty his jacket. It was cold and dark—his annoyance had become anger.

Cracks in the shed's wooden front wall let him see the building stoop. He could hear everything they would say while remaining hidden. He put on thin gloves, pulled the pistol from one pocket, attached the silencer, and waited.

His phone vibrated. Soon after, he heard the front door open.

"It was kind of you to talk about Norm Lyons and the things you did together," said a familiar voice. "I'll pass your words on to his family. His widow will be grateful. Thank you so much, Teodors."

"I ... thank you. Is good to ... remember Norm."

"Goodbye," the man said, and started down the steps. The front door closed.

Pavlic slipped the silencer though a hole and sighted toward the stoop. It was Gary Kemmerman, the man who'd gotten into Lyons' car, who'd appeared at the widow's event with the witness. The man he'd warned to back off.

But this meeting may have been legitimate. Lyons and Medved had been friends.

The man reached the sidewalk and turned right. The sight was on his neck. Shooting Kemmerman on the street would be messy and against Serge's rules, but he could explain it—he'd pull the body

161

inside, carry it away after dark. There would be blood to clean up.

Before he could act, Kemmerman moved out of view. Irritated, Pavlic decided to follow his instincts, kill him now. Shoot the man once his car was open, get the keys, fold him into the trunk, drive car and body to a deserted building a few blocks away. How long before an abandoned, unlocked car, with keys in the ignition, was stolen? The corpse would be carjacked. It would become someone else's trouble. Teo would be around for the plucking.

He pulled in his pistol and was about to step out when another car appeared and stopped right across from him. He clenched his jaw when he recognized the other passenger and knew he couldn't leave his hiding place now. He seized his cell phone and speed-dialed.

It picked up on the third ring. By then, he heard Kemmerman's vehicle start up and roll away.

Upstairs, through a gap in the drapes, Medved had watched Gary walk to his car. It'd seemed moments ago he'd stood there waiting for him to arrive. Everything had changed. He wondered if he could handle waiting any longer, appearing to work on Arman's tasks. He must lie well this time.

He wouldn't check the program. Then he could say he wasn't aware of intruders. Arman would know intruders were there only because of his carelessness.

He must stay calm, behave as always, so no one would suspect. When Arman appeared in front of the house at six in the morning, he'd be the same Teo, hours away from providing the complete program.

And, he hoped, fewer hours away from freedom.

Arman did not understand that any program based on Consolidated's setup must fail elsewhere. For access links, machine codes, or line lengths to work invisibly, they must mimic the individual computer system. Some things were in the programmer, not the program.

~28~
9:12 A.M.

Morning sunlight peeked through the bedroom blinds and warmed Malini Nivas' arm. She stretched under the quilt. It was Thursday morning, she was in Suresh's bed, and it was late. Blinking, she pushed up on an elbow, the quilt slid down, and she saw Suresh beside her, naked on top of the cover, wide-awake, and watching.

When she visited his apartment after work three days before, he'd been so full of himself, and that had led to her being in his bed this morning. On Monday, he'd met Consolidated's president and had been told he might be rewarded. She'd read between the lines of his excited account and had focused on what he'd overheard. She'd gotten him to repeat it twice. If those words were reason for the president of such a large company to offer a reward, Suresh must have stumbled upon something useful.

Tuesday, bored and daydreaming at her job in the bank, she'd considered the circumstances, and all had become clear. He'd eavesdropped his way into a secret that involved millions of dollars. The other programmer would surely be willing to share a bit of it. Suresh had called the man Teo and said he was a close friend. The friend would hear them out, and she bet he would help.

Malini would never marry a man who earned so little, held so lowly a position as Suresh. But he came from a good family, and he was pliable. After work Tuesday evening, she'd brought in dinner, which always put him in a good mood. She'd labored to convince

163

him. He'd said no, and no again when she'd called the previous day.

So she'd slept over and let him make love to her, breaking her rule once more. He'd gotten her clothes off and done it twice, and here he was, hours later, grinning. Mother had warned her about young men. Once they got you, they didn't want you any longer. But if mother understood what Malini had set in motion, she'd be proud. Using those hormones to your advantage, that was wise.

"We slept late," she said, allowing him to stare at her small breasts. "Yes."

"Today is the day you agreed to speak to your friend about what you heard." She brushed her hair back with her free hand, posing. "For us, that could open a new world. Are you not excited?"

Suresh held out his arms.

Malini sighed, slipped off the bed, and held the pillow in front of her. This place was cramped. They took turns in the bathroom, and she'd be first. Before she stepped in and locked the door, she flung the pillow toward him. He liked that.

When she emerged, showered and dressed, Suresh wore trousers and was using the kitchen sink to wash up. She opened the refrigerator. "Nothing is here to eat."

"I have juice, cold cereal, and milk." He turned to her, wiping himself with paper toweling. "I didn't know you would stay."

Malini had an idea born partly of her dislike for cold cereal. They'd both called in sick. This had been the first day since he'd told her about the millions that she'd felt comfortable missing work. The weather was crisp and clear, perfect for venturing out.

She closed the refrigerator, leaned against it. "Would you like us to eat lunch at a diner?"

He beamed. "Good idea." The crumpled paper went into the sink, without his looking. "Then we can come back."

She chuckled and pushed upright. "Then we can visit your good friend Teo, and as you promised, you can speak with him about the money."

He frowned, took a half step back. "Is that wise? Are you sure? I think it is better we don't." As he spoke, he retrieved the toweling and tossed it into the basket beneath the sink. "I promised the president I'd tell no one what I heard."

She tried not to react to his whining. "If your co-worker Teo is as good a friend as you say, would he not want to help us, at least a little? Am I not right? You would do that if you had millions, and a good friend asked you for help."

"Well, yes, but …."

He'd crossed his arms, a sign, she knew, that he wanted to dig in his heels. She moved away, busied herself at a mirror and did not look at him as she said, "With help, you and I could look for one larger apartment." She would have preferred to withhold such a commitment.

"Oh, I would love that, but …."

She turned back, almost stamping. His arms had dropped. "Why do you hesitate? This good idea will cost you nothing, and all it requires is talking as a friend to your friend." Annoyance spiked her tone.

He shrugged. She knew he did that when she backed him into a corner. "You make it sound safe," he said.

"Tell me, please now, just what about this would be dangerous?"

"Pavlic would be upset. We wouldn't want that."

Pavlic meant nothing to her. He was a boss, like every other boss. "But he won't be in your friend's rooms, will he? Would he not be at the office during working hours? Why do you always worry?"

~29~
2:45 P.M.

MALINI parked her car across the street from the house Suresh pointed out, the building with the stoop. She turned off the engine and waited, wanting him to make the first move, to make this excellent plan his own. Initiative would build his confidence. They sat quietly. Finally, he turned to her, so she faced him.

"I don't know about this," he said.

She sneered. "*You promised.*"

His right hand scrabbled over the armrest as if he'd like to grip it. "Well, I guess saying hello and asking can't hurt."

He left the car, dragged himself across the street, struggled up the steps, and rang the bell. Malini saw an old lady answer. Suresh and the lady spoke. He turned and motioned for her to wait. Foolish boy, what else did he think she would do?

The door closed behind him.

Bending, hidden in the garbage shed, Arman watched his programmer and the girl in the car. He changed position to avoid cramping in the cold.

"Teo has visitors," he said when Serge answered. "One before, now my other programmer, Rahman. In a car out front."

"Why are *you* there?"

"Ana called about earlier visitor." In the background, he heard

166

the ripping whine of a lug nut tool. Serge must be in his shop.

"That man still there?"

"No." He shifted his weight. Stooping had become most unpleasant.

"Can programmer see you?"

"No."

"Anyone with him?" Serge asked.

"A young woman drives. I don't know her."

"Then I make arrangements. When programmer goes in, you return to office. Make meeting, for alibi. Short. I have task for you." Arman heard phone noise, but then it sounded as if Serge had closed his office door. "Who was other visitor?"

"Gary Kemmerman." Arman spat the name.

"Why?"

"At door, he said what Teo told would comfort Lyons' widow."

"Convenient. Go to office. Wait for call." The line went dead.

Arman pocketed the weapon and phone, waited until Rahman was inside with the door closed, and left. Tomorrow morning he'd question Teo. The boy was a bad liar. He'd reveal why Gary had visited.

Suresh waited in the vestibule while the old lady went up to see if Teo was in. Despite his concern, he was resigned to do as Malini demanded. She was a firebrand. He kept it secret that he loved it when she was angry with him, but he sensed much to gain from making her happy now.

The small vestibule was claustrophobic, with dark drapes covering its single window and a gray-painted ceiling. He closed his eyes and re-ran the night before, no longer considering the delay. When the old woman returned, she interrupted a daydream.

"Oh, I am sorry," she said, in a singsong lilt. She wore a Victorian-style dress with ruffles at the sleeves and neck. "The young man is not there. I checked carefully. He must have gone out."

Suresh frowned. "But he told me he rarely leaves. He must be there." If Malini became angry with him about this, she would not be friendly.

The old woman shrugged, looking helpless. "Sometimes he goes for pizza, or ice cream. Or to read a book on the grass. I don't know."

This woman is confused, he thought. Ice cream in February? On the grass when it's covered with snow? Maybe Teo was upstairs. He rose. "Why don't I go up and wait?"

She blocked the entry and her right hand reached behind her. "Oh, you cannot. He made me promise. I would have to call the police."

He was not eager to meet the police, especially with his girl parked outside. It did seem logical that Teo's disks would be confidential. So, loony or not, the landlady was just doing her job. "I'll come back later."

"I'm sure he'll be glad to see you," she said, clasping her hands primly in front of her. "Goodbye."

He left. He'd tried. Walking down the steps, he knew Malini would get him to come back. Maybe that could work. He'd tell her the truth, the old lady had checked, and Teo was out. They could spend time at his place before he returned.

Worst case, he'd speak with Teo tomorrow, at work. That might be best. For that, he might get her to stay over again. But he could already hear her saying, "And you believed that old woman?"

A cable truck was parked in front of the house. Suresh crossed behind it and noticed Malini wasn't in her car. From the other side of the truck, a small man, wearing a black watch cap and pointing a pistol, stepped in front of him. He stopped, confused.

"You go in truck." A wave of the gun demanded it.

"Take my wallet." Suresh raised his hands. *Was Malini crouched down, hiding?*

A second man, much larger, appeared beside the first. "Open, Lev," said the man with the gun. The large man swung the single back door open.

Suresh glanced inside. She lay on the floor. "No!"

The small man raked the gun barrel across his face. It didn't knock him down, but he felt his cheek tear. Pain blossomed, blood spattered. In shock, he pressed a hand to the wound.

"In truck, *now!*" The gun poked his ribs. He climbed in. A strong hand gripped the back of his coat, stopping him. "Phone," the larger man said. "Give."

He handed it over. The back door slammed. The section he and Malini occupied contained no windows, no shelving, parts, or equipment. A few feet behind the front seats, a metal grille divided the space. The larger man slid into the driver's seat and started the engine.

Suresh heard Malini's car start, too. The smaller man must be driving. Why was this happening? He felt pain from his cheek and thought past his shock. Millions of dollars, and they'd gotten in the way.

"Where are we going?" he asked the driver. The big man said nothing. The truck lurched forward, and he fell hard beside her. She lay in a fetal position, knees drawn up, eyes glazed. What had they done to her? His head throbbed.

As the van careened along unseen roads, it came to him that this was not her fault. It was his. He'd known better. They were here because of his weakness.

The vehicles rolled onto New Jersey highways.

Riddock picked up Kathryn's call on the first ring. He listened as she described what had kept her at the window, snapping images of the hidden man with the silencer, the grey-haired man who almost got shot, and the young couple being taken by armed men from a cable company van. She said she'd caught everything close up, from faces to weapons to license plates. She apologized for not calling sooner.

He told her to wait ten minutes and then, only if the street was all clear, put on her disguise, pack up, and return to the office with the camera.

If the street had any other visitors in the next ten minutes, he told her to call him back and wait for him in the room, away from the window, door locked, gun in hand. He would come to her.

He made a mental note to discuss the poor security of cell phone conversations. But he wouldn't use that to scold her. She'd done well. His fear was hearing her so close to guns, and dangerous men, and he'd sent her.

~30~
3:10 P.M.

GARY yawned. He was exhausted and wouldn't tempt fate. He unzipped his coat and lowered the driver's-side window. Cold air poured into the car, clearing his head. He breathed deeply and turned on the radio.

After Sarah's death, he'd begun listening to baroque music. It had never been his preference, but for months the rationalities had calmed him. Then, without conscious decision, he'd backed off all music. Bach was on now, a station he'd chosen what seemed a lifetime ago. He pushed a different button, got and kept a Beatles song.

He'd used to walk for exercise early in the morning, before he showered and went to work. He'd worn earphones that played tunes like these. He'd also stopped going to the gym. Why bother? Who wanted to talk to gym buddies with real lives? Maybe soon he'd return. You reach an age, he knew, it was either use it or lose it. Whether he was there yet, he wanted to stay vigorous.

For Becca, he realized, and laughed aloud.

Ragged clouds covered the low sun and delivered an early twilight. Where the weak light was blocked from the highway, the car rumbled over washboards of frozen tread marks.

He needed to think about his day but found himself enjoying the music. Oldies, rock and roll, emotional tags to other times vying for attention. Yes, he wanted to hold her hand. However he tried, by degree, his immersion in the Lyons affair faded before the desire to talk to her about it, about music, about anything.

170

By the time he moved from his driveway to the Alegrettis', pulled open the storm door, and knocked on the wooden front door—knock, don't ring, as Vincent had said—he was awake.

Angela greeted him with a finger to her lips. It was the second time today that had happened. "They're sleeping," she whispered as he entered.

The house was silent. Melanie faced him, fast asleep, head on a pillow, lying on the couch under a quilt. She looked young. He wanted to tuck in the cover where it had slipped off a sock-clad foot. But he wouldn't go near for fear he might startle her.

Angela waved him into the kitchen. The low sun fanned through the window like a laser show. "Becca's in the guest room." Angela still whispered. "Mel fell asleep here. Seeing her asleep did Becca in."

"I won't wake them."

"Better not. They were wired until mid-afternoon. Couldn't even lie down," she said, pouring water into the spout of a teapot. "Nadine visited. I haven't shared girl-talk like that since college."

He silently thanked Nadine. The kitchen smelled like cooking, but nothing was on the stove or in an oven. He bet Vincent's dinner was already cooked, and chilling. "Where's Vinnie?"

"In Edison. He called my cell. It's on—"

"Vibrate," he whispered, along with her. They laughed in pantomime. She put the pot on the stove, lit the burner.

"He said he'd be back by eight at the outside. We've kind of called off dinner."

"I'll bet that upset Dalton."

"He's with Vincent." Angela reached into a cabinet for two mugs, and caught his eye as she turned back. "We keep doing this to you. But these women are bushed, they'd better sleep through until tomorrow. How 'bout I make you something to eat? At least coffee?" She waggled the cups.

"I need sleep."

"Want to peek in the guest room?" She set the mugs down on a countertop, ready to lead the way.

With all his soul, but—. "Then I'd want to stay in the guest room."

Angela surprised him, reached out and pressed her palm onto his coat, over his heart. "She'd want that, too."

"You're sure she's there?"

She pulled back and smiled.

"So I'll be home. Have Vinnie stop by, if he wants. Wake me anytime. I'm getting used to it."

"Home where there's no food." She shook her head. "Becca's surprised you survived."

"All my secrets." He turned to leave.

"Something quick to eat? Or take along?"

Gary leaned against a wall and spoke without looking at her. "I'm too tired. But thanks. I'll wait for the promised dinner."

"Soon."

He reached out and touched her cheek in gratitude.

Minutes later, at home, he stretched and turned under the shower, loosening the day's tension. His wedding ring caught on the bar of soap as it often did. He was forever sliding the ring to wash under it. This time, when he twisted the gold band forward, it slipped off.

Might be weight loss, but he suspected there was more to it. He looked at the ring Sarah had given him, that vow, that part of his life. He reached out of the shower enclosure and set it on the countertop. It was time. He would save it along with the memories.

Afterward, lying in bed, too weary to hear the wind or notice it was still twilight, he wished it would not be like last night—phone ringing in the dark, Becca sobbing, blizzard raging.

He'd left her early that morning, and she hadn't changed her mind, decided what she felt was false, taken her daughter and gone from his life. She was real. They'd both found second chances. What they'd make of it was up to them, the two of them … three of them.

Part of him held back still. The next step was hers.

Hannah had been right: they'd met because of Norm's tragedy, and it had brought them to Pavlic's attention. He'd spent the day chipping at Pavlic's world—when it collapsed, how would the man lash out? Gary's spine tingled. But his eyes were heavy.

He turned over, slid a hand beneath the pillow, and slipped into a trance-like sleep. It seemed timeless: His parents walked up, standing close, young and healthy as he could only imagine, Dad's arm around

Mom, and details of her face clear beyond what he'd remembered. Kind brown eyes, freckles—he blinked awake when they smiled at him, and they were gone. But he knew there was a reason.

"You'd like Becca," he said aloud, the words painting the bedroom.

Thinking of her, he considered the Lyons affair. He'd wanted to stir the pot, and he had. It was a witches' cauldron, churning bits and pieces of events, people, and possibilities; edges of things appeared and were sucked back into the bubbling stew. In his exhaustion, thoughts wouldn't come.

While he slept, the cauldron churned.

~31~
4:06 P.M.

RIDDOCK sat at his office desk, feet up, stretching his bum right knee. When he worried like this, he knew it was a call to action.

He'd quickly debriefed Kathryn, reviewed the images she'd brought, and printed a dozen. All but two, along with the memory card, were in a manila envelope on the desk.

The top photo he held showed a large man, a sick smile on his face and a pistol holstered at the small of his back. He had lifted a young woman off the ground with his left arm and had his right fist buried to the wrist in her midsection. The agony on her face spoke to the power of the blow.

He studied her expression—and she began to fade, the whole office plunged into shadow as the sun vanished behind the neighboring building. He lowered his legs, anticipating the twinge from his knee, and switched on the desk lamp.

Kathryn sometimes used burst mode, capturing images in rapid-fire succession. When he was a kid, he and Everett had drawn stick figure scenes on a small pad, lined the sheets up and flipped them to animate their awkward creations. Kathryn had caught the man repeatedly punching the poor girl before he threw her into the back of the van. He looked like he'd enjoyed it.

The second photo showed a smaller man tearing open the right cheek of the woman's male companion with the muzzle of a pistol, and blood spattering.

Riddock pulled a magnifier from a drawer and examined the weapon. It looked like a Stechkin APS, a favorite, he knew, with special Russian law enforcement teams because it held a twenty-round clip, ammunition was readily available, and set on automatic, it could accurately fire 600 rounds a minute.

Other photos showed Pavlic entering a blind beside the front stoop, and pointing a pistol, with silencer, at Gary Kemmerman, who was walking off after saying goodbye to Medved. Whatever the two said may have given Pavlic pause. He'd had time to shoot, but didn't.

Would he have killed Gary if the other car hadn't arrived? Gary must be right about the Medved kid and he'd almost gotten shot for it.

Five minutes before, Everett had taken Kathryn out for a late lunch. Riddock had printed the images while he listened to her. He'd retrieved her weapon and locked it up.

The office was still, except for his growling stomach. The photos gripped him. They suggested murder, identified faces, license plates, weapons. The cable van was likely a sham. The images hinted at a well-run, well-armed criminal operation.

He was a private investigator charged with respecting client interests, keeping his dealings confidential. But he had evidence of a serious crime. He knew what he had to do, and quickly.

"Let's not bring in the Feds 'till we know what we have," Lieutenant Alegretti told Riddock over the phone. "Tap the state police instead. You say you got faces—we got a database of faces, and we know where the clowns live. Trust me."

"We need to move—"

"Get those photos to Warnke right now. I'll tell him to expect you. Don't want him to let his people go. He's close to you—AG's office, green-glass building beside the Hilton Edison. I'm on my way, but you don't have to wait for me."

"You're sure?" Riddock asked.

"Speedy delivery. Then go home, buddy—good job. I'll keep you in the loop."

Twenty minutes later, in the cloud-induced twilight, Riddock turned the small blue SUV in toward the Edison Hilton. Its parking garage served the hotel and the adjacent office tower housing Warnke's office. There were acres of outdoor parking, but as usual during the week, closer to the buildings a vehicle sat in every slot.

He was about to turn into the garage when a car backed out of a visitor's-section space around the side, blocked from general view but close to the entry. Another driver spotted the opening, promptly turned the wrong way into the one-way lane, gunned his black BMW and tried to get there first.

The PI beat him fairly, if by only a few feet. He got no angry honk. Invisible through dark-tinted windows, the other driver pulled slowly away.

As soon as Riddock was announced, Franklyn Warnke appeared. The assistant prosecutor was thin, spry, and bald, except for a fringe of gray. His large forehead looked as if he'd shined it along with his shoes. His eyes and shoulders sloped at the same burdened angle, and he offered a Mona Lisa smile as he waved the PI along back to his office.

Ignoring Riddock, the AP spread the photos across the wooden desk. He pulled a lamp from the credenza, set it alongside, and used a magnifying glass to study the images. He needed it: the tinted windows dimmed natural light.

"How long have you had these?" he asked when he glanced up. Riddock sat across the desk.

"You see the times and date—took awhile for the action to unfold and my partner to get back. I've had the card under an hour."

Warnke scanned the spread-out photos again, absently lifting the phone before he'd finished.

Riddock glanced around the tidy office. Beside the photos, the desktop held a six-inch stack of folders and several message slips in a wooden box. Three framed documents hung on the wall to the left, above a long credenza holding five piles of folders, one of them almost two feet high and in danger of toppling. The stacks were at equal intervals with a single gap, which he bet was the one on the desk.

The other wall held a floor-to-ceiling wooden bookshelf, oddly filled. Higher shelves showcased pristine leather-bound volumes in sets, packed tightly together. Below, the books were thicker, eclectic, some upright and others flat, all looking well thumbed.

He turned back when someone knocked on the door and Warnke called, "Come in." A state trooper, a uniformed sergeant, stepped through.

Warnke stood, pushed back his chair and waved the man around behind the desk with him. "Look at these, Milt."

The officer bent, scanning the images slowly, left to right. The sergeant was well muscled, maybe forty, his steel gray hair trimmed short. His uniform looked sprayed on. Riddock had joked about the FBI having a machine that stamped out almost-identical clone agents; perhaps the state police also used the machine, he thought, just with different settings.

"Damn," the officer said.

Warnke shuffled the photos together and handed them over. "These work for you?"

"Sure do." The trooper glanced toward Riddock. "He bring 'em?" With the AP's nod, the cop gave the PI a thumbs-up. "Good images—clear, detailed, repetitive enough for backup, different views. We'll identify these suckers."

"Milt Thompson, Riddock Maguire," Warnke said, waving a hand between them. "Riddock's ex-FBI."

The trooper smiled and nodded.

Riddock would have to thank Kathryn. The praise would make what happened easier on his brother.

"Milt, go at this quick," Warnke said. "An all-nighter. We think they're locals—and that they killed a cop, a sergeant. Gave him no chance." He paused, watched as the sergeant's face shut down into a mask. "You don't get hits, come back. That may be Fed time."

"I got ways," the trooper said, and was gone.

"You think they shot the uniform in Starbucks?" Riddock asked.

Warnke tilted his head and looked at the PI before answering. Light from the angled lamp reflected off his skull. "Tall and short. Little guy holding a foreign-made automatic pistol. Fits. Wish your camera recorded the voices, so we could pass it by the clerk who heard them. The cop killing will make Milt bust his chops." The AP lifted the magnifier and dropped it, with irritation, into a ceramic mug printed with 'Best Dad'.

"No family photos?" Riddock asked, to forestall what was coming.

Warnke opened and closed his mouth, sidetracked. He looked at the cup when he spoke. "Too many visitors I'd rather not see them. Maybe I should lose the cup." He looked up at Riddock. "You already knew what your photos meant."

"What's with the books?" Riddock waved toward the shelves, more to change the subject than to satisfy his curiosity.

Warnke didn't turn away. "The fancy ones came with the office—bet no one ever used them."

"Anything more I can do?" Riddock asked. "Vincent said not to bother waiting. Probably wants to keep me out of it."

Warnke snorted. "Well, you gave us photos, memory card, a statement, and phone time with your partner—Kathryn, is she? Sounds sharp. You get a gold star. Not every PI would do that." He scratched a cheek—he needed a shave—and shook a fist at Riddock. "Obstruction of justice applies only when we can prove it."

"Oh?"

"Who the fuck you protecting?" Warnke switched off the extra lamp, and leaned forward onto his arms. "Why were you watching Medved in the first place? You got a client involved. You didn't tell me about that, and I gotta know. Talk however you want to your friend Alegretti, but *I* gotta know."

Warnke went on when the PI said nothing: "Your client is Morgan Westbrook. I'll squeeze *him*."

Riddock sat back, unconcerned. "I *was* hired by Westbrook—to look into Norman Lyon's death. You guys ruled it an accident." He smiled. "Westbrook's hiring me was prudent, don't you think? He knows nothing about my watching Medved, or the images. Go ahead, pull him in. You'll gain zippo, and maybe reveal too much."

Warnke's fingers curled. "Your partner was at Medved's because?"

"My idea. I learned he does programming, and had been Lyons only friend at the company. Vincent brought you printouts, didn't he?"

Warnke slapped his hands on the desktop. "You sound like a fed."

Riddock stood. "You need anything I *can* provide, just ask."

The AP looked up with a wry smile. "Vincent says I should shake your hand."

~32~
5:07 P.M.

RIDDOCK knew he'd done the right thing. Now it was up to larger powers. When he triggered the hotel's sliding doors, it was black outside, colder than before, and raw. There were parking spots available, even close to the hotel. Meetings were over, guests gone home or off to other restaurants. The roads would be crowded.

He'd decided not to eat dinner at the hotel. Minutes before, standing by a restaurant, he'd convinced himself it was too expensive. But out in the cold, he admitted that sitting alone, surrounded by couples, would have disheartened him. February blahs or his lack of social life, he was lonely.

He'd stop off for Chinese. Maybe tonight, the girl of his dreams would be waiting at the take-out counter. Gary'd met a woman because of a death—probably a murder—so stranger things did happen. For sure, no one was waiting at home for him.

It was quiet as he walked toward the car; the wind kept him company, tugging at his coat, ruffling his hair. He'd come to terms with his knee and the painful shift it had brought to his life. It had taken years. None of the quick answers had worked. So many things you think you know, but they take their own time maturing inside.

The front of the building was ablaze with light, but when he turned the corner, only courtesy fixtures along the edge of a snow-covered flowerbed lit the path. Parking lot pole lights were aisles away. The hush after being inside, feeling the breeze in the semi-darkness, suited him.

Riddock pushed the button on his remote. His car chirped, Hello, I'm here for you. He reached for the door handle and barely felt the blow to his head.

~33~
7:05 P.M.

"WAKE UP! You be fine."

Riddock heard that. Awareness brought pain cascading through his head. When he tried to move, he found his arms were bound behind him. He was sitting, leaning against something. His shoulders and arms ached. He couldn't feel his hands.

He blinked, squinting. Bright lights were beating at him, searing his eyes closed. His face felt sandpapered. They must have taped his eyes and mouth, then yanked it off.

He'd been hit before, but this … things inside resisted coming together. A damage report: He pushed the pain aside, regained memory, a degree of control. He blinked again, saw double, narrowed his eyes, but kept them open.

Car headlights: a vehicle had been pulled into the building, engine off, lights on, telling him whatever was going to happen wouldn't take long.

"Good, you wake," said the stranger, watching, nothing in his hands. "Want drink?" The man wore brown trousers and a shiny, cream-colored shirt so loose that two of him might have fit inside. He was bald, with a round face, fleshy nose, and thin lips set in a menacing smile.

Riddock nodded, the slight motion freeing the pain he'd willed contained. He recognized the Russian accent, saw the stranger look to his left.

"Mihran," the bald man said. The PI tried to swivel his head, got nauseous, and had to close his eyes. He found if he moved very slowly, he had a limited field of vision.

A smaller man, this face familiar, appeared from the right holding a cup. He handed it to the stranger, who stepped closer, and lowered it.

"Hands?" Riddock asked, meaning to say more, not moving his head to sip. The word came out thick and slow. He needed medical attention.

The stranger nodded and spoke to someone he called Lev. A third man, much larger than the other two, half again Riddock's size, his face also familiar, appeared. He had an oversized knife with a serrated blade. The PI saw a pistol holstered at the small of his back. The large man dropped to a knee, reached behind, and cut through the bonds.

Blood returned, attacking Riddock's fingers with a thousand needles, making them useless. He tried to move his hands. Muscles screamed when he drew his arms forward. The stranger held the cup patiently.

He heard dripping to his left; the drops were splashing, and he realized he was sitting in wetness. The room was unheated. He saw windows missing. There was no furniture. The floor was broken cement. The doorway looked as if sledgehammers had worked it over—it had burst open beyond where the frame might have been. An abandoned place. But it had walls and a roof. The vehicle had been driven in under the roof, where its headlights would be less visible from outside.

The other two men were in the photos he'd given Warnke. They'd kidnapped the young couple. The large man had beaten the girl. He filed the names, Mihran and Lev, wished he could phone them in. He'd worried about the kidnapped youths in the photos, didn't know he'd be joining them.

How long had he been out? It'd been dark when he was taken; it was dark now. He reached for the cup, grasped at it with both hands and shook, some spilled. He sipped clumsily, found it was water.

"Why here?" he whispered, intending to say more, but finding it difficult to put thoughts into words.

"To answer questions," said the stranger.

"Anything," Riddock whispered. The pounding in his head came and went, easier when he didn't move. His hands tingled. He couldn't hold the cup, it spilled on him, he couldn't help it, but the stranger took no notice.

He couldn't mention Merle—that would get the man killed. Same with Gary. He couldn't mention the photos. How could they know about them? Raising them would neuter Warnke, let these people cut and run. There might be other things he could offer to make him a fringe player.

Could they let him live? They wouldn't believe anything he said, at first. They might hurt him again. Deep inside, he laughed at himself, there was so much less of him to feel pain. He remembered when his knee was shot, that pain dissolving his future.

"Good," the stranger said. "Cooperation will make it easier."

"No need ... for this," he whispered. "Not rich." That wasn't what he thought, but the best he could do.

"Call me Serge," said the bald man.

He knew that name but didn't show it. Serge was the criminal Merle was running from. He'd found Merle's nightmare. Or been found by it. Merle wouldn't let him shoot. Now Merle would have to do his own shooting.

"Who do you work for?" The tone was no longer gentle. The leader bent forward, but not for the cup.

Riddock concentrated—not an evasion, he had an answer in his head—but because it was difficult speaking. He forced his thoughts into sounds.

"Consolidaa ... hired ... for dead employee—"

"That would be Lyons." The man made it a statement.

Riddock nodded. Painful, but easier than speaking.

"When did you get job?"

"Morning ...."

"What have you learned?"

He'd need more than a nod for this. He fought to speak. "Ineview ... presden ... poleee ... jus star..." He didn't know whether it was sweat or blood dripping down his forehead. He couldn't continue. Nothing would come out.

Serge shook his head. "What was in the envelope you carried?

Who did you visit?"

Crafting the answer was easy: he'd met an attorney to help him renew the office lease. "New ... offccc ... leeee—"

"Bull," Serge said. "Lev." The big man stepped forward, hands free until he effortlessly hoisted Riddock off the floor and smashed a knee into his groin.

Before this new pain, the hurt in his head went away. For a long time he was agony curled on the floor. Before he recovered—partway was all he would recover—he understood the pretty girl by the take-out counter would have to meet him in another life.

But he wouldn't take anyone down with him. One small win in this sea of agony. Talking would prove torture worked, he'd earn more pain. He'd be just as dead for telling them what he knew. And then, he could barely talk, which they didn't understand.

"Lying *bad* for you," Serge said. "Who else you work for?" Riddock stayed hurt. "Merle Kingsley ring bells? Before we ring yours again."

So they did know. "Boyguar," he said, but he had trouble understanding what came out. Some bodyguard job I'm doing, he thought. He concentrated on Everett and Kathryn.

Serge nodded. "You say Lyons' death is investigated by police as homicide. House fire as arson. You did not tell *me* that. What else do you know?"

He wondered if Westbrook had passed that on to Pavlic, or directly. What was the difference? What was the man fishing for? News the authorities knew of the theft? "Polee ... tell me." His stomach hurt, low down, the pain directional as feeling returned, he wished it wouldn't.

"You offer police information too soon," Serge said. "You were involved before. I need to know everything."

Riddock tried to speak. "Was as ... arrang ...."

Serge bent close and frowned, not understanding the PI's efforts to say he was supposed to know those things, it was as arranged, Westbrook had required he be plugged in.

Pain crumpled the images in his mind; look how he'd wound up. Others, he'd worried about others. His eyes were tearing.

"You are not being honest." The voice dripped with disgust.

He looked up, helpless. No uncle, he'd never be an uncle. He wished Everett and Kathryn a good life.

"Lev!"

Riddock floated in an acid sea, somewhere in that journey, he missed a beat and when part of him tried to return, it couldn't talk, and he hardly felt the shots.

"Lev. Mihran. As usual."

Serge left the room and the building, got into his car on the asphalt outside, and drove off. He was certain, if that man had known about the theft, or Merle's involvement, if he had known anything he might have bargained against his life, he'd have somehow raised it. That was what people did.

One dangerous snoop was gone. They would close up shop at Consolidated, at least for a while. They'd wind down this operation tomorrow. But they could introduce their new man and be prepared to come back once the waves died down. One more missing person, and they were home free.

It took about forty minutes for Lev and Mihran to erase all traces of the bodies. It would've been quicker without the frost. They had to warm up the backhoe, and deal with frozen earth. But it was work they'd done before.

They carried Riddock's body out of the trucking terminal, decaying behind a chain link fence in that isolated, forsaken section of the Meadowlands. Lev dumped the corpse into the front of the Indian couple's car, which already contained their stiffening bodies in back. They returned to the room, wiped away bloodstains, tossed rags into the car.

They opened the driver's-side window, and Mihran steered from outside while Lev pushed it into one of the empty below-grade tractor-trailer loading bays that lined the rear of the abandoned facility. The backhoe had wide treads, and Lev rode it down the ramp, onto the auto, flattening it, popping out windows, crumpling doors. Then he machine-filled the bay up to ground level, using earth from a mound behind the facility. He rolled the backhoe over the gravesite, packing it tight.

Mihran raked the fresh dirt and spread assorted junk over the surface. The season's fourth major snowstorm was forecast for early the following week. It would cover everything. Weeds would grow in springtime. It was too deep for animals to dig up. No one would come looking.

When they finished, Mihran peered along the row of bays. Memories were exhausting. All but two of the bays had been filled in.

He'd have to speak with Serge about additional space.

~34~
10:15 P.M.

"ONE cup only," Serge said to Arman. In public, he never used Russian. They both liked strong coffee. Arman knew what the one-cup limit meant.

They were sitting in an all-night Dunkin' Donuts, in a strip mall. After the lone employee in view poured, Arman had followed Serge back to the rear of the shop, to a booth that kept them mostly invisible from outside. Serge, wearing a suit and tie—unusual for him—and a long coat he had unbuttoned, faced the door. His shiny bald head, bulbous nose, and wire-rimmed glasses made him look, Arman thought, like Nikita Khrushchev.

It was late for such a meeting. Serge had called unexpectedly, demanded Arman be waiting in front of his darkened house, and then driven here without explanation.

The shop's lighting glared. Both men would have preferred darkness.

Arman ignored his coffee. "What is wrong?" He'd worked with Serge long enough to be alarmed. While Serge drove, Arman had considered the events of the week. Every task he'd been given—Lyons, the man's house, Rahman, and the private investigator—had been handled well. Serge could not know about his attack on the witness. That would never be reported. He wasn't aware of having made an error.

"Several things," Serge said.

Arman watched the bald man lift his coffee, stare at the steam

188

rising from it, and set down the cup without drinking.

"You know why Rahman and the girl visit Teo?"

The tone alerted him that he was supposed to, but he didn't. "No."

A radio, turned low, was playing hip-hop music in the rear of the shop. Its metronome beat overwhelmed its words and provided an odd counterpoint to their conversation.

"You *do*," Serge said, hunching forward on his elbows. "Stop being stupid. Rahman want money from Teo because of what you say."

That stunned Arman. "I told Rahman nothing!"

Serge was distracted. In a mirror, Arman saw the man in a gas-station uniform, who'd been sitting up front near the server, stand and leave the shop. The young woman who'd poured their coffee leaned half asleep on the counter. Arman straightened, backing away from Serge.

The bald man went on. "Rahman say you yell at Medved, tell him he jeopardize millions, risk what we do here. You do it Monday. Rahman tell me that today before he die. It was the truth—the girl say the same thing before she die."

Arman recalled his loss of control and grew angry. Stupid, indeed. He was the stupid one. "Sorry. It—"

"I know. Will never again happen. Rahman only tell girl and Westbrook. Pain made him honest." Serge smiled at something, and offered it up: "The girl call him a blabbermouth." Then he frowned. "You put us in danger."

Arman nodded. What else was coming?

"The police find C4 at Lyons'. Now they investigate fire *and* death."

"I did those well." Arman suppressed a shudder. Serge always smelled out the truth.

"You did." The bald man toyed with a coat button, then rubbed his head as if he were smoothing hair. "But this is my worry come home. We make waves, they look. We must protect ourselves." He caught Arman's eye before he added, "We will shut down at Consolidated."

Arman couldn't hide his disappointment. "We *get* complete

program for elsewhere. Teo promised, for tomorrow."

Serge glared. "You believe visitor and Teo spoke of the dead man?" His tone made a lie of it. Arman remained silent. "New broom will sweep clean. Westbrook will toss you out, bring in new computer director to clean up the mess. That is best way."

"I—"

"Listen, my friend. Consolidated's return to lawful operation is good. We start again when authorities tire and look elsewhere. I find you another company."

Arman nodded, squirmed on the hard plastic seat, sipped his coffee as much for cover as taste.

Serge watched him and went on. "We need Medved's disks and drives. Early tomorrow, pick up Medved as if you bring to office. Be normal, so he is not suspicious. Take him where you can kill him, leave body in usual place. My people handle it. You go back, get his computer things." Serge looked down at his coffee. "Use gloves."

Arman flinched.

"Wipe clean Medved's computer in office—Rahman's, too," Serge said. "Do it tomorrow, while you still there. We must not leave a trail. Medved will vanish, so blame him for difficulties. You are injured party, betrayed by your people. That will make you easier to relocate." The bald man finally reached for the cup. When he bent, his coat bloused in front of him and he brushed it back with irritation before sipping.

"But Teo *promised* to finish program copy tomorrow," Arman said. "One day—"

"We cannot wait. We deal with what is left."

Arman felt the blame wash over him, looked across the table, and knew Serge had picked it up.

"My friend, be clear." Serge held the elevated cup in both hands. "You do this well. Whatever is suspected cannot be proved without Medved and computer." He sipped again. "We need not enter Consolidated system—without Medved to tell, we were never there. Others build program from boy's disks."

He nodded, certain Serge would always blame him for the lost printouts, for the failure.

"Arman, *can you do this?*" The bald man spoke through his teeth, clipping the words. "Medved does not know me. I make you rich. But if you question orders …."

"I know, you kill me."

"No. You are friend." Arman felt the bald man's smile twist inside. "I have others kill you."

A magnified electronic voice from the shop's kitchen joined the muted hip-hop beat, stilling both men. The noise ceased as abruptly as it had started.

Arman nodded. "Teo will vanish. You will have disks." Then he smiled. "May I make a request?"

Serge rubbed his head again, a motion his underling knew he sometimes made when he was thinking. "Something you enjoy?"

"Yes."

"Tell me." His smile might be because he'd guessed.

"We need Kemmerman dead," Arman said.

"Why?"

"Lyons spoke with wife. Kemmerman spoke with Lyons, and then with widow. He met witness to Lyons' killing. He spoke with police. He met private detective. Detective worked for Westbrook and Kingsley. He met Westbrook and raised Kingsley's name. Then he met Teo. He is everywhere."

Serge had begun nodding before Arman finished, but he remained silent for a moment. "We need Kingsley soon," he finally said. "He will be receptive now. Can you find Kemmerman?"

Arman nodded.

Before the leader spoke, he sipped again. "Then kill him. Bring him to usual place. Now get sleep."

"No. I eat, have coffee, and wait for Teo."

Serge rewarded him with a smile.

Arman hoped he'd find Kemmerman and the woman together. He'd have his way with her while the man was helpless and forced to watch. That man had been making everything worse, as if his mission was to disrupt Arman's life.

"You have Teo before sun rises. Kemmerman will be dead by mid-morning."

Neither had cause to notice the car parked in darkness across the street.

PART THREE
§
SAY GOODBYE

~35~
10:19 P.M.

WHEN he thought he heard the cell phone ringing again in darkness, Gary panicked, heaved out of bed, blind and unbalanced, bashing the edge of the mattress, and almost fell down before he realized it was his doorbell.

He squinted at the clock radio. 10:19 P.M.—too late for casual drop-bys.

He pulled on his robe, belted it, flipped on the living room lights from the upstairs landing, and padded barefoot down the carpeted steps. Switching on the outside lights, he peered through the small stained-glass window in the front door, and there was Vincent, bent close to look in, face distorted by the tinted panes. Gary opened the door and stepped back, away from the blast of cold air.

Vincent entered, and behind him was Becca. She was wearing boots and carrying a shopping bag. The collar of her blue coat was turned up, her hair was messy, there were rings under her eyes, but she smiled at him as she leaned against a wall and unzipped her right boot.

"Gary?" Vincent said, swinging the door shut.

He forced himself to look away from her. "Why'd you bring her? She could be in danger here."

"Down, boy." He patted Gary's shoulder. "Don't worry. The state police have a tail on Pavlic. He's home, the house is dark. They'll watch him all night. Looks good for tomorrow."

"Angela told me Dalton was with you—he do well?"

"They may make him Official State Hacker."

"So you believe me—and Norm—now?"

Vincent nodded.

"What about the Medved kid?"

"Warnke said it's a done deal. He thanks you, by the way. He'll call me early in the morning. We'll arrange pick-up. Will you help? You're the only one knows him."

"Sure."

"What else do I need to know?" Vincent asked.

"Guys, can you do this later?" Becca said. Both men looked at her, standing there in white socks, still holding the bag. "Gary, you shouldn't worry about me. Vincent carried his high-tech pistol, in case squirrels attacked us during our walk. Everyone wants to protect little me." She tilted her head. "It's good to see you, too."

"I—"

She raised a hand to cut him off and faced Vincent. "Enough. It's late. Angela said Gary *has* to be hungry. I know I am. Angela already cooked dinner for you." She turned back to Gary. "I woke up and wanted to say hello. I was gonna call, but Angela asked Vincent if it was safe for me to visit. Then she sent him out to get food for us. She said you'd never eat otherwise. We'll be dining on Hunan Gourmet takeout. I know you favor that place. If you want to ask, Mel had dinner, and she's asleep again." Becca hesitated before adding, "Out for the count until tomorrow."

When she said that, she dropped her eyes, and he came awake. He turned to Vincent.

The lieutenant smiled. "You wanna return, Becca, you just call me, anytime, and my squirrel gun and I will come collect you."

Or not, Gary thought. "Thanks, Vinnie. We'll go over the rest in the morning."

"It can wait?"

"It's gonna wait."

Becca shooed Vincent out and pushed the door closed behind him. "How do you lock this?"

He came close and showed her.

She looked at him and grinned. "We have to leave the front light on for him."

Gary reached and turned it off.

She slipped past. He followed. She set the bag of take-out food on the kitchen island. He reached for it, to help her unpack. His left hand touched hers. "Where's your ring?"

"I don't need protection from you, silly." She frowned at something, and her voice grew deeper. "Gary …?"

"What?"

"Do you usually sleep without *your* ring?"

It took him a moment to answer. "Just—uh, I just now put it away. It … it signifies a time of life … that's past."

"This is scary," she said, frozen in place.

"You did the same thing?"

She nodded.

He was still holding her wrist. She pried his hand free, studied it one last time, brushed his palm with fingertips, and let it go. "You hungry?" She didn't sound frightened now.

"Yeah," he said, voice thick.

Her eyes twinkled. "I mean for Chinese food."

He steadied himself with a hand on the countertop. "No."

"Me neither." She turned away before he could read her expression. "Maybe later." She opened the refrigerator, pulled containers from the shopping bag, and piled them in.

He heard the refrigerator door sigh with pleasure and remembered it laughing at him.

"This is way too empty," Becca said. She closed it and turned back. "We have to do something about that."

"Do you cook? You asked me, but I never asked you."

Without looking, she pushed the refrigerator door to ensure it was shut. "Is that important to you?"

As if a puzzle was falling into place, he understood. "You asking if I require meat and potatoes on the table every evening at 7:18 P.M. sharp?"

She looked surprised.

"You *know* the answer," he said. "You know *all* those answers."

They stood a few feet apart, looking at each other, and she put a hand over his on the countertop, as she had in the diner, when he asked her to marry him. She laughed, lightness again. "Bet I cook better than you do."

"Can I take your coat?" he asked.

She shook her head. "I'll do it." He watched as she unbuttoned. "You like to watch women undress?"

"Only you."

She held the coat closed until she finished with the buttons, then playfully moved as if she might flash him. "Guess what I have on underneath?"

Below the hem, gray slacks reached her socks, but he would've answered the same if he hadn't seen that. "I know Angela—she wouldn't have let you out without wearing everything short of a chastity belt."

Becca laughed and performed the promised flash. "Count on you to guess right."

The light green sweatshirt complimented her hair and eyes. He saw the outline of a bra. "Can we do something about the clothes?"

Her eyes melted him. "*You* know the answer. But I'm so glad you asked."

"Wow." Becca reached down, grasped the sheet, pulled it up and dropped onto her back, centuries of evolution at work to allow the little fishies to swim upstream.

He tugged, and she let him pull the sheet away. "Not wow yet."

"Do I lack something?" she asked, speaking at the ceiling.

"You lack nothing."

"Then what?"

He lay naked beside her, knowing what he wanted, not knowing how to get there. "You didn't join me."

"Oh, the orgasm thing." She faced him. "I don't have them. I gave up faking a long time ago."

"You said your husband abused you."

"Do we need to go there?" He saw a flash of irritation. "What happened happened, and that man isn't here. He's as far gone as your Sarah. I hope."

"No problem on that score."

"But you don't look happy."

"How about I try a flanking maneuver?" He reached around, and tickled her ribs until she squirmed and giggled. He'd already learned that much about her body. But the tickle wasn't what he'd meant. "Did you ever have orgasms?"

"Oh, silly, sure. Don't worry about it, please."

He couldn't let it pass. "We're full partners, right?"

"We are."

"Good." He moved on the bed.

"Gary—what are you doing?"

"This." He nuzzled, made clear what he wanted to do, and then lifted his head.

"That's—"

"My right as a partner," he said, softly.

"But ...."

He couldn't force her, wouldn't interrupt again. He saw her lips scrunch, heard the resignation in her voice. "I'll disappoint. Nothing will happen."

"It's okay."

She stiffened. Her arms reached down with hands clenched in little fists, as if she'd beat him away. But after awhile, her fingers opened and gripped his arms. When she lost all control, he moved up and entered her again.

"Wow now," he said, spent, lowering himself onto an elbow beside her, looking at her, he'd never tire of that.

She reached down and pulled up the sheet. She stared beyond the ceiling, breathing deeply; a breath caught, and emerged as a long sigh. She lowered her right arm onto him, palm up. They lay quietly.

"Becca ...."

"Hmmm?"

"I want us to make up for ... what happened to you."

Except for her breathing, she was still, eyes swimming, thoughts private. "Gary ...."

He waited. When she didn't continue, he fished for her happy little laugh. "What, I pause, you pause?"

Staring at the ceiling, looking as if she'd surprised herself, she whispered, "I love you."

He watched her. Time passed silently. When she finally turned, she said, "We must have woken your neighbors."

"They'll have to get used to it."

~36~
10:25 P.M.

LEV liked the bar. Dark wood, low light, rough male conversations—many of them in Russian—a broken television, and the smells of cigarette smoke and stale beer brought back memories of places by the docks in Riga. He cradled the open bottle of vodka in his thick right hand, staring at the scarred countertop without seeing it. It had been good then, but he was pleased to be here. He had plenty of money, and no one was hunting him.

He laughed at the comparison between Riga and Rahway. His movement rocked the rickety barstool. He raised his glass, drained it to the difference. Here he had decent rooms, friends, and women. Here, his pack did the hunting.

Mihran sat on the stool beside him. He'd been talking to someone for quite a while. Lev glanced to his left, bent forward, and found him speaking with a slim stranger wearing an expensive coat. Two rows of shots were lined up on the counter in front of them. They must be downing shot-for-shot.

Lev knew that Mihran, even with his hollow leg for vodka, only matched shots for a purpose. When the two of them were called to action, often without warning, as they had been yesterday and twice today, only sharp ears, eyes and aim kept them alive.

Lev looked down at his glass. He had been drinking too much. How many times had Mihran saved him? he wondered. Still, he filled the tumbler from the bottle, spilling only a little, and downed the vodka in a silent thank-you.

He wanted to better see this person Mihran was talking to. He peered at the mirror on the wall, but it was broken in places, the gaps covered by posters, and the man was sitting in a blind spot. So Lev twisted on the stool, extended his muscular arm and pounded his partner's back.

Mihran acknowledged him without turning. "My friend?"

"Who have we?" Lev asked.

For a moment, Mihran didn't know how to handle the question, because this stranger might be more than a good mark—he might be the road to months of riches. He owned a fancy car and did not mind getting drunk beyond good sense. But Mihran felt he had softening up to do before they led the man outside.

He raised his left shoulder and spoke to Lev softly—the stranger was dazed, wouldn't hear. "A friend who will give us a ride soon, but not yet."

"Let me talk to him." Lev's voice was deep and threatening.

Lev usually sounded like that. Mihran turned on the stool. "Lev ...." He saw his partner's eyes, and backed off the shaky seat, giving up his place. Lev could be violent. He'd protected Mihran for years. Perhaps they'd protected one another, Lev the strong one, the man of action, and Mihran the clever one, slower to anger—but he was losing hair, sleeping poorly, and felt tired all the time.

Lev switched stools with little grace, banging the one he'd left upright when it threatened to tip. He glared at the well-dressed man beside him. "Where you live?"

The younger man took no notice of the switch. His reaction to Lev's question was to screw up his face in thought. Lev noticed his hair was well cut, his hands clean, nails done, shoes shined and expensive.

"Man-hattan." The man finally said. His speech was slurred. "My name is Fedor. Please to meet you." The hand he extended shook.

Lev would have ignored it, except for the feel of Mihran's imploring hand on his back.

"Where you from?"

"My parents ... from Moscow. They dream of ... going back," he said, as if the wish was very funny.

Lev might have laughed, because it was humorous. But he wanted to know how good a mark Mihran had stumbled upon. "How long they here?"

The question caused the slim man to frown, as if thinking had become a chore. "Ohhhh, two years."

"What they do?" Lev leaned closer, had to look down.

The slender man fired back the answer as if it was something he repeated frequently:" Dad's a bi-ig doctor." That, too, made him chuckle. "As if there's other kind." He breathed deeply before continuing: "But he makes lots money for Mama. Buys art. For me, expensive cars."

The young man's head drooped with the effort.

Lev smiled. Mihran would come up with a way to get the money, the art, and the car. Noise exploded in the back of the room: a chair fell, angry voices sounded. Lev didn't turn. Moments later a bartender growled, and that was it.

"One more shot—let us have one together," he said to the stranger, raising the glass that had been in front of Mihran.

The slim man spilled much of his vodka on the bar. The glass rolled when he finally set it down. He leaned forward against the wood for support.

"So, Fedor, what is doing?" Lev asked.

It took a few moments before the other man spoke, and then he drew a breath before each short sentence: "Want to ride? Let's find woman. You drive. I drunk."

Lev and Mihran caught each other's eyes, and both almost laughed. Fedor's wish was another joke. With all the vodka he'd consumed, he'd never get it up.

Mihran imagined them returning this drunken Fedor to his grateful parents. A fine gesture. Then taking what they wanted.

Perhaps Fedor's mother would be Lev's woman tonight. She'd have dyed blonde hair, a face-lift, boob job, body toned by her personal trainer. They were all Lev's type.

Lev smiled, maybe thinking the same thing.

"Sure, sure," Mihran said to Fedor. He turned to Lev. "Ready?"

They found their coats. Half-supporting the stumbling drunk, they pushed through the door.

Instantly, sounds and smells changed. It was dark and bitterly cold. Streetlights had burned out, or been shot out, and those in the distance shimmered in the brisk wind. What light there was came from the crescent moon. The sidewalks were broken concrete. Empty lots surrounded the bar. The street contained old, low buildings, fronted in brick or stone, in blatant disrepair.

Fedor staggered to the right, choosing a direction, and they moved past an alleyway.

"Your car?" asked Mihran.

Fedor motioned ahead, and they continued, propping him up.

Mihran heard a noise and was about to turn when he felt a gun press his spine. He glanced toward Lev, and saw that he, too, had an armed man behind him. Mihran saw Lev grow angry, and knew what he was thinking. *Who are these fools who think they can take me?* Lev said that often when he was drunk. He was hotheaded, but Mihran hoped he would be steady now, and not risk getting them both shot.

Were these men robbers, or others from the bar who coveted Fedor? He and Lev would give up what they had, and escape from this.

He looked for Fedor, who had slipped away, and found the slim man several paces in front, holding a nine-millimeter pistol with a steady hand.

"You're under arrest. State police. We know you're armed, and we will shoot if you resist."

Police. They had broken away from police before. Surprise them. They're trained not to shoot unless they have to. Even then, when they get excited, they aim poorly. But there were three of them, close, guns drawn.

Without warning, Lev reached back for his gun and tried to

lunge forward. The man behind banged hard into him, knocking him onto the pavement, smashing onto him with his knees. Lev's arm bent behind him and the gun, spun free, skidded across the sidewalk. When he tried to rise, the man on top twisted his arm cruelly and kneed him in the back. The big man's face smacked the pavement with an ugly sound. Lev cried out and stopped resisting, breathing in painful rasps.

Mihran noted the cop who'd put Lev down had holstered his gun rather than use it. He turned forward and found the slim man closer, the gun still in his hand, but lowered. He didn't move. The man behind grasped Mihran's arms, laced his wrists together with that impossible plastic cord. No one had fired a weapon. The loudest noise was Lev's moaning.

Mihran realized these police wanted to capture them without others knowing. He stood still as they frisked him. They removed his pistol and knife, even found his razor.

Two unmarked police cars arrived, rolling quietly, without sirens or lights. Already cuffed, Lev was hoisted into the first car. Mihran was folded into the back door of the second. He was surprised to find another man waiting across the bench seat.

As the car started forward, Vincent Alegretti read Mihran Grinko his Miranda rights and held up photos.

FRIDAY, FEBRUARY 20

~37~
4:26 A.M.

"FOR YOU," said Angela, tapping the cordless phone against the lump her sleeping husband made under the quilt.

Vincent groaned, not moving. "Becca want me?"

The humor in that woke her up. "Hell, no." She pushed the phone into his hand and dropped back onto her pillow, chuckling.

It was pitch black even after he forced his eyes open. The bedroom was warm, but he was chilled from exhaustion. "What time is it?"

The clock and phone were on her side of the bed, useful when their kids lived home. They hadn't changed much in the house, and that order remained, which made no sense because now demands at night were always for him.

"After four." She turned away and pulled the covers over her head.

He fought the quilt, sat up before he put the receiver to his ear. "Alegretti."

"Something's going on, Vincent. Sorry to wake you."

It was Warnke, and he sounded wide-awake. "What's up?"

"Man picked up Arman Pavlic around ten. They went to a Dunkin' Donuts, talked, drove off. Our tail followed back to his house. Pavlic went inside, lights out. Our guy came in so we could process his photos. Took a while but we made the man Pavlic met with as Serge Yukovich."

"Who's he?" Vincent reached down for his slippers, didn't find them beside the bed.

"Nothing's ever stuck to him before," Warnke said. "Now we have witnesses. Yukovich is Pavlic's boss, uses an import-export business and an auto repair shop to launder money. More important, the pigeons you brought in say the man had Lyons and Schroder killed, and three people murdered yesterday. All related to Consolidated." The line was silent. "Vincent?"

"Who were they?"

"The two kids in the photos you saw. One of them worked at Consolidated. They were trying to visit Teodors Medved—the Consolidated programmer you told me your friend met with. Our pigeons say they'd been protecting him."

"Please don't tell me Medved's the third." Vincent swung his feet onto the carpet.

"No."

Vincent heard something in Warnke's voice. "Not Gary?"

"Riddock Maguire. Sorry."

"Bastards!" He rose, wanted to be shooting someone, not standing undressed in his bedroom. He knew he'd have to call Merle, who was wrapped up tight these days. How would he handle this? Maybe they could get together soon as the run was over. What did Gary know? He and Merle were supposed to have met, but Gary'd never said anything. "Let's pick up Pavlic now," he said.

"Can't. He left before our guy got back. Car's gone."

"We *lost* him?" Vincent yanked a pair of briefs from his dresser. The bedroom door was closed in deference to Melanie, whom he hoped was fast asleep in the guest room.

"Yeah," Warnke said. "And his gun with the silencer."

The words triggered a reaction that leaned him against the dresser. He knew what must come next. "Let's get Medved outta there right away. He's our Rosetta Stone for the computer fraud, and that's the reason for all the deaths. I were them, I'd kill him quick."

"Right," Warnke said. "Go for it—you'll need firepower. Get Kemmerman to call Medved—he's never met us, and he's involved up to his ears. Call me with what you arrange. Bring Medved to me—we know how to treat a rat."

~38~
4:39 A.M.

Gary's phone rang again in the dark. It was the cell this time—easy to identify, since he wasn't sleeping soundly. Every time he moved and touched her, found her there, he woke with joy.

He reached out and felt her sleeping—warm, soft, breathing deeply. He traced the curve of a hip, moved to her waist. He did not want to leave the bed. The ring sounded again.

Slipping from under the covers, trying not to wake her, he stumbled to the dresser and flipped open the phone with his eyes closed.

The phone spoke: "Gary? Gary!" Vincent shouted.

"Yeah?"

"You up?"

"No."

"Well, get up. We have to move fast." Vincent paused for a response. There was none. "Gary, you got us into this, and now we have to save Medved's ass—the kid you wanted to help, remember? We're goin' there right now. You, me, Larry, and a SWAT team. We don't get there first, they'll kill him. You're the one knows him best. Get moving."

Gary was still fuzzy. "Right now?"

"If we want him alive. Quick. No shower. You said you had his cell number. Bring it. Get to the station."

He heard rustling from the bed, turned away and tried to speak

208

softly. "What made this urgent?"

"Man Pavlic met with tonight has an auto repair shop and a history of murder—three just yesterday. If they're killing to protect themselves—"

"You at the station, or home?"

"Good idea. Get your ass to my house. I'll get Larry to pick us up. Five minutes. Move."

"Vincent?" Becca asked, when he lowered the phone.

"Yeah. What day is it?" He headed for the closet.

"Friday, I think," she said. "Vincent wasn't calling for me, was he?"

"Me." He opened the closet, turned on the small light, and searched for clothes.

She sat up, swinging her feet over the edge of the bed and pulling the sheet with her. She watched him in the full-length mirror inside the open door.

It felt strange. But she'd explored his body earlier, moving around to inspect, nurse's privilege, she'd said, touching him, laughing when he'd reacted. They'd talked for hours, nestled, beyond sex, each wanting to learn more about the other.

"I'm a fallen woman," she said.

He climbed into his briefs. "Fallen Beccas' are my specialty. Marry me. No one cares about your past."

"Are you serious? It's 4:30 in the morning." She leaned toward him and the sheet slipped. She pulled it up.

He stepped into khaki cargo pants. "You bet. Want a proposal every two minutes 'round the clock, you got it. Starting after I get back. But you'll find that annoying. We won't get any sleep."

"No need," she said. "Okay."

He leaned sideways against the doorframe, frozen for a heartbeat. "You'll marry me?"

"Don't fall. Yeah, I'll marry you. But I'll get a divorce first." The sheet slipped again; she didn't seem to notice. "You'll protect me?"

He nodded. "These decisions okay with Melanie?" He zipped.

"She knew you'd ask. She wishes you were younger."

"You need me younger?" He forced himself not to look at her, wrestled into a tee, pulled on a heavy green shirt. He made sure he started with the button in the right hole.

Becca laughed. "She does. She wants you for herself. But I put my foot down." She leaned forward. "In our whole lives, we've been asleep together maybe two hours, and you're up and out already."

He found socks, put a shoulder against the doorjamb to make it easier. "World's been a bit off balance this week."

"Can I tell Melanie, Angela, Nadine ... and other friends?"

"That we slept together?" He buckled his belt.

"That we're engaged, silly."

"Tell the world. Please. I will if you don't." He decided on shoes without laces, and reached for a shoehorn. "Vinnie said if we don't get Medved fast, they'll kill him. I've got two minutes to be at his door. We're meeting a SWAT team. I've never done that before." He couldn't help looking at her. "Lot of firsts for me tonight." He stepped into shoes.

"Is this what life will be like with you?"

"I hope not. Not the dressing and going part." He looked out again. "I'd choose you even over a SWAT team."

"High praise," she said. "Will you be careful ... *please?*"

Her eyes reflected light spilling from the closet. He nodded. "Wait for me?"

"Okay. Either here or at Angela's." She smiled playfully. "You'd better wash your face before you go."

He thought she'd stay in bed and let him pass, but when he stepped out of the closet she ran to him, into the light, sheet gone, hair matted, face puffy, arms out, irresistible.

~39~
5:34 A.M.

Pavlic sat in the BMW, darker for its tinted side and rear windows. He'd been waiting almost five hours, making sure Teo Medved would not slip away.

He patted the pistol and tubular silencer. The weather forecast was good: cold, clouds, but no snow. It would be easy for him to get around and do his killing. No tunes played in his head. They were for after, a reward.

Serge had ordered him to pick up Teo without raising suspicion, so it was too early to get the boy. He usually appeared at six, and Teo was always ready. This morning, he'd ring the kid ten minutes early. He drew back his sleeve, and peered at his watch. 5:39. Eleven minutes. He forced himself to be patient.

Once Teo answered questions about yesterday's visitor, he'd strangle him. He wouldn't use the gun; there was no reason to get the car bloody. He touched the switch and his driver-side window slid up with a murmur, closed with a thunk. He didn't need the chill any longer.

Parked at the curb, several doors down from Ana's building on this sorry street, he watched with eyes slightly out of focus, as he'd been trained, seeking movement of any kind. He glanced at his watch again. Nine minutes.

Was this not like old times? No. Events had shaken him before, but never had he brought disaster upon himself. He'd learn from what had happened. He'd lost control. He wouldn't make that

211

mistake again.

5:46. Enough. It was time, right now.

He reached for the door handle before he sensed a vehicle pulling close behind him in the street. It was almost alongside by the time his hand grasped the gun. But the black van rolled right past, slowly, without lights.

It was a police vehicle. It stopped in front of Teo's stoop. A second, similar vehicle followed, pulled beyond the first, made a U-turn and parked at the other curb—facing the wrong way on the one-way street, pointing at him. Doors opened and closed without interior lighting.

He drew the night-vision scope from the boot. In its green haze, he saw three SWAT officers standing on each side of the street, clad in body armor, helmets, radio microphones. They were carrying little machine guns and wearing night-vision goggles. They scanned the street, windows, and rooftops. Another policeman remained behind the wheel of each vehicle. The small trucks were probably armored.

He was fortunate he hadn't stopped in front of the building. At this distance, in the darkness, they couldn't easily see into the car. Frayed nerves betrayed him, and he jumped when his phone vibrated. It had to be Ana, telling him about the police. He didn't answer.

Startled again, he swiveled in the seat when flashing lights appeared behind him. A police car had stopped across the intersection, blocking it, probably to prevent traffic from entering the street. Lights flashed as a safety measure.

The tinted rear window saved him. He pressed against the headrest, willing himself invisible, turning back slowly—and thirty feet away, a trooper was moving toward him, flashing a light into the alleyways and parked cars. They were going to find him.

He'd have to shoot down the trooper, use surprise to escape. He'd have to run. He'd never make it out in the BMW—he'd move toward the patrol car with flashing lights, there would only be two of them, without machine guns. He switched off the inside light, hunkered down, pistol aimed upward through the front windshield. He'd shoot the man in the face: no armor there. One silent shot might not be heard.

He'd steal a car, slip away before reinforcements arrived.

At 5:52, when he should have been walking Teo down his stoop, moments before he'd have to kill the trooper, the man turned and headed back toward the house. Pavlic pushed up, watching. The blocking vehicle allowed two additional police cars, one unmarked, to enter. They passed the BMW and stopped in the middle of the road by the stoop.

Before he thought to focus on them in the darkness, four men ran up the exterior stairs and into the house. The boy must have unlocked the door. Three minutes later—fast, this must have been prearranged—they emerged with Teo. Spiky hair, skinny, wore no coat; he was the only one Pavlic recognized through the scope. One of the men carried a sack.

He tried, but could not identify faces.

If he emerged and fired, it would be suicide, and he was not likely to hit the boy, who was near invisible between police in body armor. Other men crossed in front and behind. Guns pointed everywhere. The group descended the stoop as one animal, reached the sidewalk, and the cars.

They had beaten him. He had been there first, but he waited too long. How could they know about the boy? Only Kemmerman had met him. Serge had been right.

Did Kemmerman know Pavlic himself had been there yesterday, waiting beside the front door? *Had those final words been staged?* His instinct to shoot had been correct. He contained his fury and swore he'd kill this man who was always in the way.

Serge would not consider his orders—keep things normal, raise no suspicions—as reason for failure. Arman was on-site, it was his job to act. Minutes, again minutes. He felt a wave of anguish.

The greater it grew, the colder and more grounded he became. He'd use this hatred to think clearly, act boldly, wreak vengeance. He watched all but the SWAT team disappear into the two late-arriving police cars. Accompanied by one of the SWAT vans, the cars pulled away with the boy in the lead car. Medved was in protective custody, but Kemmerman was probably not.

He itched to follow. He might have a chance for a drive-by shooting if they got out of the car without protection. But the unit with flashing lights and the second SWAT vehicle held their positions for more than five minutes, freezing him. By then, his target had vanished. He had a police radio, but he dared not turn it on. They wouldn't broadcast their destination anyway.

There were still things he could do here.

By the time the final police vehicles pulled away, the roofs of buildings showed darker against the graying sky, and the length of the street was visible.

He ran into the building, up the stairs to the boy's rooms, gun out against a leg. He found the door half-open and paused, wary, stood to the side and pushed at it with his left hand, the gun leveled in his right. The door bumped something, and stopped.

He froze, listened, saw scratch marks on the floor. He entered the room. Teo's heavy clothes dresser stood at an odd angle. The boy must have pushed it along the wall until it blocked the door, then shoved it partly aside when the police arrived.

That told him what he would not find. The only things missing from his visit yesterday were precisely what he sought, those disks and the hard drive. The computer had been taken apart. Teo must have done that in advance—his visitors had no time to play with tiny screws, disconnect parts, wires. It all must have been in the sack he'd seen. The boy had left only his mess—the useless books, random papers, dirty clothes, empty soda cans.

The rooms felt deserted. He found Teo's winter coat, toothbrush, even his keys. The boy had been in such a rush that he'd left everything except his computer materials.

So Pavlic couldn't go back home, or to his office. Serge would not be able find another role for him. He would have to go to ground, run to save himself. Serge owed him that much.

Kemmerman must have done this.

What could he do? The police knew this place. He'd been compromised, but Serge hadn't. Once the police got around to her, though, Ana might lead them to Serge.

He crept downstairs and knocked on Ana's door. She opened at once, that insipid smile on her face. He shot her twice. She fell like a rag. With his left foot, he pushed her back from the doorway. She was weightless. For good measure, he bent and shot her in the head.

Pffht. He retrieved her cell phone. Before he left, he reloaded.

He strode back to his car, imagined he was in combat in order to focus. He had to get the BMW out of the neighborhood, and he needed real information before he reported his failure to Serge.

He had precious little time. He brightened when he remembered where Kemmerman lived. He'd go there. The police wouldn't expect that. If he left now, he'd get there just after seven.

Let Serge do the questioning. The man would tell what he knew. If the woman was there, Serge would let him deal with her. He wanted that.

Kemmerman would save him. Then he'd kill him, but only after he watched his woman raped. Just how would he kill her?

Recalling her figure brought back his smile.

~40~
6:15 A.M.

"THIS IS ... adventure," Medved said, from the darkness in the back seat of the unmarked police car. The other three in the vehicle laughed. Vincent headed toward Warnke's office in Edison, in the building beside the Hilton, where Fraud Unit specialists were waiting.

Gary had spoken to Warnke at length, by phone, during the ride to pick the boy up. He'd given his word to Medved and felt responsible for him. It'd taken some convincing, but the fraud people were grudgingly prepared to treat Teo as an escapee from evil not of his making.

If the programmer turned out to have criminal motives, his status would change, but dealing with him as a cooperating witness cost nothing. It was all Gary had asked for.

"You've been running your scheme through Arman Pavlic, right?" Gary asked Teo. He sat beside the boy. The car bounced over a mound in the roadway—a worn left front shock absorber jolted with every bump. Gary's back didn't complain.

"Yes, yes." The boy nodded. "But is his scheme, not mine." Medved had rings under his eyes that Gary hadn't noticed the day before.

Vincent reached for the radio and asked his office to update Warnke and to issue an APB on Arman Pavlic. The man's home and office were already being watched.

Medved heard that. "You are Gary's friend? The policeman, the

216

one he called from my rooms?"

Vincent nodded. The sky was lighter. Even that early in the morning, thickening traffic slowed them. Too many cars and SUVs sped past, drivers oblivious to police vehicles in the semi-darkness. Sirens and lights would only draw attention. They were not interested in being followed or in handing out speeding tickets.

"Arman is not at home," the boy said. "His car was on my street. Very early, before you."

Gary looked across at Medved.

"I peek through drapes," the kid said. "Sometimes is better than Internet."

"How early?" Gary asked.

"I could not sleep. First time I peek was almost four. He waited already."

"Is that when you pushed the furniture to block your door?"

"No," Medved said. "I need to keep him out only after you called."

"Otherwise you would've gone with him today?" Gary asked.

"Or died in my rooms."

Gary shifted on the worn bench seat, trying to find a place between the springs. "Has Arman ever been there so early before?"

"No." The boy spoke with his hands, too; Gary saw them moving in the flicker of highway lights. "I am ready when he comes. I watch so I can be downstairs. He has always arrived near six."

"Was he driving a black BMW?" Vincent asked.

"Yes, yes."

"Vinnie, Teo told me yesterday that the people who live downstairs in his house may be linked to Arman," Gary said.

Vincent grabbed his radio again and asked the troopers who had been at Teo's to get back there as quickly as they could and check for the BMW. Its driver was armed and dangerous. He also asked them to search inside, beyond Medved's upstairs rooms, go through the entire small house and detain anyone they found.

"Did Arman tell you what you'd be doing before he brought you to America?" Gary asked.

The boy laughed. It was the first time Gary'd heard him laugh naturally. "Working with computers. Not stealing. Would you come to America if you knew?"

Gary shook his head.

"Not me," said Medved. "But once here …."

"Y'had no options," said Larry Goldstein, turning around from the front passenger seat, where he had the bag of disks and hard drives between his legs. "My buddies and I need to talk to you about this stuff."

"I would like to help police," said Medved. "What is your name?"

"Larry Goldstein."

"Ah, that is good." The boy settled back in his seat.

Gary couldn't resist. "What makes his name good, Teo?"

"It is not Russian."

Minutes later, they were still riding, mostly silent, when Vincent's radio crackled. He flipped a switch and raised it to his ear. "Too bad," he said, shaking his head.

~41~
7:12 A.M.

BECCA was so happy, her exhaustion didn't matter. She slipped out of bed early, too excited to sleep, missing him. She'd listened when she first woke—the voices in this house had welcomed her.

Her fears and doubts had gone into in a box that she taped, and packed away inside. She felt like the teen-ager she had never been—a forty-eight-year-old adolescent.

She found her panties and bra, put them on, raided his closet, and pulled on his sweatpants, his sweatshirt. They smelled clean. She wished they smelled like him. She'd shower later, at Angela's.

She called the hospital, told Personnel she'd be in Monday. She'd hidden from phantoms long enough. She'd need time off for their honeymoon. Where would they go?

Megan would absolutely not believe this. Two days before in the hospital corridor, she recalled, Megan had urged her to visit him.

She boiled an egg, made toast and jam, ignored the empty dishwasher, and washed her dishes. No others had been in the sink. Did that man ever eat?

She looked at herself in the mirror over the bathroom sink. Except for the well-earned rings under her eyes, she looked the same. But she didn't feel the same.

Gary wouldn't want her to lose herself, as others had. Three days, they'd met only three days before—but she felt his love, strength, and softness.

His bathroom provided nothing she could use but a comb. That would do. She turned on the cold water, bent her head toward the sink and splashed her face over and over, washing so much away, wanting to start fresh.

The blow to her head was completely unexpected.

She couldn't focus her thoughts or open her eyes, had no idea where she was or what had happened. She felt motion, and something confining. She moaned.

She was smashed across the nose and eyes. Again she went under, slumping against constraints. The nurse in her knew her nose had been broken.

This woman would know what Kemmerman had been up to. She would tell everything, Pavlic was convinced. He would break her bones until she told him what he needed to know. Serge would understand then why he had focused on Gary Kemmerman.

He had waited several minutes with the unconscious woman in his car, hoping the man would return. But he couldn't risk being spotted on the block. She'd have to do for what he and Serge needed.

He'd take her to a place neither Gary nor the police knew about. He and Serge would question her, have her, kill her, and dump her naked on some street.

There were many ways to destroy a man.

~42~
7:58 A.M.

WHILE Vincent and Gary stood behind one-way glass, watching and listening, Medved answered questions in an interview room. Franklyn Warnke, Larry Goldstein, and three fraud unit specialists probed into what Arman and the boy had done. Two cameras recorded the session, one capturing an overview, the other focused tightly on Medved.

Vincent shook his head, and whispered to Gary—he didn't have to whisper, but watching this way made them both feel like voyeurs. "He was part of a criminal enterprise." But he, too, was moved by Medved's quandary.

During the questioning, it became clear the young man wanted to stay and succeed here. He had no interest in being a criminal. Medved described Arman's pressure to get a copy of the entire program, and his certainty that once he turned it over, he'd be killed.

His interviewers were as appalled by his story as they were fascinated by the way he'd been able to circumvent every audit and control procedure, and provide the thieves with a portal into corporate coffers. Though criminal, it was impressive.

There was no copy of the entire program, Medved explained. He was afraid to put everything together, and after each run he deleted sections otherwise stored only in his head, so Pavlic could not simply bring in another person.

But for all his technological wizardry, he had no answer to Pavlic's looming deadline. Shortly, patience would have frayed and he would

221

have gone, program or not. He admitted that Gary Kemmerman, and the policemen he was talking to, had provided his way out. A way he wouldn't have had without them. He thanked them.

The police recognized that Medved's delay, and final disobedience, had been vital. A half-hour into the session, they all wanted to help him.

Vincent and Gary left when the questions grew technical. They waited in Warnke's office. Vincent used the AP 's phone to make a call. He was talking when Gary's cell phone vibrated.

"Kemmerman," he answered.

"Gary?" It was Merle Kingsley. Gary knew what they had to discuss could not be said in front of Vincent. It felt odd, having to keep secrets, but he said, "Hold a minute. Be right with you."

He stepped into the hallway, away from other ears, and found a deserted alcove before punching back on the line. "Do you know your friend—Riddock—was killed?" Vincent had told him. He expected a strong reaction from the small man.

"Yes," Merle said, without emotion, and asked, "Where are you?"

"State AG's Corporate Fraud Unit in Edison."

"Because?"

"Vincent and I went and got Teo. He implicated Pavlic. Your referral." Gary glanced around for a seat. There was none. He turned his back on passers-by.

"This is the Medved kid you told us about yesterday morning?" Merle asked.

Gary heard an edge, wondered what was coming. "Yeah."

"Can he identify anyone else?"

"Only Pavlic."

"Have you told anyone about me?"

"No." The little man was cloaked in secrets.

"Good. Don't. Even Vincent."

What was Merle up to? "If that's what you want."

"Did Vincent tell you what Riddock did? Because of what you asked."

"No."

"He staked out Medved's house with a camera. His people took photos of you emerging, with Pavlic standing beside the house aiming a pistol at you."

Gary's skin crawled. "How do you know that?"

"Vincent. He had Riddock give the photos to his prosecutor friend, Warnke."

Gary leaned against the wall, hoping he hadn't contributed to Riddock's death. "Is that why—?"

Merle interrupted. "Riddock also turned over photos of Serge's men kidnapping a young couple who tried to visit Medved after you."

"Serge?" Who was he? What was Merle asking him to do?

"The police are holding back on you," Merle said. "Serge is the one I've been trying to avoid. He's older, meaner, and he runs the group that includes Pavlic. Riddock's photos allowed the law to pick up two of Serge's men. They talked, said Pavlic brought Riddock to Serge. Serge killed him. The police are searching for Pavlic. After Medved's processed, they'll pick up Serge."

Gary straightened, couldn't help pacing in the small, shadowed space. "You'd rather not have that happen?"

"Not alive."

"Vincent's the one—"

"He knows nothing about my relationship with Serge."

For moments neither spoke, there was only static on the line.

"Why tell me this?" Gary asked.

Instead of answering the question, Merle said, "The three of us were supposed to check in about now, remember?" His tone was bitter.

If there is a tomorrow, Gary recalled Riddock saying.

Merle brought him back. "If the police aren't keeping you in the loop, they won't let you near Serge."

"Why didn't they go for him first?"

"No reason for the man to run. He doesn't know his guys were picked up, or that the police have connected him to Arman." Then Merle asked the question Gary understood was his reason for the call. "Why'd they go after Riddock? Was that a warning for me?"

"Been thinking about that," Gary said. "When Riddock and I met Consolidated's president, Westbrook had hired him to look into Lyons' death—but Westbrook seemed frightened when Riddock already knew of the arson and the police investigation into Lyons."

"If I were in Morgan's shoes, I'd thank Riddock for sharing that," Merle fired back.

"Yeah, but Riddock asked to look into corporate fraud. He told Westbrook the arson and auto fatality, a day apart, opened that avenue. He wanted names at key financial institutions Consolidated uses."

"He wasn't supposed to do that," Merle said, in a growl.

"Westbrook reacted badly when I raised the possibility of financial fraud. If—I know you don't want to hear this, but if he passed his concerns on to Serge, that might have been enough for them to target Riddock."

"Why'd you mention theft?" The little man was biting his words. "I thought we weren't going there. But you and Riddock both dipped into it."

Gary breathed deeply, determined to keep his voice at a whisper. "Don't know why Riddock did. I raised the possibility of a crime Lyons uncovered being cause for his death to get a better settlement for his widow. It worked. I also figured it would give Riddock a chance to gauge Westbrook's reaction. You two were certain he's trustworthy. I wasn't sure. Right now, I wouldn't give you odds."

"You may have helped get Riddock killed," Merle said.

Sending Riddock to Medved, and Schroder to Consolidated, he may have helped get two people killed. "When can we meet?" Gary asked.

"Why bother? I'll send you a payment."

He couldn't keep the whisper. "Don't do that."

He could barely hear Merle's response. "You have anything more to contribute?"

"Don't see what's left to do."

"Well, I've got one last detail," the small man said. "Then, whatever happens, I guess we're done with each other."

Gary turned toward the wall. "Stay out of it, Merle. You can't help Riddock now. This is a police investigation. Those guys killed a cop, they'll kill you."

"More good advice." Merle hung up.

Gary heard bitterness in his sign-off. He was about to return to Vincent, when his phone vibrated again. Was it Becca? Was she awake yet? She'd be tired, too. He was smiling when he answered. "Kemmerman."

"Gary, is Mom with you?" Melanie asked.

~43~
8:14 A.M.

H E HEARD the panic in Melanie's voice, and for an eternal instant everything stopped, his chest constricted. "No," he heard himself say.

"Oh, Gary," she sobbed.

He forced himself to breathe. "What happened?"

"Mom called, said she'd wash up, be right over. When she didn't show, I walked to your house, rang the bell. No one answered so I went around the side." She gasped and went on. "A window's smashed, the door's open, someone broke in. I went in, I couldn't help it, I called for her. She's gone. Find her, Gary, please find her." The girl was near hysteria.

"I will, I promise," he said, his heart breaking for Melanie, for Becca, for himself.

"Gary?" Angela came on the line.

"Yeah."

"You get that?"

"Yeah."

She lowered her voice. "Mel says there's blood in your bathroom."

His heart stopped. "Anywhere else?"

"Only there, but I don't know how accurate a reporter she was after she found it. It tore her up. Should I tell this to Vincent?"

"I'm with him. We'll deal with it. If Becca contacts you, call me. And Angela—"

"What?"

He was about to cry, break down himself, but he couldn't afford to, tried to keep it out of his voice. "Tell Melanie we'll find her mother. I promise. Tell her I'll bring her home safe. Please, Angela, comfort her, give her hope. I'll find Becca and we'll get married."

"I will ... married?"

"You heard. Gotta go." He broke the connection. So many promises.

He banged Warnke's door open, waving a hand in Vincent's face, stopping the other conversation. "That was your wife and Melanie. Becca's gone missing. My side door's been forced, blood's in the bathroom and I'll bet Arman Pavlic has her."

Vincent's face stained with pain and guilt.

The Lieutenant hung up and had Gary repeat his conversations word for word. Then he made two calls from the desk phone, pocketed his cell and stood. "Let's go."

"Go where?" Gary asked, running down the corridor behind Vincent. For a large man, Vincent was fast—or motivated.

"Pavlic's house," the lieutenant called over his shoulder, without breaking stride. He flung open the stairway door. "For starters. A team's on the way to your place, too. Maybe we'll find something, maybe they will. Troopers are surrounding Pavlic's now. We'll figure what else to do."

At the foot of the stairs, Vincent opened the door to the police garage and Gary followed him through, wondering how many other gateways today would bring.

But no one was home at Pavlic's large, new house, except a Russian-speaking woman named Svetlana. She didn't know where Pavlic had gone. The police noted bruises on her face, neck and arms, but she refused assistance.

Pavlic may have built big, but the furnishings inside were sparse and colorless. Thermostats had been set at sixty, and whole rooms were empty except for thick carpeting, an ice-blue color that added to the chill. Gary paced the first floor, trying to stay out of the way. Police were everywhere.

He knew there was no time. Arman would dispose of Becca once they'd forced her to answer questions. It would be ugly, revenge. Gary had dragged her into this. He'd exhausted her, told her all about the criminals, put her at risk. It was his fault. Such joy they'd shared hours ago. The memory was crushing. He pushed guilt away. There was no time for that, either.

Or, he'd have the rest of his life.

"No time," repeated in his head as he wandered about, crazed. *If he were Sherlock Holmes, what would he be looking for?*

He walked into the garage because it seemed the only space in the house where there were no police. The doors were down. There were slots for two cars. One was there, a gray Lexus—no black BMW. Some tools, concrete blocks piled in a corner. A thick rubber square hanging on plastic straps on a wall.

Where would Pavlic take her? Somewhere safe, a controlled environment. Somewhere he could question Becca, presumably with his boss Serge.

Gary focused on the black rubber mat. It was deeply scarred. From hanging over the passenger-side fender of a black SUV, he guessed, from killing Norm Lyons. He'd learned that from Becca. Scrapings on the mat must prove the murder. The industrial-grade material might have come from an auto repair shop. Pavlic's boss owned one. He'd learned that from Vincent. And neither Pavlic nor Serge, he'd learned from Merle, had reason to suspect they'd been connected.

What better, if they wanted to interrogate Becca, for Pavlic to take her directly to his boss' shop. "Vincent," he shouted, running inside, "I know where they must be."

~44~
8:40 A.M.

GARY knew it was personal for Vincent, too. Even with howling sirens and blazing lights, he drove too fast. He led a caravan of three vehicles. The other two held the SWAT team the lieutenant had called out. Six related murders this week, including a police sergeant, had law enforcement livid.

Without mentioning Merle, Gary had carefully connected the dots for Vincent, who'd phoned and pulled Warnke from Medved's debriefing. The AP had provided the address of Serge's business, Wharfside Auto Body, and agreed to the raid into Kearny. The lieutenant had spoken with the local precinct, asked them to provide backup and, covertly, ensure no one left the building before he and the SWAT team arrived.

The car recoiled from a pothole and shuddered, but tires and axles held, and Vincent didn't slow. Sitting beside him, Gary wished he'd never again have to ride in a police car, never again feel like this, a passenger in the collapse of his own life. Rocking in a seat belt, sick, hands clenched, symbols of futility. He'd come full circle. Lost Sarah, found Becca, and now—was he going to lose her, too?

The question returned, the one he'd avoided last insane car ride, spinning in the blizzard. Sarah had died despite science and prayer. Her illness had defeated everything doctors' had tried, all he'd pledged to God. He recalled curdling anguish, vision of a life not worth living. Could he survive Becca's loss?

Was he God's punching bag? Or had he met Becca for a reason, and been given, along with the second chance, the wisdom to save her? He was the one who'd declared war—if he was still breathing, he wasn't done fighting. He would not be a victim again. Noise around him, the panic inside, faded.

Vincent, the SWAT team, the entire US military couldn't make him whole. He could rely on good intentions and overwhelming firepower, but their methods were not designed to achieve his goal. Becca would die in a firefight. There must be another way.

He considered options. There were more than he would have embraced yesterday. He ran through actions, alternate videos in his head. There was no time for delay. He'd have to decide and run with it.

"Vinnie."

"Yeah." The lieutenant blasted through an intersection. The vehicle trembled.

Gary didn't notice. He looked at Vincent and spoke calmly. "Turn off the sirens and lights, all our vehicles, and slow down. Do it now."

Vincent glanced across the seat. "Why? Take us longer."

"Serge has no idea we know about him, right?"

"Probably."

"Then we have the advantage of surprise."

"Even so—"

"Startle them, and they'll kill her." If they haven't already, he feared.

Vincent grimaced, but saw where Gary was going. They were minutes from the target anyway. He nodded and spoke into his radio. Lights and sirens went out. He slowed the car.

Gary flexed his fingers, white from pressure. "How long do we have?"

"Maybe six minutes."

He cringed over the delay, reviewed his plan a final time. He had to share it with Vincent. SWAT team actions were critical. They wouldn't do as he wished without instruction. But Vincent might not buy into it. He'd have to make it happen.

"Listen, Vinnie. You want to capture Pavlic and the other guy. So do I. But I need to save Becca. You understand—"

"I want that too!" His friend sounded desperate.

Gary heard the guilt. He'd use it. "Shoot-'em-ups won't be healthy for anyone, especially her." The lieutenant nodded. "Threaten them, they may use her as a hostage. And those guys, with all they've done, know better than to negotiate. I've got a way that might bring her out alive."

"The downside?"

"Puts me at risk."

"No!" the lieutenant barked. He hunched forward, staring out the windshield as if Gary were not there, ending the conversation.

"I need your help, Vinnie."

"Don't talk crazy."

"Hear me out. I got Becca into this, refusing to take their warning. Now *I'm* the only way to save her. Pavlic knows me. Serge must know of me. I've had negotiating experience. I can do things no one else can."

"No," Vincent said again.

"Then you'll have to shoot me. Time's short. Hear me out."

Vincent's ears reddened and his jaw worked. He wouldn't turn around, but he listened.

Gary spent precious moments scribbling in the small notepad he carried. Before they arrived, he called Angela and asked for Melanie. "Calm down," he said to her. "This'll work out. We know where your mother is, and we'll get her out safely. I promise." It was easy to promise. If she didn't make it, neither would he.

"Angela said you said—"

"You can give her away to me, Melanie. You just can't come on our honeymoon."

She wept and laughed at the same time.

"Stay by the phone, don't give up hope."

"She trusts you, Gary." The girl broke up. "Please take care of my mother …."

He disconnected. That was all he could say.

"You two getting married?" the lieutenant asked.

"Vinnie, what's mine is hers. Melanie's, if we don't make it." He placed the note he'd written on the dash. "I wrote that out. I want you to witness it and make it happen—if you need to."

Vincent worked his mouth, wiped a sleeve across his face.

The vehicles stopped, out of sight, before they reached the target building. Following Gary's plan, Vincent had the SWAT team approach carefully from different directions, and position themselves to block every door and window of the detached structure.

The men in helmets and body armor stealthily moved behind whatever objects they could find to give them cover, but they did so in ways that left them clearly visible to anyone inside. That was vital to Gary's plan. No one, nothing would leave that building unless the SWAT team allowed it to, and that would be apparent to anyone inside, looking out.

In the building's parking lot, hidden from the street in front by a solid fence, were several vehicles, including a black BMW with tinted windows. Vincent identified it as Pavlic's.

So we were right, Gary thought. One way or the other, it ends here.

He and Vincent moved as close to the building as a nearby fence allowed. Vincent got confirmation the team was in position.

Gary heard it. "Come in fast only if you hear shooting," he said. "Otherwise, wait for me. If they try to deal with you without me, all bets are off." He handed his cell phone to Vincent. "You'll call Melanie? Please—"

"I know." Vincent cut him off, took the phone, and stared at it, not his friend. "Good luck," he said, eyes averted.

Gary saw Vincent's haunted look, and moved before the lieutenant could change his mind. He raised his hands and walked rapidly forward. Any of the SWAT team would have put themselves in harm's way, run out, tackled and dragged him back to safety.

As tactical coordinator for the team, Vincent spoke softly into the radio.

Gary traversed the seventy-five feet, and stepped through the single open garage door of the cinder block and brick building that housed Wharfside Auto Body. Pavlic and his boss were in here somewhere. Maybe with others.

And Becca, he hoped still alive.

~45~
9:18 A.M.

A WARNING buzzer sounded when Gary entered the garage. The space had an oil-spotted concrete floor, a high ceiling, and two bays with lifts, both down, empty. Tools lay on aluminum cabinets. Parts hung on a side wall, and tires, some with rims, were piled along a back wall broken by small windows alarmed with wired glass. An open door mid-way along the left wall, leading to another part of the building, revealed a vestibule with linoleum flooring and the first steps of a stairway. Further back, a second, gray metal door was open to what looked like a small office.

There were no cars, just Arman Pavlic, emerging from the office and approaching fast. He looked like the devil, in black shoes and trousers, a shiny black shirt with a large collar open at the neck, revealing gold chains. Fury had twisted his features. His eyes, and the pistol he gripped, were locked on Gary.

Gary stopped and kept his arms up in a non-threatening pose. "I need to talk to you," he said as the killer closed.

It wouldn't have mattered what he said. Pavlic swung the gun viciously at his head. Gary twisted away and blocked the blow with his left shoulder, but its force knocked him to the floor. Concrete tore the back of his right hand. Pavlic stood above him about to do worse damage. The man frisked him.

"It's that meddler," Pavlic shouted. "The idiot is harmless."

"Who?" asked someone else.

"Gary Kemmerman."

"Good. We want him, he's come to us. Bring him."

Pavlic kicked Gary above the left hip. A blossom of new pain, but nothing broken.

"Bring him now." The words had been spoken softly but with menace. The stranger must be Serge, Pavlic's boss, the man Merle had found frightening. Gary's face pressed the floor. Pavlic seized him below the shoulders and yanked him upright.

He heard the garage door rolling down.

They headed toward the office. Through the doorway, Gary saw two beat-up wooden chairs in front of a desk that contained a phone and an electronic organizer, but no cash register. Pin-up calendars from other years hung on the walls. From outside, he noted the two long fluorescent fixtures above the desk that provided lighting. The glare illuminated grime.

Pavlic shoved him through the doorway. He stumbled and found Becca sitting on a third chair beside the desk, duct tape covering her mouth, circling her neck and the back of the chair. Blood oozed from a wound somewhere beneath her tangled hair. Lines of tears had tracked channels on her cheeks through the blood. Her left cheek was red and swollen. Effort had been made to wipe the blood, now streaked and clotting, beneath her broken nose. Her arms lay across her lap, the left hand cradling her right forearm, which was bent at an odd angle.

One of Gary's towels lay blood-soaked on the floor beside her. He knew it was the reason her daughter had found blood only in the bathroom. Becca wore his sweatshirt, his sweatpants, his clothes. He bit his lip to keep steady.

He saw she'd given up, except now she stared at him, fear in her eyes for him. He felt a strange relief. She was alive. He leaned toward her.

The stranger waved an automatic pistol at him. "You like this woman?"

"She's why I came," Gary said in the calmest voice he could muster.

Another wave of the weapon. "To die here with her?"

"To save her." The stranger was almost as tall as Pavlic but much older, with a round face and thin lips locked in a menacing grimace.

He wore brown trousers and a tan-and-green patterned shirt, both so baggy that Gary wondered if he was healthy. "I brought a SWAT team with me," he went on. "Your building is surrounded."

The older man looked to Pavlic.

"I will check," said the other, and vanished.

Gary took a half step toward the stranger. "We need to talk alone."

"Have you information in exchange for your lives?" The old man asked that as if he didn't believe what Gary had told him about the SWAT team.

"May I put my hands down?" Gary said. "I won't fight or run. I think I have a way out of this for you. You alone."

The old man waved the weapon toward Becca and offered a wicked I-can-kill-you-both smirk, curling his almost-invisible lips. "What can you offer? I kill your woman right now."

Gary met the cold eyes. "Not if you expect to get out of here a free man. The room's freezing. May I put my coat over her shoulders?"

Puzzled, the stranger looked at him, weighing what he'd heard, and nodded.

Gary moved slowly. He didn't want to startle the man with the weapon, and his left side ached from shoulder to stomach. He had trouble lifting his left arm. It took longer than he wanted for him to shrug out of his jacket. He lowered it over her. He heard her shallow, frightened breathing. Below his sweatshirt, on her whole arm, he touched her.

The older man used the gun to motion him away. Gary complied, moving a step closer.

Pavlic returned. "Is as he says."

"Armed men?" the older man said, and when Pavlic nodded, asked, "Where?"

"Every side."

"Can we shoot to escape?"

"No. They use cover, wear armor, and carry machine guns. Others must be behind."

The old man's thin lips squeezed into an angry line. "Why you bring his broken woman here? She know nothing. Now we have army against us."

Pavlic didn't reply.

Gary glanced at Becca. Her head stayed down, but her eyes glinted. She'd told them nothing.

The boss swung his gun in short arcs, growling at his underling. "How they find us?"

"Ask *him*." Pavlic waved his pistol at Gary.

"I ask *you*," the older man demanded.

Pavlic stood his ground. "I don't know."

Abruptly, the older man leaned back, offering an ugly smile. "Perhaps you were followed."

"I was not!"

Gary saw Pavlic's finger had slipped into his pistol's trigger grip.

"But your car is in my lot," Serge whispered, with a look that pinned his underling like a butterfly on a board.

It was working, but Gary wouldn't say another word—he'd already told Serge all he dared. *Think: you can die, or talk to me.*

The old man studied Gary, and then said to Pavlic, in a different tone, "We must decide based on fact. Go look from second floor, from all sides so positions and numbers are clear. Careful at the windows—and no shooting. Why provoke our deaths? Come back, and we plan."

Pavlic didn't like it, but he nodded and left.

Gary's attention wavered toward Becca.

The leader turned to him, pistol up again, mouth tight. "Never mind woman or I *will* shoot." His words were clipped, and he spat. "Your plan is?"

"Pavlic kidnapped this woman because she saw him murder Lyons. He came to you because you previously loaned him a vehicle. He needs another to get away. You don't know why he needs to flee. He held me at gunpoint."

Without the coat, the chill of the room numbed him as he went on. "I am here, and the police are here, to rescue the woman and to arrest Pavlic, who has been identified as the key figure behind financial fraud at Consolidated Brokerage. In addition to murder and theft, he is possibly guilty of arson—the police found C4 residue at the Lyons home fire, and Pavlic was in the home that day.

"When you refused to give him a car," Gary whispered, "he tried to shoot you. But you were able to kill him. She and I will both say this to the police."

He knew it didn't matter what he and Becca said. The two men the police had captured would condemn Serge. But the old man could not know that because Becca hadn't told him.

Serge looked into the distance, considering. "Why you say that? What guarantee you will say that when police come?"

"I want this woman to live." He hadn't planned the answer—he spoke from the heart. "Yes, I'll say that, as often as they ask me. I'll be grateful to you. So will she."

The man looked at Gary and nodded.

They heard a muffled sob from Becca.

And then, "Bastard!" Pavlic spat the word and fired once. He'd been listening. Serge had no time to react. A red stain blossomed on his shirt. He went down in slow motion.

A tubular silencer was screwed on to the weapon Pavlic had used—no cavalry to the rescue.

Pavlic checked the fallen man and turned away, pointing his pistol at Becca and Gary, and smiled oddly, as if something pleased him.

"You didn't go upstairs," Gary said, numbness spreading.

"No. Better not to. Now your bitch die. First you watch me shoot her in stomach, so she have time to watch you die."

He had to force himself to speak. "That won't get you out of here. I can help with that."

"There is *no* way out for me." Pavlic's eyes flared, but the smile remained. "You know that."

Gary glanced around, found Becca's eyes were closed. He turned back. "Spare her. She had nothing to do with this."

Pavlic's smile widened as if he'd been waiting for that. "She is *vengeance*. Triumph over *you*. You did this to me. I do worse to you." He sounded pleased. "Then I go shoot police."

The pistol was leveled at her, too far away for Gary to reach in time. He stepped in front of her. Gunfire exploded in the small space.

For an instant, Gary saw the old man up on an elbow, blood staining his shirt, eyes glazed, gun hand propped, firing at Pavlic.

237

Then he felt slugs tear into him. He wasn't aware when he fell.

When the SWAT team blew the door and raced in, they found two dead and two dying.

~46~
11:55 A.M.

MERLE Kingsley slid into the passenger seat of Westbrook's Town Car, and pulled the door shut. The wind faded; all he heard was the purr of the engine and a faint whine from the heater.

The small man, in thick glasses and a bulky green parka, turned to Westbrook in the driver's seat. "Good to see you," he said to the much-taller president, as he dropped the hood and unzipped his parka halfway.

Kingsley had driven into Consolidated Brokerage's parking garage, where he knew no attendant would be on duty. He'd rolled up the ramps to Level Five—the top floor—and around the curve to the small section that elevator-machinery rooms blocked from building windows. The eight parking spaces, bordered by half-walls and open to a sky strewn with chunky clouds, had been empty except for the president's car. Kingsley had left his Volvo and joined Westbrook.

From that level, over the wall, they could see low hills, a scattering of commercial buildings and townhouse communities on the slopes, evergreens folded among mostly bare trees, and a segment of Interstate 80 in the distance. Only occasional, far-off airplane noise interrupted the almost-silent universe within the large car.

Years before, Kingsley and Westbrook had held many impromptu exchanges in that deserted place. The president had on the long, tan cashmere overcoat he generally wore to business lunches. He reached out and patted Kingsley on his left shoulder. The sun poured from

239

behind a cloud and lit up the scene. Glare off the hood glinted on Kingsley's thick glasses. Westbrook blinked as he asked, "To what do I owe this honor?"

When Kingsley spoke next, he knew he sounded as sad as he felt. "I wish life was back to when you and I ran the show and had to meet here if we wanted *any* peace. Company trucking along?"

Westbrook ignored the question and dealt with the tone. "What's got you down?"

"My buddy vanished," the small man said. "You know about that?" He saw surprise on Westbrook's face.

"Riddock? Hell, he'll appear and tell us he's been busy in the field. Probably with the Lyons thing. I asked him to look into it, as you suggested." The president shifted in his seat, turning toward his visitor, squinting in the brightness.

"He was supposed to meet me this morning, but he didn't show," Kingsley said. The parka bunched as he shifted to face Westbrook. "His brother told me Riddock didn't get home last night. Everett said he's never out without letting them know. They found his car in the hotel lot where he'd parked last evening. He's not registered there, and the staff didn't recognize his photo."

"I'm sure he's okay." The president grinned. "Yesterday, he came as the exterminator, in the uniform right down to the hat and a spray-tank on his back. His getups are worth his fee."

"He's one of a kind, but this time I'm worried, Morgan. You think his involvement in Lyons' death caused him to go missing?"

Westbrook leaned away, lengthening the distance between them. "Shit—you and I go back too far to do this tap dance. Yeah, if we're talking possible arson and murder, and he got too close, that might be enough." The president lowered his right arm from the seatback to his lap. "If anything's happened to him, I wish *we* hadn't sicced him on Lyons."

Kingsley heard the "we"—it was true. He lowered his head and spoke softly. "Been a while since you and I leveled in this corner. You telling me you had nothing to do with his going missing?"

"*Damn right!*" Westbrook threw up his left hand to emphasize the point. "How can you think otherwise?"

The man in the parka shook his head. "I guess we gave up being truthful sometime between then and now."

"What in *hell* do you mean?"

Kingsley's hands were in thin gloves; he kept them in plain sight on his lap. He looked up and caught the other's eye before he asked, "Why'd you need to have him killed, Morgan?"

"You're nuts!" Westbrook spat the words, furious. "I didn't, didn't, didn't! That make it any clearer?"

Kingsley knew he might have a big apology to make. He wavered, recalling their closeness over the years, Morgan's rock-solid integrity. But no one was left but him to answer for Riddock. He had to know.

"Remember me, Morgan? I hooked up with Serge long before you did."

"Who in Christ's name is *Serge?*" Westbrook seemed puzzled.

Kingsley said, so softly that the man in cashmere had to bend forward to hear, "I don't know if he told you about me, but I made peace with him early this morning. I agreed to recommend that programmer you want. Serge and I were talking—rare for him—and he told me about you."

"Told you *what?*" Westbrook's hands waved. "How can a man I don't know tell you anything about me?"

"Let me explain. It may come as a shock. I learned this from the police, and I wanted to tell you before they did. It's the real reason for our meeting."

The little man watched Westbrook shift. His gun, if he had one, was in the oversized housing beneath the steering wheel. Kingsley spoke with an ease he didn't feel.

"It's complicated, so listen, I'll try to get it right." While he spoke, he sat perfectly still. "Someone talked. The cops know about the murders of your programmer Suresh Rahman and his girl. They know your employee was killed because he overheard what Arman Pavlic told the other programmer, Teodors Medved—and how Rahman tried to visit Medved to ask him for money. The cops have Medved in protective custody—they've cracked the program Serge used to steal from Consolidated."

As he listened, the concern on Westbrook's face turned to alarm.

"Don't worry, Morgan," Kingsley went on, "I'm told Medved can only finger Pavlic. It's all moot anyway, because Pavlic and Serge were both shot dead hours ago. A SWAT team raided Serge's office. It's just you and me now."

Westbrook turned white. In a motion so smooth it had to be practiced, he reached beneath the steering wheel with his left hand, grasped a pistol and leveled it at Kingsley. His features had turned nasty; his voice rasped. "You didn't need to go there. I'd rather not do this, but you're leaving me no choice."

The small man's eyes flicked toward the snub-nosed .38 in the president's hand. This close, it would make a mess of him, first shot. He forced himself to relax. Westbrook's expression was cold, but he'd wait for a response before pulling the trigger. He owed him that much. Then he might shoot anyway.

"You don't need the gun, Morgan. This is *me*. How about I still recommend the programmer, you cooperate with the law, and when the cops go we pick up where we left off. I came to warn you so you wouldn't be surprised. Pavlic got himself and Serge killed. The cops linked Norman Lyons' death and the fire at his house. They tailed Pavlic, took photos when he and Serge met last night. Those, plus what Medved said, triggered the raid. They tried to take on a SWAT team. It's better for us they're dead than talking." The man in the parka tilted his head. "Hey, I thought my police info would help."

Westbrook glowered, the revolver steady. Then the tall man lowered the weapon to his lap. Not losing it, just not needing it so urgently.

"I'll check what you said. Sorry about the gun. Better to be careful. You taught me that." He frowned. "Serge said you wanted no part of him. He hadn't decided what to do about you."

Kingsley relaxed, leaning back, smiling warmly across the seat. "Serge was scary. It's hard to work with threats, and he took most everything, left crumbs. With you, it would be a pleasure. I still have contacts. And I'm not greedy. What say?" He swung his left arm over the seatback, exposing himself to the pistol, and waited.

Westbrook also seemed to relax. "If what you've told me is fact, fine."

"The police will prove it out soon enough. And we'll be back in business." A cloud came and went past the sun, leaving both men blinking. Kingsley asked, "Was Serge giving you much?"

The pistol came up. "Why do you ask?"

The little man pulled off his glasses and wiped a lens on the back of a glove, ignoring the gun. "Think of all the money you'll have now, Morgan. You'll be in the big time, world-class."

"And you want how much?" Westbrook's tone was icy.

Kingsley laughed, and fit the glasses. "Oh, you name it. I have more money than I need. Other things I care about."

"Perks." Westbrook nodded. "Sure. We can work something out."

"So much at stake, guess it *was* worth taking out Riddock," Kingsley said.

Before he answered, Westbrook checked the little man's expression. "Yeah, he was too close. To everything."

"No other way?" Again, Kingsley's sadness came through. "You had to kill our friend?"

"That much money," the man with the gun said, "is worth protecting."

"Besides, Serge did it, right?"

"Arman brought Riddock in," the president said. "When he wouldn't talk anymore, yeah, Serge did it."

The sun faded like house lights going down. This time it stayed darker, and Westbrook looked forward, out the windshield, thinking of something.

Kingsley imagined them trying to break Riddock—he'd *died for him*, the little man knew. He kept his elbow down, slowly raised his right hand.

Westbrook turned back, glancing toward the motion, freezing when he saw the small pistol inside the parka's sleeve.

"This was never about money," Kingsley said.

Westbrook watched the muzzle flash. The .25 caliber shell tore into his skull, shredding his brain. He slumped against the drivers'-side door, gun still in his hand, hand still in his lap.

Kingsley plucked the billfold from Westbrook's breast pocket, careful not to get blood on his own coat. He pulled the bills from it, and tossed the wallet on the floor. He turned off the engine, left the key in the ignition, and climbed out. The raw air was bracing.

Before closing the door, he bent back toward the corpse. "Riddock taught me how to do that."

~47~
4:05 P.M.

THE whole area was a crime scene. Franklyn Warnke had organized the cross-jurisdictional effort. State Police had the entry road, the dilapidated trucking terminal and the surrounding snow-covered, garbage-strewn weed fields well secured. A helicopter sat motionless on the old cracked-asphalt parking lot, a sharpshooter on point just in case. Armed perimeter patrols had gone out two-by-two in an early, cloud-induced twilight. They moved slowly, afraid they'd fall into pits—or worse.

Aside from occasional wind-whipped voices, Vincent could hear the metallic whine of vehicles speeding along the distant Pulaski Skyway, and intermittent jet-engine shrieks from planes approaching the airport. The back of the terminal was illuminated by portable spots, set up on poles and fed by a fluctuating generator. The cracked and fallen walls, uneven against snow mounds streaked by humped earth, turned the scene into an archeological dig straight from a horror film. Three of the below-ground loading bays, two unfilled and the third being excavated, looked like freshly-dug graves and cast eerie shadows.

Standing beside Warnke, hands deep in his pockets, the lieutenant had his eyes on the small, red, freshly dug-out auto, crushed and dirt-encrusted, one of the vehicles in the photos Riddock Maguire had turned over.

Mihran Grinko, flanked by two federal marshals who towered over him, stood on almost the same spot he'd left twenty hours before. The men remained silent, watching the forensic team moving like black ants in and out of the site. One of them stepped closer, pointed at Warnke, nodded and gave him a thumbs up, confirming they'd found what Grinko had told Warnke to expect.

Grinko had nothing further to do here. A federal task force would take him and Lev, question them about other matters, and hand them over to witness protection.

Warnke had told Vincent that when he asked the feds how they could let a pair of vicious killers back into society, all they'd say was not to worry about it.

"Franklyn, keep us informed," said a marshal in a southern twang.

The lieutenant knew the futility of Warnke's asking the same.

"Will do, Tobey," Warnke said. "Take good care of our boys." They watched Grinko led away.

Vincent turned from the retreating backs. "How many others are buried here?"

"Grinko said three other cars he knows about are underground." Their breath made steam. The AP jammed his hands into the pockets of a black cloth coat. "This was done over decades. I wonder how many of these people just went missing? Grinko doesn't know everything."

"Aren't the Meadowlands where all mysterious disappearances wind up?"

Warnke just stared.

Vincent rubbed his hands together, stamped his feet on the frozen ground. "Been a tough week."

Warnke turned to him. "Shame about your friend and his girl."

The lieutenant hadn't been home since he left, with Gary, this morning. He couldn't face Angela and Melanie.

He'd radioed for an ambulance the moment Gary had walked into that garage. His team had burst in at the first sound of shooting, EMTs along with them. The EMTs had taken Gary and Becca away.

"Her daughter's staying with us," Vincent said. "Ain't easy."

"Kind of you, though." Warnke's gaze trailed back to the scene. "Makes it rough when the vic's a friend. Profession's a bitch. I need sleep."

The lieutenant knew Warnke hadn't since Riddock brought the photos to him the previous afternoon—before dinnertime, one of the meals he and Angela had cancelled on Gary.

"What I don't understand is what happened to Westbrook," Vincent said, stamping his feet. "Robbed and murdered *in* his car, *in* his parking garage, at the same time all this shit's flying around his company. Has to be a connection."

"Logical assumption, but there doesn't seem to be." Warnke retrieved the briefcase he'd set down. "None of the players were left to bother him. Just a robbery gone bad. Random violence."

"Yeah," Vincent said. "Time to go home." He rubbed his eyes. "Whether I want to or not. Angela used to complain she didn't remember what I looked like. Now I walk in, I'll get it good from two women. And they'll both be right."

Warnke started toward the cars and glanced back, trapped by the scene. "Stayed home," he said. "That's what Lyons should have done three days ago. Taken that snow day. You think any of it would have happened if he had?"

The terminal might have been a meticulously constructed stage set, acutely lit by spotlights against the oncoming darkness. Blood-red clouds, in keeping with the day, were fading into a bruised purple.

The generator rumble joined the roar of construction equipment beginning to excavate a second filled-in, garishly shadowed bay. It would still be going on tomorrow.

The lieutenant and the assistant prosecutor, both numb, turned toward their vehicles. It was Friday night, start of the weekend. They'd find heavy traffic on the roads.

SATURDAY, FEBRUARY 21

~48~
5:10 P.M.

IT HAD grown dark by the time Vincent was finally allowed to visit Gary. He stood beside the hospital bed, looking at the tubes and wires. Liquid flowed, a pump clicked softly, things dripped, monitors pinged.

The nurse had said he might be awake, but his eyes were closed and his breathing shallow. What showed above the blanket was ashen, and the patient didn't seem aware of his visitor.

"Norm dead, you hurt—we must live on the wrong block," said the lieutenant.

Gary heard him and wanted to agree. Instead, he groaned and opened his eyes. They stayed open and began to focus. He tried to swallow. It was white all around him, like heaven, except Vincent was standing there.

"Nurse said you might be awake." The lieutenant bent close, checking Gary's eyes, and then went on. "Don't talk. You'll live. I still have a job because of that, so don't ever make me offers I can't refuse."

Gary tried to concentrate. *There was something he had to know.* He just stared.

"Your shoulder's broken, you were shot three times, side and thigh. You stopped the slugs before they got to Becca, so she's alive.

You don't get away free, but the doctor says you were fortunate—no vital hits. Arteries, organs, bones—he talked at me, but all I remember is that, with physical therapy, he said you should recover. They'll brief you tomorrow. You're a celebrity. You saved a Ridgetop nurse. People stop me in the halls, everyone wants to come to your wedding."

"Becca?" Gary sounded like a frog.

The lieutenant took a cup, held it so Gary could sip. He put it down and continued. "They broke her arm to make her talk. Didn't work. Tough lady. Gotta tell you, if she survived and you hadn't, I think she'd have killed me for letting you in there. She also has a concussion, a broken nose, and bruising from when Pavlic kidnapped her. But she's very pleased you're alive." The man shook his head. "She's splinted, stitched, bandaged, and … smiling. God, so is Melanie. She's been holding your hand—for hours, you feel it?—and thanking you. She walks around crying, can't wait to give her mother away."

Vincent paused and leaned closer, brows knit, probably waiting for a reaction. When he got nothing except Gary's eyes, he went on. "She told us what happened. You must know that Pavlic is dead—Serge got him. Serge also died. Pavlic used fragmentation loads. The slug hit nothing vital, so Serge had time. Becca doesn't think he meant to shoot you, but that's immaterial. Gary, I feel responsible. But she insists that what you did saved you both. Maybe you knew best."

"What else?" Gary mumbled. Talking scratched his throat.

"We found bodies behind an old trucking terminal Serge owned. Warnke tells me they'll be digging all weekend. And then—well, *this* one's weird. Westbrook was killed in his car, in his building's parking garage, shot resisting a robbery." Gary recognized the cop look, but Vincent gave it up and asked, "You know anything about that?"

Gary slowly shook his head. But he wondered.

"That's what I figured. Oh, and Hannah says she knew you'd help solve Norm's murder, but she didn't mean for you to get shot. She's getting smug about predicting you and Becca were an item. It's a help to her, having something positive in her life."

"Teo?" Gary asked.

"You'll love this. The fraud unit took a shine to him. They like his talent and attitude—and he'll work cheap. He may be the only geek besides Bill Gates who's a born salesman. He's staying with the Goldsteins."

Gary nodded, tried to smile, but couldn't.

The lieutenant threw up his hands. "Kid skimmed over four hundred grand from the others. Called it his survival fund. We saved him, so he wants to give it to us. Proves he's honest. We'd never have known about the account if he hadn't told us. Of course, the money goes back to the company. The fraud group has Medved trying to track down the rest of it, but with Pavlic and his boss gone, it's a long shot."

Fuzzy as he was, that reminded Gary of his conversations with Riddock and Merle Kingsley, and he connected the dots between Westbrook and Merle. Lucky for Hannah he'd come away with Westbrook's commitments in writing. For Merle, it'd been payback. That was not for Vincent to know. For Becca? He grasped she was alive. "Becca ...?"

Vincent motioned to Gary's right. He pulled back the privacy curtain. Becca lay under a sheet facing him, bed pulled close, exposed right arm encased in an elbow-down cast. He saw a gap in her long hair: inches of her head had been shaved and bandaged. He wondered how many stitches she'd needed. Another bandage went across her nose, below two black eyes. But she smiled at him.

At least one of us can smile, he thought.

For a moment she turned toward the lieutenant. "Vincent ...."

"Later," the cop said, and lumbered off. Gary did not see him signal a nurse, who stepped close as soon as he was gone.

"Any longer and you'll start to feel pain," the nurse said. "We don't want that." She worked a separate machine by the edge of his bed. "I'm cranking up your pain medication. You'll be able to do it yourself soon."

She smiled at Becca and left.

He saw Becca's eyes were twinkling despite her wounds. "How's your arm?" he whispered.

"I'm getting a button nose." She sounded nasal. "I hope you like that."

Any nose would look good on her, he thought. He drifted away, forced himself back. "You didn't tell them anything, did you?" He was out of energy.

She knew what he meant. "I hate people who hurt me."

He was in love with a tiger.

"One of your friends came by," she said. "Vincent got him in. Merle Kingsley, you told me about him. But I didn't let on. He insists he's paying for our honeymoon. Odd, he said just don't tell Vincent. Wherever we want to go, for as long as we want. I told him we couldn't accept that, but he said it was part of your fee. He wants you to work for him. He said something about Consolidated calling him back. Did you do anything for him, besides those two meetings you mentioned?"

He lay quietly, except for his machines, looking at her.

"It's Saturday," Becca said. "I met you Tuesday, and you've gotten me kidnapped, beaten, and shot at. The other guys I dated were easy compared to you."

He saw her try to grin, heard her question from far away. "How'd you find me in that garage?"

"Melanie asked me … take care of you," he whispered, wishing he could smile. A wave of weariness rolled over him, but he managed to murmur what he wanted to, what he knew summed up this past week, and all the weeks to come: "Love you." In the moments before he dozed off, his eyes held hers like a lifeline.

"We'll take care of each other," she said. But he didn't hear it.

COMING SOON FROM E. J. RAND
PERFECT COVER

§

PROLOGUE

*W*HY *was Janelle screaming?*
Despite the shrieks, Rosa curled up and would have slipped away, but she felt her head being lifted and something soft pushed beneath it.

"Wake up!" She'd heard the deep voice before but couldn't place it. Her head throbbed. She squeezed her closed eyes, concentrating, and knew she and Janelle were at Ridgetop Hospital, cleaning Five Medford, everyone asleep but them and the nurses. Why was she lying on something hard and cold? She was freezing. She heard Janelle whimpering. What was going on?

Gray and black squares rippled like waves when she blinked. She smelled disinfectant. The dented metal cabinet below the slop sink split into two, then merged. Had she been drinking? No, with effort she remembered—she'd come in to get rags. What was she doing on the floor? Her left arm was pinned; she shifted to free it, groaned from waves of pain in her head.

"Doctor's on the way, you'll be fine." Rosa recognized Nurse Safrian's voice. "Lie still—talk to me."

Why would she say that? Rosa turned her head and flinched.

253

Lieutenant Reed was in her face, staring. She felt fingers squeezing her right wrist. The nurse was taking her pulse. The security man bent closer. She wanted him gone, the nurse gone, wanted to be back cleaning without anyone's attention.

"*Madre del dios!*" Janelle wailed, "*Aiee!*"

Startled, Rosa glanced up. Her head spun, eyes closed, and then she saw Janelle staring, eyes wide, mouth open.

Heart pounding in her throat, she fought dizziness and glanced down. When she saw the blood, she began to scream.

~1~
WEDNESDAY, APRIL 26
8:50 A.M.

Wıᴛʜ the envelope he'd been hiding in one hand and his coffee mug in the other, Gary Kemmerman padded downstairs barefoot. He saw the Oriental rug Becca had chosen to replace the living room carpeting and, as he reached the landing, smiled at the photos on the mantle above the fireplace of their recent Bermuda honeymoon.

They'd just finished breakfast; he still smelled pancakes. Thinking she'd be in the kitchen he turned that way. When he didn't find her, he poked his head in the dining room. The mirror told him he needed a haircut—at least, at fifty-eight, he still had hair. He'd lost the sallow look, gained back to his normal 193 pounds, and knew it wasn't just Becca's cooking.

There she was, standing behind a couch, tall and curvy in her sleep shirt, reddish hair tangled. When she was ready, he knew, she'd tell him why she'd been wearing that cryptic expression.

"Happy two months' anniversary," he said, offering the envelope, making no effort to hide his smile.

"Won't work," she grumbled. She leaned toward him without taking it, hands on the back of the couch.

Drawn white curtains filtered the early-morning sun, brightening the room. The house was still, free of the noise from the planes, trains and cars that moved through the northern New Jersey suburb.

"I got the date wrong?" He doubted it, but set the mug down on the coffee table and started around to her side, holding out the envelope, toes curling into the new rug, free hand rubbing at his cranky back.

She shook her head and turned to face him. "Course not."

Her tone was combative and he wasn't used to her frown. He hesitated.

"You almost got shot again, didn't you?"

So that was it. Vincent told his wife Angela everything. "No, I didn't—well, not exactly. Please." He waved the envelope until she took it.

She pulled at the flap without looking down. "Do we need to be on vacation to keep you from poking your nose where it doesn't belong?"

"You guessed about the vacation?" How could she, he wondered? During the arrangements, the only phone number he'd given out was his cell.

Becca frowned, glanced down, and smiled at the inscription on the card. She pulled out the photo. "What's this?"

"Our summer vacation." It *had* been a surprise. It was almost impossible to keep secrets from her.

"Masts? Sails? Are we going on a sailing ship?"

He stepped close and craned around, peering. "It's the *Waveskimmer*—they call it a five-mast, stay-sail schooner—I think it's the largest sailing ship in the world for cruise passengers. The brochure says the sails unfurl in two minutes: a computer does it. It has engines, too."

She couldn't help smiling at him. "How did you *find* this?" She studied the photo, angling it to better catch the light. It showed the white-hulled ship, sails unfurled, gliding on blue water before a green island and beneath ragged clouds embracing a rainbow.

"On the Internet," he said. "You told me you want us to go somewhere memorable every chance we get. Probably because I'm nine years older than you, how many trips can we take before I fall apart—but I remember your words exactly."

Her expression changed; he wanted to take back that last word.

"What'd you mean before, 'not *exactly*' shot?"

The last time they'd talked about this had been in the hospital, when he would have said yes to anything she wanted. He knew where she was heading and it made him uncomfortable. "Well, Vinnie asked if I'd help him with——" he shrugged, and his arms came up—"if Angela squealed on me, you know it all." He reached out, nestling a hand at the curve of her waist.

For a moment, the picture held her attention. Then she looked up. "Our favorite police lieutenant promised he wouldn't let you get shot again. Remember? I married a retired crisis consultant, not a cop. 'Creative' and 'intelligent' are not résumé items for risking your life. We agreed, you and I—and Vincent, too—that you were done with sleuthing."

The room was remarkably quiet when she finished. Back in February, Becca had witnessed an auto crash that'd killed one of his friends. When he promised the widow he'd look into it—the police had called it an accident; she'd insisted it was murder—he'd met Becca. He'd helped solve the crime, but he had indeed been shot, and she'd been badly beaten.He glanced at the mug, didn't want to retreat, and turned back with determination. "You're a nurse, you hit Ridgetop most days, you won't retire from what you like." He held up his free hand before she could reply. "And ... I understand."

What she'd barely held in came out. "That's different." The photo was down now, her attention on him.

Tires squealed as a vehicle took the nearby corner too fast; he waited the moment. "I don't want you on the night shift, but you take your turn. Two months this time—doesn't matter how I feel."

Her head tilted the way it did when she was annoyed. But her tone was ordinary. "Megan does it, too. Nursing is not life-threatening."

"Well, neither is what I do. I was just helping Vinnie. I don't carry a gun."

That upset her. "I still remember"—she shuddered—"a muzzle flashing and you falling. I don't want you on either end of a gun."

He remembered, too, and sought her eyes. "I ... I respect that. Vinnie wouldn't involve me in anything where I'd *need* a gun, is what I'm saying. We *both* know what he promised."

For a second time her head tilted, and the look pinned him.

"Then why did Angela tell me you risked your life?"

He raised both hands, palms out. "Gotta talk to that woman. She's blowing it up. Here's what happened. Vinnie threw incidents, facts, at me, asked for an opinion. We talked about it. Nothing dangerous—"

"That's not what I heard." Her eyes were keen. Neither of them heard the shriek of a commuter jet curling above, headed toward Teterboro Airport.

He shrugged. "I figured it out, thought it would be best if I handled it myself."

"Vincent didn't send you?" She leaned closer. "You didn't tell him what you were going to do?"

He breathed in and shook his head. "He wouldn't have let me. The boy who says he did the robberies—he's a kid. I knew he wouldn't shoot."

"But he had a gun."

"I came out of his house with the kid and the gun. I drove him to the police station. No biggie."

She scrunched her mouth. "I don't want you taking risks like that. Angela told me you confronted the boy because you didn't want *him* to do something stupid. What *you* did was!"

He didn't know what to say. "Vinnie's pissed at me. But there was no reason anyone had to get hurt."

The closest photo on the mantle showed them holding each other, smiling, with the ocean behind them. A day to savor, complete, no need for words. His hand moved onto her hip.

With the card, she slapped at it. "Three months ago you almost died on me." The exasperation was gone when she added, "I don't want to lose you."

"… There's more to it than that. What is it?"

She blinked and took a gasping breath while he waited. Her eyes focused on his chest. "Uncle Hal was a policeman."

He bent forward, leaning closer so she had to look at him, and pressed both hands onto her waist. "Don't be frightened. It wasn't dangerous. I wouldn't—"

"I want you to promise—" she had started with intensity, paused, glanced at the photo and then at him, stooped before her, and her eyes grew tender, along with her voice—"to be more careful."

She stood waiting, photo in one hand, card and envelope in the other.

"I promise." He straightened and wrapped his arms around her, squeezing hard.

"You're not old," she said, breathless, and then, "Where are we going?"

FOR MORE OF

PERFECT COVER

PLEASE VISIT

www.reluctantsleuth.com

WITH SPECIAL THANKS

Deep appreciation to those who've helped shape SAY GOODBYE:

Friends Walter and Judy Distler, Julie and Sherman Frankston, David M. Grant, Neil Guiney, Dave McCaw, Judy McKay, and Jordan and Kathy Wouk.

The Sometimes Vagabond Writing Group, headed by Dr. Allan Lazar and usually starring Elisa Chalem, Dan Karlan, Susan Moshiashwilli, Jeremy Salter, and Eileen F. Watkins.

Barry Sheinkopf, mentor extraordinaire, who runs The Writing Center in Englewood Cliffs, NJ.

Debby Buchanan, of my publisher Deadly Ink Press, for her seminal conferences and for sharing my love of this story.

Rebecca Kandel for creating a wonderful cover design.

My son Matthew, who created the series' website.

My wife Ellen, who is always with me.

~E. J. RAND

Printed in the United States
201151BV00034B/1-6/P

9 780978 744212